Praise for

'A sparkling, heartfelt romance that will have you racing towards happily ever after. I devoured it!'

STEFANIE LONDON, *USA Today*
bestselling author on *Meet Me in a Mile*

'Hrib successfully tugs at the heartstrings.'

PUBLISHERS WEEKLY on *Meet Me in a Mile*

'A swoony, often laugh-out-loud read about believing in yourself and taking chances and not giving up at the first obstacle to success.'

LIBRARY JOURNAL on *Meet Me in a Mile*

'A fun and sexy love triangle that goes the distance! Heartfelt, fun and steamy – my favourite kind of rom-com!'

JENNIFER SNOW, *USA Today*
bestselling author on *Meet Me in a Mile*

'*Meet Me in a Mile* is filled with humour, heart and the kind of love that lasts a lifetime – it captivated me from start to finish…sizzling chemistry with laugh-out-loud adventures and tender moments that made my heart melt.'

MICHELLE MAJOR, *USA Today* bestselling author

Elizabeth Hrib was born and raised in London, Ontario. She studied nursing in university but fell in love with storytelling and dreaming up happily-ever-afters, so she decided to make it her day job. When she's not writing, she can be found playing the piano, swooning over her favourite books on Instagram or buying too many houseplants.

The Best CHRISTMAS CHOIR Ever

ELIZABETH HRIB

All rights reserved including the right of reproduction in whole or in part in any form. This edition is published by arrangement with Harlequin Enterprises ULC.

This is a work of fiction. Names, characters, places, locations and incidents are purely fictional and bear no relationship to any real life individuals, living or dead, or to any actual places, business establishments, locations, events or incidents. Any resemblance is entirely coincidental.

Without limiting the author's and publisher's exclusive rights, any unauthorised use of this publication to train generative artificial intelligence (AI) technologies is expressly prohibited. HarperCollins also exercise their rights under Article 4(3) of the Digital Single Market Directive 2019/790 and expressly reserve this publication from the text and data mining exception.

® and ™ are trademarks owned and used by the trademark owner and/or its licensee. Trademarks marked with ® are registered with the United Kingdom Patent Office and/or the Office for Harmonisation in the Internal Market and in other countries.

First Published in Great Britain 2025 by
Afterglow Books by Mills & Boon, an imprint of HarperCollins*Publishers* Ltd
1 London Bridge Street, London, SE1 9GF

www.harpercollins.co.uk

HarperCollins*Publishers*
Macken House, 39/40 Mayor Street Upper,
Dublin 1, D01 C9W8, Ireland

The Best Christmas Choir Ever © 2025 Elizabeth Hrib

ISBN: 978-0-263-39761-1

1025

This book contains FSC™ certified paper and other controlled sources to ensure responsible forest management.

For more information visit: www.harpercollins.co.uk/green

Printed and Bound in the UK using 100% Renewable Electricity
at CPI Group (UK) Ltd, Croydon, CR0 4YY

One

Charlie

Snow in December wasn't a surprise, but the ankle-deep slush that soaked through Charlie's boots and into her socks the moment she got out of the car? That was a step too far. There was nothing she hated more in the world than wet feet, and she curled her toes as she tried to shake the slush from her boots. The sooner they got inside, the better.

"If I knew it was going to be this frigid, I would have picked a different day to move in," Gram muttered from inside the vehicle, her breath fogging. She sat in the passenger seat, soaking up the last of the car's warmth.

Charlie peered in through the driver door. "If I'd known it would be this cold, I'd have demanded my payment in hot chocolate."

"Forget that," Gram said. "I'd have gone straight to the Irish coffee."

"Now you're talking," Charlie said. Nothing like a little

whiskey to take the edge off a day that started with movers blasting her out of bed at the crack of dawn.

She looked up at the hulking building next to them. It rose ten stories, consisting of brown brick and glass balconies. Most of the railings boasted green garland or twinkle lights. Even the front door was decorated with a holly-filled wreath.

Charlie wrinkled her nose. The Christmas spirit was strong here.

Besides that, the grounds were well manicured under the dusting of snow. Old rosebushes had been pruned back to protect them from the winter winds, and the sidewalks were cleared and salted to prevent ice buildup. A whiteboard sat just outside the entrance. Welcome Home was written across it in bold black letters.

"It's nice, isn't it?" Gram said, finally climbing out of the car. A silk scarf was wrapped over her head to protect her ears from the chill.

Charlie offered her a hand for balance. Doris Bender was a tall, slender woman with short gray hair and impeccable taste. She wore a dark blue peacoat that always smelled like Chanel No. 5 and carried around a Louis Vuitton handbag she'd bought back in the '80s. When Charlie was young, Gram had taught her three things: how to sing scales, how to play the piano and how to spot fake pearls.

Charlie had taken the music to heart, the facts on pearls not so much.

"It looks just like the pictures you sent me," Charlie said diplomatically. At twenty-nine, she was about forty years too early for admission. So what did her opinion matter anyway?

Gram hummed in agreement. "Wait until you see inside. Homey. Quaint. Exactly what I was looking for."

"Exactly what the brochure promised," Charlie said. *Glendale Retirement Village: The Best Because You've Earned It!*

Gram hiked her purse up her arm with a nod and started down the sidewalk.

Charlie closed the passenger door and surged after her. "Careful!" she called. "It might be slippery."

Gram waved her off. "I've survived worse than a little ice."

That was what worried Charlie. She'd always thought of her grandmother as poised and ageless, but a recent fall and a trip to the emergency room had reminded them all that at seventy-four, Gram was not invincible. Luckily, nothing had been broken, and Charlie's parents hadn't been forced to rush home from their month-long European culinary tour.

But getting Gram moved into Glendale while they had a unit available was a priority that couldn't wait. So the task had landed on Charlie's reluctant shoulders. Returning to Elm Springs, to the place where Tom had…

Well, this was the last place she wanted to be. A twisting ache tightened in her stomach, and she sucked in a shaky breath.

"Hey! This all headed to the fourth floor?" a voice called.

Charlie turned to greet one of the movers that had rumbled up in the truck behind them. He stepped out of the cab, a clipboard in his hand.

"Yes." She removed her gloves so she could unfurl a piece of paper from her pocket. "Suite 402. I called ahead, and a woman at reception said it would be unlocked for you." She glanced into the back of the moving truck as the mover opened the doors.

Gram had only brought a fraction of her belongings from the four-bedroom Victorian she owned. That was all that would fit in her new one-bedroom apartment. Charlie was already dreading having to deal with the rest of the house until her parents got back. The plan was to be ready to sell by the new year, which only left a month to get things sorted. But the thought of being stuck in that house, where Tom had received his palliative care and the memories were heaviest, was a crushing weight to bear.

Gram has no one else, she told herself. *Because your brother is dead and your parents are in Europe. So, tag, you're it.* Whether she liked it or not.

"Sounds good," the mover said, and Charlie shoved her feelings back into the dusty box she'd stuffed them in two years ago. "We'll get an elevator put on Service and start taking things up to the suite."

"Thanks, Pat!" Gram called, walking up and looping her arm through Charlie's. "Come inside. Let me give you the grand tour."

Charlie was more eager to get out of the cold than she was to tour a retirement home, but she didn't complain. Truthfully, she'd already been on the home's website, scoping things out. She'd even ended up on the staff landing page and had spotted an old fling from her college days.

Julian Guerrero was Glendale's activities director. It must have been eight years since they'd last seen each other, and though Charlie wasn't thrilled about digging into her past—one that belonged to the version that still had Tom— she figured it might be nice for Gram to have a familiar face around for this transition. From what Charlie remembered, Gram had always liked Julian. He'd been polite and sweet, and sure, Charlie recalled being a little bit infatuated for those seemingly endless weeks. But summer had come to a close, and the fling had eventually fallen off.

Gram strolled through the front doors, dragging Charlie into the lobby. She was pretty spry for someone who was still healing a nasty bruise to her hip.

A string of glittery, hand-cut snowflakes hung along the reception desk. A woman greeted them. She had a name tag pinned to her jacket—Erin—and the softest voice. It was like she spent her days speaking to toddlers instead of people who were hard of hearing.

Most people remembered names or faces, but Charlie remembered voices. She noticed inflections and tone, accents and vibrato. The voice was like a fingerprint, and Charlie absorbed this one, committing it to memory.

"Erin," Gram said. "Good to see you again."

Erin grinned. "I hope the move is going well."

"Excellent. I went with the company you suggested. Pat and his team have been wonderful so far."

"Minus the wake-up call," Charlie muttered.

Gram nudged her forward. "This is my granddaughter, Charlene."

Charlie rolled her eyes. Charlene was so *formal*. Charlene belonged on a stage in a sparkly gown with a mic in her hand. Whereas Charlie rocked holey jeans despite the temperatures outside and salt-stained boots and an old knitted hat Gram had stuffed on her head this morning. She mustered a smile. "Please, call me Charlie."

"Nice to meet you," Erin said.

"I was actually hoping to give Charlie a bit of a tour," Gram said. "Just while the movers do their thing."

"Sure thing. I'd be happy to take you around if you like?" Erin waved her arm down the hall, leading them through the building.

The space was old but well-kept, boasting more of that Christmasy decor, though Charlie appreciated the way most of the staff stopped to welcome Gram. As the tour continued, she was greeted by a series of delicious smells, reminding her that she'd only managed to cram a piece of toast in her mouth while the movers were unloading their packing equipment. Her stomach growled as they came upon a large dining room.

"You can certainly opt to have your meals brought to your suite," Erin said. "But most residents enjoy coming downstairs. It gives them a chance to mingle."

Gram raised her eyebrows teasingly, and Charlie smirked. Knowing Gram, she'd be on husband number four by the new year. "Go easy on the mingling."

Gram fixed her hair in the reflection of the door. "Gotta play the game while I still can."

"Pretty sure by my age you'd already been divorced twice," Charlie pointed out. "I think you've used up your game."

Gram liked to tease, but for most of Charlie's life, at least as far back as she could remember, Gram had been happily single, living in her big house next to the Hudson River. Charlie and Tom had visited almost every summer as kids. She could still remember the sound of Gram's piano filling the living room as she and Tom gave midnight performances dressed in old costume jewelry. It was their favorite place in the world.

Had been their favorite place.

Her chest tightened uncomfortably at the memory. She shoved it away.

Next, Erin swept them past an outdoor patio that was currently covered in snow. Charlie could see the vision, imagining ivy and greenery climbing trellises in the summer. There were pots at every entrance, which Charlie assumed were usually filled with flowers. Now they were filled with tall birch sticks and evergreen garlands and tiny red berries. Someone had even made a miniature snowman on one of the tables. It looked back at Charlie with a crooked smile.

Erin moved them along to the elevator and up to a common room on the third floor. "We keep this room stocked with books and games. We've got some remarkable chess players in the community if you'd like me to introduce you."

Gram hummed thoughtfully.

Chess? In all honesty, Charlie had been uncertain when it was decided that Gram would be moving into a retirement home. *You're far too young*, she'd thought. *Far too adventurous.* But she also hadn't bothered to visit these past couple of years, and if she squinted, she could make out the limp in Gram's gait, the new laugh lines by her eyes and the snowy patches in her gray hair. Maybe chess wasn't so bad. With Charlie off avoiding things and her parents traveling more and Tom... Well, there were fewer people around. And Gram needed people.

"You'll certainly never be bored," Erin was saying. "Our activities director is excellent."

Charlie perked up at the mention of Julian.

"He's always organizing programming and trips to local

events. Speaking of," Erin said, approaching a door, "this is his office. We'll see if he's in and say hello."

She went to knock, but the door flew open at the same time, revealing a man. They both jumped, Erin giving a little yelp while the man scattered a stack of papers across the hall.

Charlie's gaze locked on him as recognition bloomed in her mind. The Julian on the website had been the one she'd remembered. Youthful, smile brimming with mischief. This Julian was…different. She swallowed hard, feeling a long dormant thrill surge through her, warming the tips of her ears and the back of her neck and the space beneath her breastbone. Well, he'd certainly grown up, hadn't he?

Yeah, grown up gorgeous, some unfamiliar voice inside her said.

"Julian! I'm so sorry," Erin said, scrambling after the papers on her hands and knees. "I didn't mean to startle you."

"Totally my fault for rushing. I was just on my way to a meeting," he said. "I should have been paying more attention."

His voice greeted her like a fuzzy recollection, and Charlie's heart flip-flopped strangely in her chest. It was deeper than it had been, rich in a way—like hot chocolate spiked with booze. A flush of heat rushed through her. It was a feeling she hadn't expected upon seeing him again.

She didn't want whatever it was.

It needed to go back into the stupid box and stay there.

Julian hunched over, collecting all the papers in reach.

"Julian Guerrero!" Gram said excitedly. "What a nice surprise."

Julian looked up for the first time, and Charlie registered the confusion that crossed his face as he clocked Gram and then her. His eyes lingered for an extended beat, widening, his brows arching.

Was he suddenly reliving the same memories Charlie was? That hot, sweaty summer fling. Days camped out at the river's edge in very little clothing. Late nights on Gram's porch. Staying up to odd hours of the morning just so they could kiss under the stars. God, she'd been such a romantic back then. Or at least young. Young and silly and unaware of how fast the world could rip things away from her.

"Sorry," he said, dragging out the word while he searched their faces. He got to his feet. "Do we know each oth—"

"Charlie?" she cut in before Gram could respond. Was he serious right now? How could he not remember? *"Charlene."*

He gave her a slow blink.

"We met the summer between third and fourth year of university... When I came to town to visit?"

He laughed politely. "University? God, that was a lifetime ago. I hardly remember what I had for dinner last night."

"You and me both," Gram said, and they chuckled.

"You really don't remember?" Charlie continued, a spark igniting inside her. It grew stronger with every passing second, the feeling like a burn that she wanted to wrench away from. She'd become so good at burying things since the moment she'd learned what grief was, shutting down her feelings and locking them away. That was how she'd kept herself from being overwhelmed by Gram's fall and losing the house she'd once loved and having to come back to this town. Her hands curled at her sides. So what the hell was all this warmth and confusion and affection flooding her? "You were working at Mackey's Diner. I came in with some friends, and you asked me out in front of the whole table?"

She remembered thinking he was rather bold. She could have easily turned him down in front of a crowd, but he'd been cute and funny. She'd fallen for him easily.

Julian gave a wry grin. "I'm sure I asked out a lot of girls like that."

"A lot of girls," Charlie said flatly. *Really?*

"Probably improved my odds."

"We spent an entire summer together," she noted.

"So clearly my plan worked. Someone took pity on me." Gram and Erin laughed at his self-deprecating joke, but Charlie's blood ran hotter, irritation fanning into exasperation. How had she ever been remotely attracted to this... jackass?

He caught her eye for the briefest moment, and she glared back, hard, stamping down the rush of sensation that sent her heartbeat spiraling. Screw her own traitorous pulse.

And screw Julian Guerrero!

"You know what," Julian said, rubbing his forehead, "I think I might have a vague recollection of that."

"Excuse me, *vague*?"

"Mm-hmm." His mouth twitched.

Had he just called her forgettable? Someone not worth remembering? Charlie didn't know if she should be offended or mortified by his answer. Maybe both? She couldn't believe she'd ever thought it might be good to reconnect, even just for Gram's sake. Tension coiled like an elastic band around her tongue. She didn't think she'd be able to get another word out even if she wanted to, so she simply narrowed her eyes, daring him to keep going.

"I guess there's no need for introductions then," Erin said, cutting through the awkwardness that filled the hallway like an avalanche. "That makes my job easy."

"Yes, we go way back," Gram agreed. "Though it's obviously been too long." She patted Julian's arm like he was a beloved friend and not an ex-fling from Charlie's past.

Charlie grimaced at the sight. Hell no! Gram needed to choose any other retirement home where the chances of running into Julian were zero.

"I had no idea you were working here," Gram continued. "It truly is a wonderful surprise."

Wonderful *isn't the word I'd use*, Charlie thought, considering he was acting like she was a clingy leech he'd accidentally picked up in the river that summer.

Julian might claim to only vaguely remember her, but she certainly remembered him. They'd both been about twenty-one. Her gaze dragged up and down his body before she could stop it, her eyes almost too eager to take him in. Julian hadn't been the first man she'd ever slept with, but from what she remembered, he was certainly the first man she'd really enjoyed sleeping with. A hot blush crept across her cheeks, and she scowled, frustrated with herself. She couldn't be blushing over this man.

"You're looking well," Julian finally said to Gram. It was the most neutral thing he could have possibly said.

"Fit as a fiddle," Gram replied. "Or so I told them when I applied here."

Julian chuckled. It was so frustratingly polite. His eyes flickered toward her, and Charlie blushed even harder. Her whole damn face was on fire, but she couldn't tell if it was from annoyance or that tiny wisp of attraction that flared like an ember in her chest.

So tiny it didn't even count.

Blah!

"Took a bit of a spill the other month and knocked the old hip, but I'm bouncing back," Gram continued.

"I wouldn't have known," Julian assured her.

Gram preened and fluffed her hair as Julian kneeled to collect the rest of his papers.

Charlie bent down to help, giving herself something to do other than stare at him. She picked up the first paper she could reach, surprised to find sheet music. She picked up another, studying the Italian words on the page. It was music she recognized. What was a retirement home doing with an aria from *Gianni Schicchi*?

"Here," she said, handing over the papers.

"Thanks." Julian stood. Up close, the height difference was obvious—and familiar—as he towered over her. She remembered spending a lot of time pressed up on her toes, entwining her arms around his neck to pull him close enough to reach his lips. He looked down at her through dark brown curls, his eyes so green Charlie couldn't stop staring. He was still boyishly handsome beneath the mask of age, and she remembered that his cheeks dimpled when he smiled. Those dimples had gotten her into a lot of trouble that summer.

"Are you planning on staging an opera?" she asked, distracting herself from those thoughts.

His face shifted through confusion to amusement. "What?"

"It's just that I'm surprised to find sheet music for an opera in a retirement home."

"Is that what this is?" He flipped through the pages in his hands, a smile curling up the side of his face, showing off those dimples she'd been so fond of. Charlie tore her eyes away. "Someone donated a bunch of sheet music the other day, and I finally got around to clearing it off my desk."

"It's *O Mio Babbino Caro*," she said. "Probably one of the most famous arias out there."

Julian's brows arched. "You could tell all that just from a few pages of notes?"

Charlie nodded. If he only knew how many months she'd spent in her dorm room perfecting the octave leaps only to realize she wasn't in fact meant for opera. After some soul searching and with Tom's guidance, she'd let go of a dream she thought she wanted and transitioned into Juilliard's Drama Division, finding her way back to musical theater, which she'd always loved, and eventually to a Broadway stage.

"Oh, right. Juilliard," he said, nodding. Charlie tilted her head slightly, studying him. Maybe he remembered her more than he was letting on.

"Does Glendale have a music program?" Gram asked, intrigued. Charlie knew that the most important thing packed on the moving truck today was Gram's piano. The same piano she'd taught Charlie and Tom to play on. She said it was coming with her whether there was room in her suite or not. "If you're getting sheet music as donations—"

"It's not a full-time program that we offer right now," Erin cut in.

"I am working on it, though," Julian said, grinning. "So don't count it out just yet."

"We never do," Erin said. "But we didn't mean to keep you. Just making the rounds while Doris gets moved in."

Julian tucked the sheet music under his arm. "Well, I look forward to catching up with you both."

That was a lie if Charlie had ever heard one, and she was completely fine with that. She didn't want to catch up with Julian Guerrero. She didn't want to pass him in the hall. She didn't want to make small talk. Frankly, she didn't want to have to think about him ever again.

He checked his watch and started down the hall, lifting his hand in farewell. "It was good bumping into you."

Another lie. Charlie watched him retreat until he disappeared into the stairwell. She only realized she was staring when Gram took her by the arm, steering her after Erin.

"Julian is great," Erin said as they passed the common room again. "The residents love him."

"How long has he been working here?" Gram asked.

"Oh, it has to be six…no, seven years almost? Longer than me at any rate. He really gets to know all the residents and their interests. I think that's why he's so good at arranging activities—"

"Lord, he's even more handsome than that summer you two dated," Gram said, leaning over to whisper.

"Gram," Charlie hissed, not in the mood to talk about how handsome Julian was. She was still too busy being annoyed. And even though Gram wasn't *wrong*, the last thing Charlie needed was Doris Bender getting involved in her love life. Because when Gram wanted something, there was nothing and no one that was going to stop her. But Charlie wasn't looking to get reacquainted with Julian, especially after that interaction. All she wanted to do was get Gram settled, get the house sorted and then get the hell out of here. "Don't start meddling."

"I never meddle."

"Oh please, it's your middle name."

Gram tutted. "You can't just turn down every good thing that comes your way. Especially when he's practically hand delivering you an opera."

Charlie scoffed. She had, in fact, made quite the habit of turning down anything that came her way lately, especially when it came to music. It just wasn't the same without Tom by her side. "It was one aria with a side of couldn't-be-bothered-to-remember-my-name."

"We all need a little memory jog every now and then," Gram said.

"I don't need anything jogged." She was perfectly fine letting this blast from the past come and go. The past only linked her to Tom and the grief she'd been outrunning, and she knew better than to open those floodgates again. Locking it all away, including her ex-flings, was the only way to keep herself from drowning.

Two

Julian

Julian practically tripped down the stairs in his haste to get away from Charlie. Away from the blood rushing in his ears and his pulse jumping at the base of his throat and his chest tightening as she'd glared at him with those familiar hazel eyes. Eyes that he swore used to take his breath away when he caught her staring at him from the steps of her grandmother's porch.

But that wasn't what was happening now. Nope.

He was out of breath because he was rushing, not because of Charlie. That would be ridiculous.

Julian made his way across the building, sheet music (to an aria, apparently) tucked under his arm. He hadn't planned on bringing the aria to his meeting, but now he was running behind, replaying that disastrous interaction on repeat like an unfinished melody. He wanted nothing more than to scrub it from his mind.

And the look on Charlie's face.

And…well…the look of Charlie's everything. Because he'd be lying if he said she wasn't still gorgeous as hell. But that was not how he was supposed to be looking at family members of residents. Or thinking about them. Or wondering…

God, what had it been? Eight years since he'd last seen her? Since they'd… Well, *hooked up* wasn't quite the right term, though there'd been a lot of that.

Julian shook his head, banishing those thoughts. What did any of it matter? It was only one summer. And clearly three months of flinging hadn't meant anything. Because at the end of it all, Charlie had set off for Juilliard, he'd returned to college, and eventually she'd stopped returning his calls and his texts… He sighed. None of that should have surprised him because he was a pro at being left behind. But it had surprised him. And the hurt that came from being left behind by the people you cared about stung somewhere too deep to forget.

He knuckled the space between his ribs as he dragged his thoughts back to the safety of work. To the job he was good at, a job he loved—the longest and most reliable thing in his life. Every day he counted himself lucky that he got to wake up in the morning and truly enjoy what he did.

"Afternoon, ladies," he said, nodding as he passed a group of elderly residents in matching pastel jumpsuits. The paint splotches told him they'd just come from the art room. "Looking snazzy as always."

They tittered at him the way they usually did. Being fortyish years younger than most of the residents relegated Julian to the status of endearing and adorable and even, on occasion, *cute*. Those kinds of comments never ceased to make him feel like a ten-year-old playing at adulthood.

Julian had only grown up with one grandparent. His grandma Sofia. She'd been the one to take him in while his parents dragged out their messy divorce, but she'd also battled dementia for a lot of his life. Moments like these reminded him of her: patiently enduring the overzealous compliments about his dimples and the nosy investigations into the status of his nonexistent love life.

Which brought his thoughts back to Charlie. Exactly where he didn't want them to be.

Seeing her again, his first reaction had been to panic, to pretend he didn't recognize her. He thought maybe she'd let it go. Then when she'd pressed, he'd doubled down and pretended like that summer had been a blip hardly worth remembering. *I'm sure I asked out a lot of girls...* God, what was wrong with him? He should have just said, "Hi, good to see you, too." Her grandmother had moved into Glendale. It wasn't like he was going to be able to avoid them.

Plus Charlie *had* to know he was lying. It must have been obvious in the way he'd looked at her. At the disbelief written into his features and the confusion that wavered in his voice. Because beneath that, somewhere deeper, a flicker of betrayal had ignited.

No! He didn't need those feelings surging through his blood right now. Even back then, he'd known better than to get close to people, but Charlie had slipped past his defenses, and in the end had ghosted him.

Whatever her reasons then, it didn't matter now. He'd learned his lesson, and he didn't need to dwell on thoughts of summer sun against his skin or the way she used to hum against his lips right before she kissed him.

Julian swallowed hard. Charlie had knocked him completely off his game, and he suddenly felt like anyone who looked close enough would be able to see the flush in his cheeks or hear the unsteady beat of his heart.

"Frank!" Julian said, greeting an older man who was working his way toward the dining room in his wheelchair.

Frank lifted his hand for Julian to shake like he did every day. "Short rib today," Frank said.

Frank was the keeper of all things. The time. Glendale's weekly menu. Room assignments. If you wanted to know what dinner would be three days from now, he could tell you. If you wanted to know where Mrs. Abernathy's suite was, he could point you in the right direction. He wasn't the greatest conversationalist, but if you wanted to know the score of game six in the 1987 World Series, he could also tell you that. Which was pretty remarkable as far as Julian was concerned.

"Want a ride to lunch?"

Frank lifted his hands into his lap, and Julian pushed him the rest of the way to the dining room. Frank pointed at a half-full table of residents, and Julian wheeled him over, nodding and lifting his hand in greeting as people acknowledged him.

"Julian?" Maggie Shiplake, busybody extraordinaire, called. Nothing happened in this place without Maggie knowing about it first. As a former high school secretary, she made it her business to be in everyone's business. "How's the outing to the community center looking for tomorrow?"

"It's a go as far as I'm concerned," Julian said. Maggie sat with Harriet Childs. He could never be sure what would come out of her mouth. Right now she was stuffing it with a raspberry Danish.

"Won't you join us for lunch?"

"You know I'd love to, Maggie," Julian said. "But I am most definitely late for a meeting." He clapped Frank on the shoulder in goodbye.

"They work you too hard," Maggie said.

"You tell Diane that the next time you see her," Julian said. "I also wouldn't mind a raise if you want to start dropping hints."

"We always do," Maggie called after him.

Julian hurried out of the dining room and down the hall, pausing outside an office that belonged to Diane Clark, Glendale's executive director. She was the constantly-frazzled-but-excellent-at-her-job type for which she blamed going gray in her midforties. Besides her actual children, Glendale was Diane's baby, as was evident by the very old, very worn sweater she donned every day with an image of Glendale on the back and her name embossed on the arm.

Diane was in charge of the facility's financial health, managing staff and making sure Glendale met local and federal regulations. Today Julian was most interested in the financial part.

He knocked on the partially open door and waited to be invited in before pushing the door open the rest of the way. "Good afternoon, my favorite person ever."

Diane gave a great sigh, looking for her phone in a landslide of paperwork. "Is it already afternoon? I swear I just checked, and it was nine." She found her phone, glanced at it, then dropped it back on her desk. Looking up at Julian, her nose wrinkled. "What do you want? I don't have any money to give you."

Originally from Long Island, Diane's accent jumped out when she was exasperated. Today would probably be one of those days. Julian dropped the stack of sheet music he'd been carrying onto her desk.

Diane rolled her eyes and unwrapped a candy cane from a bowl on her desk. She crunched on the end before offering him one.

Julian declined. "Isn't it a little early for those?"

"Never." She motioned with her chin. "What's all this? More paperwork?"

"It's an opera."

"Is this your new strategy? Bury me in sheet music until you get your way?" Diane paused for a second, distracted by something on her computer screen. She started typing furiously. "If you're trying to butter me up, start bringing me coffee. Black. Like the void I want to shove my desk into."

Julian sat down on the edge of said desk. "I'm a little concerned about your caffeine intake."

"I think it's replaced the blood in my veins."

"That's the worrying part."

"Too late to go back now." She stopped typing and leaned back in her chair, regarding him over the rim of her glasses. "Now, what can I do for you? And remember you only get three asks a year. I'm like a genie. Use up all your wishes, and I'm going to stop taking your meetings."

Julian picked absently at the edge of the folder he was sitting on. "I *would* actually like some money—"

Diane flopped her arms dramatically, pretending to melt into her chair. "Julian, come on!"

"Hang on a second," Julian said before she could fully combust.

"You're trying to kill me."

"Just...look." He shoved the sheet music in her direction. "People are always donating stuff like this for the music program. Books of music, old CDs, radios. Which is so great."

"Yes?"

"But I can't run a music program with stuff. I need people. Or at least *a* person. One singular person with a little bit of knowledge on how to turn all this stuff into productive and engaging classes."

Diane clicked her tongue. "If you want a budget for music, you'll have to pull it from somewhere else. From one of your more popular programs. Art maybe?"

"Music *was* a popular program before the budget was cut." Julian had been fighting this battle for years now. There was never quite enough to go around, and like Diane, he did a lot of balancing as the activities director.

"We had the budget because of a grant from the government. You want it back, write me another proposal."

"I write you one every year! And you apply for the same grants. And nine times out of ten, it's a no. I can't wait around for some stuffy business person crunching numbers in a federal office to get their act together."

"Then cut down on travel costs."

"That travel lets the residents leave this place every now and then. It'll be like holding them hostage if I cut into it. You know how they like their day trips to the community center. Do you want a mutiny on your hands?"

Diane huffed, the sound almost a laugh. "Some of them are surprisingly spry for their age. Must be that yoga class you keep taking them to."

"Diane, come on—"

"Julian, you know I think you do a great job with what you have. But you also know better than anyone that there isn't enough money to hire someone else just to manage a music program."

Julian shook his head, hating how familiar this conversation was starting to sound.

"Look, I know this is important to you."

"Not just to me," he said. "It's important to this whole place." Sure, he'd seen firsthand the way his grandmother used to light up to the right music. She may have forgotten names and dates and places, but music stirred something in her that even the dementia couldn't touch.

When she'd looked at him in those moments, she was no longer lost to the disease. She was once again the same woman who'd made Julian feel safe after his father had stopped calling and who'd given him the space to mourn when his mother was too busy vacationing to remember she'd promised to be at his basketball game. Despite how hard Julian had fought for those relationships, they'd slipped through his fingers. And music was the one thing that kept his grandmother from completely slipping away from him while she was still alive.

"You know I focused my studies on aging in postgrad."

"I know," Diane said. "And I know the literature. Music reduces anxiety and improves sleep and memory—"

"And slows cognitive decline," Julian said. "It also builds a greater sense of community, making it easier to transition into life here at Glendale."

"I know," Diane said again. Softer this time.

"So why are we still having this conversation?"

Diane rubbed her tired eyes. "I want to help make it happen. I just can't do it this year. I'm squeezing everything I can out of the budget, and what I really need most are some more nurses."

Julian sighed. Shrugged. "I get it. Just figured I'd make my yearly plea so you don't forget about me if some anonymous donor should come knocking." He stood, accepting defeat. "Maybe I'll put out a volunteer request again. Who knows, someone might bite this year."

"Never change, Julian."

He shot Diane a resigned smile before making his way back down the hall. He skipped the stairs and headed straight for the elevator, already thinking up a sign that might implore anyone in the community with an ounce of musical talent to volunteer their time.

"Hold it!" he called as the elevator door started to slide shut.

A hand shot out, grabbing the door as he jogged to close the distance. When the door opened again, a familiar face looked back at him. *Charlie.* And Doris.

Oh, for crying out loud! Bumping into them once was bad enough but twice? That was some kind of punishment. Julian considered making an excuse about forgetting something, but then he caught sight of those hazel eyes. As if a string of Christmas lights had hooked him around the chest, he felt himself being dragged into the elevator against his will.

Dammit.

"Thanks," he said, charging straight through the awkwardness as the door closed, boxing them all in. "For holding the door. The residents like to make me walk up the stairs under the pretense they're keeping me young and fit. I secretly think they just like to torture me."

"No problem," Charlie said. "Gram still gets mad at me when I don't wear socks in the house."

"I never wore socks, and now I have arthritis," Doris said. "Coincidence?"

"Yes," Charlie said at the same time as Julian said, "Probably."

Doris clicked her tongue and huffed dramatically. "Well, excuse me for trying to save you years of pain and suffering."

Julian and Charlie laughed, the sound triggering a spark of awareness. It felt good to laugh with her, and for a ridiculous beat Julian wanted to catch her hand, to see if their fingers still felt right intertwined.

No, no, no! He couldn't want that. He couldn't want her. Because he already knew what it was like to be left by her.

The moment passed, and Julian tucked himself into the corner of the elevator before his mind could drag up other nonsense. Like her little happy wiggle when she ordered food she particularly liked or the way she stopped to pet every cute dog on the sidewalk.

Charlie took a step back, too, settling against the opposite wall next to her grandmother, avoiding his eye. He tried not to stare, but it was like opening an old photo album and being submerged in memory. She looked the same but also different. Her hair was shorter and blonder, cut above her shoulders, which suited her. And there were new curves in places that he remembered running his hands over. Those suited her, too. She'd very obviously blossomed in their time apart, and though the years had been kind to her, there was something else that had changed. There was something different, perhaps more reserved about her, as if part of her had been hidden away for safekeeping.

"How was the rest of the tour?" he asked before he could lose himself to that thought.

"Excellent," Doris said. "Charlie's had nothing but good things to say about the place."

Charlie caught his eye then, almost reluctantly, but her lips turned up at the corners. She was really quite pretty when she did that, her eyes seeming to twinkle, though maybe that was just the strange overhead lights in the elevator and his imagination. Whose eyes actually twinkled? *Get a grip*.

"Glendale does have a reputation as the place where people have nothing but good things to say," he said.

"I mean, the complimentary butterscotch candies in the lobby alone are worth five stars," Charlie said.

"Don't forget peach cobbler Wednesdays," Julian added. "A cannot-miss experience."

"And this bopping elevator music."

Julian nodded. "Have you seen the matching walking club tracksuits yet? Not even just cotton. We sprang for the poly-cotton blend."

"What?" Charlie gasped. "No. And here I thought the postcards for sale in the art room were really tipping you over the edge."

"Hey, those are hand drawn by the residents themselves," Julian pointed out. "And every purchase goes straight back into the bingo prize fund."

"Oh, well, I'll have to buy one now," Charlie said, nudging Doris. "Wouldn't want the bingo prize to be lacking."

"It's caused riots in the past," Julian said.

Charlie smirked. "Can't have that."

"You know, one day you two will understand how

riveting a game of bingo can be," Doris cut in. "I could do without the world's slowest elevator, however. I'll be seventy-five by the time we get to the fourth floor."

Charlie burst into laughter, the sound filling the tiny box like chimes, melodic in a way that made him want to hear it again.

Julian silently cursed that desire the second he had it. This was the woman who'd ghosted him. Who hadn't cared enough to even tell him that she'd moved on. She could take her smile and her laugh and her twinkly eyes and shove them—

"And how did your meeting go?" Doris asked him.

"Oh." Julian sobered, returning to thoughts of budgets and grants. "Not as well as I'd hoped. But I should have known that."

"Did it have anything to do with that aria you had?" Charlie asked curiously, catching her lip between her teeth in a way that was far too distracting for this small of a space.

Julian tugged on the collar of his shirt. "I was actually showing our executive director some of the donations we've received recently," he said. "Trying to butter her up to get funding for a music director. Unfortunately it's not in the budget this year. Or any year, judging by the way things are going." He sighed, trying not to let the defeat overwhelm him. "But that's life. Just another hill to climb. I guess I'll try going down the volunteer route again."

"I'm sure someone will jump at the chance to volunteer," Doris said.

"Problem is I think I've already squeezed all I can out of the community. At least anyone that can carry a tune."

"Oh, well, if carrying a tune is your only prerequisite, Charlie can do it," Doris piped up.

Charlie opened her mouth, looking from him to her grandmother, slightly horrified. "Um…no. I'm very busy."

"You'd do a favor for an old…friend."

"Gram—"

"Wouldn't you?"

Charlie scowled at her.

For a moment Julian thought Doris had been about to say *old flame*, and he was going to throw himself out the elevator door the second it stopped. But then he took a second to actually consider Doris's suggestion.

Charlie was a Juilliard grad. She was far more qualified to be hosting a music class than he was. If she'd volunteer, he could relaunch the program temporarily.

Then again, did he even want her to volunteer? That would mean spending time with the person who stomped on his heart all those years ago with zero regard.

He'd been hoping to avoid her and Doris, if only to hide from all the damn memories that had resurfaced at the mere sight of her, but how could he even consider throwing away an opportunity like this for his residents? If Charlie was willing to do this, then he had to put his past feelings aside. He *would*. "Do you think you'd have the time?"

Her eyes cut toward him, the heat of her stare making the space between them swelter, but he knew he couldn't look away. He couldn't give into the strangling tension that stretched between them without giving himself away, without revealing that he was remembering everything, so he locked in and held her gaze.

"She's got nothing but time," Doris said. "Isn't that right?"

"I have your entire house to get sorted," Charlie muttered. "Which is going to take loads of time."

"I don't need loads of time," Julian said. He lifted his hand, fingers measuring out a pinch. "Just a little of it."

Charlie's nostrils flared. She'd always been a little feisty, and he'd liked that spark.

"Toss some stuff in storage and sell the rest. C'mon." Doris bumped her shoulder. "You're going to need something to keep you occupied while you wait for things to sell and for your parents to get back for Christmas."

"I don't know if I was planning on hanging around until Mom and Dad got back." Charlie glared at her grandmother, and they seemed to be having a sort of silent conversation. Julian would have looked away, but where else was there to look? "All right," Charlie conceded after a moment. "Fine."

Doris nodded approvingly.

"Really?" Julian said. It wasn't the most enthusiastic yes, but it was still a yes. "I wouldn't want to put you out or anything."

"She'd love to," Doris insisted.

"Apparently I would love to," Charlie said. She gave him a thin smile.

"Okay, great." He wasn't a fool. This was definitely the last thing either of them wanted. But if he had learned anything in this job, it was to take people up on their offers, no matter how sincere they were. It was easy to ignore the elderly and to push their needs aside. So if he wanted to bring music back to Glendale, then he needed all the help he could get. Even if that came in the form of a reluctant ex who probably wished she'd let the elevator door slam in his face.

The elevator stopped, and the door opened. Julian walked out, turning to them. "I've gotta run, but find me tomorrow," he said to Charlie, "and I'll show you the music room."

"I can't wait," she muttered, her tone heavily sarcastic. The door closed as her eyes narrowed, cutting toward her grandmother.

Three

Charlie

"I can't believe I let you volunteer me for this," Charlie said, meeting her grandmother in the lobby of Glendale.

Gram caught her in her arms and pecked her on the cheek. "Good afternoon to you, too."

Charlie grumbled in the back of her throat. Was it a good afternoon? She'd hardly made a dent packing up Gram's living room, and she still had both china hutches to tackle. On top of that, now she had to…

In all honesty, she wasn't entirely clear on what Gram had signed her up for. What exactly did the role of volunteer music director consist of? Was she teaching a class? Did Julian expect her to don a black hat and tap heels and do a little dance across a stage? She probably should have inquired about the expectations, but it had all happened so fast yesterday, and she'd still been annoyed with him, never mind with Gram's penchant for getting her roped into things. Before she knew it, the elevator doors had closed on Julian's annoyingly cheerful smile.

It was a dangerous kind of smile—buoyant and maybe even a little bit cheeky. It was that smile that had convinced her to go on a date with him in the first place all those years ago.

Gah! She couldn't believe he was using it on her again like she was young and naive enough to fall for it.

"You look nice," Gram was saying as she looped her arm through Charlie's, guiding her through the lobby.

"I was forced to put on makeup to hide the bags under my eyes."

"Sure you didn't dress to impress a certain someone?"

"I will leave right now," Charlie warned, even as heat spiraled through her. Why the hell would she be trying to impress Julian? He'd made it clear that he hardly remembered their time together, so that was where she was going to leave everything. Forgotten in the past, where it didn't have any way to hurt her now.

Gram's lips quirked, the lines by the corners of her mouth deepening. "Oh, come on. Being here isn't that bad. And you didn't really think I was just going to let you dump me and run off, did you?"

Charlie scoffed. "Gram, I came all the way out here to help you move in. It's not like I'm abandoning you."

Gram stopped walking, reaching out to tuck a lock of Charlie's hair behind her ear. "Exactly. It'll do us some good to hang out. It keeps me young and all that."

"I think that's the first time I've ever heard you refer to yourself as old." If anything, Gram was the one keeping Charlie young.

"My mind is young, these bones, not so much. But

they've still got some life in them." Gram squeezed Charlie's arm gently. "Besides, you told me you had no immediate plans. So if not here, where else would you be running off to?"

Far away from Elm Springs and Tom's memory and reminders that Gram was getting older and all these damn feelings. She'd already realized it was harder to lock them away here, especially with Christmas right around the corner. Holidays had always been cheerful and festive, with the family packed in at Gram's house. But without Tom around to share in those holidays...

She needed to be gone before then. Which was why she needed to be spending her time sorting the house and helping Gram get settled instead of getting sidetracked by Julian's music situation.

"Anyway, I think it'll be good for you." Gram put her arm around Charlie's shoulders, pulling her close. "This might be an opportunity to get in touch with yourself again."

Oh boy, Charlie knew where this was headed. Gram didn't mean get in touch with herself, she meant get in touch with *music*.

"It's just a fun, no-strings-attached, little volunteer gig."

"I'm well aware of what this is, and I'm fine, Gram." The last thing Charlie needed was a pity project at a retirement home.

"If you were fine, you'd have taken that contract in New York City you told me about. That little ensemble role."

"It wasn't the right fit. I also told you that."

"And what of the numerous auditions you've been offered over the last couple of years?"

Charlie's throat felt like it was closing up. She did not

want to talk about this. "None of them were the right fit," she managed to say.

"Charlie—"

"Gram, don't—"

"It was two years ago," Gram continued, matter-of-fact. "We all miss Tom." She gestured around at the building. "But life goes on. It has to. And you have to move with it, or you'll get swept away."

Funny, that was the same thing the therapist had told Charlie, back when she'd still been going to therapy. There was a brief period of time after Tom's passing when Charlie thought therapy might make sense of the gaping hole in her chest. It hadn't, so she stopped going. "Life isn't sweeping me away. I'm just reevaluating things."

"You loved being onstage," Gram pointed out.

And yet she hadn't been on a stage since.

"I think if you'd just call Alicia, she could get you back out there performing again, and you could—"

"Gram, please," Charlie said, a little exasperated. Performing onstage, singing for a crowd... Tom had been by her side for most of her career, guiding her, steering her. He'd been a talented orchestra director, and he'd taken her along for the ride, inviting her to perform on stage with him. She caught her lip between her teeth as emotion filled her chest to the point of bursting. Tom had always been so proud of her. He'd called her his little sister with the soaring vocals. "Growing up with Charlie was a great time, until I realized she could yell at me in three different octaves," he used to joke with the audience. She didn't know how to be *Charlie Ward, Juilliard-trained soprano, concert artist, sister* without him.

"It's not committing to anything. It's just…opening the door."

"I don't want to talk about that right now. I'm tired. The bed in your guest room is atrocious." She avoided the room they'd always occupied as kids, the one that had belonged to Tom while he… Her thoughts trailed off. She hadn't even been able to bring herself to walk up those stairs to the second floor yet. "And now I've apparently volunteered to host a geriatric music class."

Gram made a tutting sound. "One, the mattress in the guest room is practically brand-new. And two, I am one of those geriatrics you're talking about, so watch it."

Charlie groaned. "You're not staying for the class, are you?"

"Of course I am." Gram looked perplexed that she would suggest otherwise. "I've been inviting people, too."

"Inviting who? You've just moved in. You don't even know anyone yet."

"Listen, if you think I'm going to pass up a chance to hear my granddaughter sing, you are sorely mistaken."

"Who said I was singing?" Charlie winced. It was like a giant fist had gripped her insides, twisting and strangling.

Gram laughed. "What else would you be doing?"

"I don't know. I thought there might be some of those little tambourines."

"These aren't toddlers, Charlie. You're going to have to entertain." Gram did some jazz hands. "Give 'em the old razzle dazzle as they say. But not too much. We're all on heart medication and blood thinners now."

Charlie shook her head at Gram's little display as they paused outside a door at the end of the first floor hallway.

"I have it on good authority that this is where the magic happens," Gram said, leading Charlie into a windowless room.

"Whose authority?" Charlie asked as she looked around.

There were a few hard-backed chairs scattered around the space, an old music theory textbook on the floor and a derelict-looking piano next to the wall.

Growing up, when Charlie had been nervous before a big performance, Tom had always told her to close her eyes and imagine a place where the music sang to her. This place was definitely not singing.

She spotted an old mic stand, and her footsteps echoed as she crossed the room. "The acoustics might not be terrible," she admitted.

"I see you've found your way to our music room!"

Charlie turned to find Julian standing in the doorway, arms crossed, the sleeves of his shirt shoved up to reveal a pair of very toned forearms. She'd always been a sucker for muscled arms. Charlie fought off a flush, averting her eyes.

"Sorry," Julian went on, "I would have met you, but I got sidetracked looking for a driver to take the bus to the community center."

"And did you find one?" Gram asked.

"Well, Bert Crenshaw offered, but he hasn't had a license for a good ten years now, so I thought I'd better look elsewhere before taking him up on his offer."

"Good choice," Charlie said, trying to think about something other than Julian's arms.

"I mean, he used to drive school buses," Julian said.

"So, if you're in a real pinch—"

"—he could make do."

Charlie inclined her head. "Might send you all to the hospital."

"And get me fired," he joked.

"But at least you've got options."

"Right." Julian trailed off awkwardly. Abruptly.

Which is perfectly fine! Charlie told herself, swallowing a bead of frustration. Because she didn't want to playfully spar with him. This was strictly business.

Julian cleared his throat and threw his arms out. "What do you think?"

Charlie took a beat, trying to figure out what to say about the state of the room.

Julian held his hands up, like he was about to beg her not to run out the door. "Okay, I know what you're thinking."

Charlie smirked. "I highly doubt that."

"It's a little rough," Julian admitted. He ran his hand through his hair, displacing the curls.

She clocked the muscles in his forearms again, eyes trailing higher, noting the way his biceps flexed beneath his shirt. Yesterday she'd remembered him as mischievous and boyish. But this Julian carried himself with purpose and confidence and experience. Charlie found herself a little overwhelmed by the desire to simply stare at him and admit that there wasn't anything boyish about him anymore. She needed to stop looking at him.

"The acoustics in the room are excellent," he was saying as she forced herself to stop ogling him. "Or so I've been told."

"Well, I'll let you two talk logistics," Gram said, making her way to the door.

Charlie had almost forgotten she was there. "And where are you going?" she asked, wanting Gram to hang around if only to be a buffer between her and the unwanted sensations and feelings and memories Julian was awakening.

"To round up more participants. If we're gonna get a show, then we should really make an afternoon of it."

"Gram," Charlie warned. She caught her grandmother's arm as she passed. "Don't go making this into something." She lowered her voice. "This isn't a performance."

"Charlie, I've never known you to be anything other than a performer, whether it was two people in the crowd or two hundred," Gram said quietly. She kissed Charlie's cheek and disappeared.

Julian watched her go. "She really doesn't take no for an answer, huh?"

"It's both a blessing and a curse," Charlie said. "And also how Gram said she ended up married three times."

Julian laughed.

But as far as performing was concerned, Gram wasn't exactly wrong. After years of living room recitals, school performances and community theater productions, Charlie had followed that performance bug straight to Juilliard. Many Broadway performances and orchestra concerts later, and she was here, in this tiny windowless room. Wouldn't Tom get a kick out of seeing her now?

"So," Julian said. "You all good here?"

No? "Is there some sort of programming I need to stick to, or am I sort of winging it?"

"Just keep the old folks entertained. How you choose to do that is up to you. We've got some speakers if you want to connect to Spotify." Julian passed between her and a chair, putting his hand on her back as he did to stop himself from jostling her.

At the touch, Charlie felt something stir in her that she hadn't felt in a very long time, and her pulse raced. She moved out of the way, putting some distance between them, stuffing the feeling somewhere to be forgotten.

Julian bent to collect the book on music theory she'd noticed. He dusted it off on his jeans before handing it to her. "You can get technical if you want." He gestured across the room. "The piano also works if you'd rather tickle the ivories."

"You're not gonna break out a box of percussion instruments from the closet?" Charlie said, deadpan. She put the book down on a chair.

"Fresh out of those," Julian said, lips pursed. "Though I have recently come into some quality sheet music for a certain opera if you're interested in casting among our residents."

"I think I'll start with something a little more manageable." Her options weren't great. Unless she was going to connect to Spotify, which felt rather lazy, she supposed Gram was right. She would have to sing a little if she meant to actually entertain for the next hour. "I'll save the opera for the advanced class."

"Too bad," Julian teased, catching her eye and giving her a dimpled grin. "I was looking forward to hearing that. I think we could really sell this place out. Charge a fortune at the door. Get maintenance to help with props. The admin team can do costumes."

"Put it on your calendar then," Charlie said. "The first entirely geriatric production of *Gianni Schicchi*, coming to a retirement home near you."

Julian laughed, the sound bouncing between them, and Charlie fought the urge to hear it again. She didn't want to laugh with him like she used to. Like they were lying out on a blanket at the river's edge and he'd just whispered some terrible joke. She didn't want to feel like no time had passed, because years had come and gone, and everything had changed. "I really do appreciate you taking the time to do this."

"Do you?" she said, skeptical.

"Of course. I realize Doris sort of put you up to it."

Charlie crossed her arms. Standing in this room, with a piano to their left, it felt like they were supposed to break into some sort of awkward duet. "It's not like you politely declined her offer."

"Is that what you were expecting?"

"I did say I was busy dealing with Gram's house."

"She didn't seem that concerned about it."

A surge of irritation flickered at the base of Charlie's spine. God, she was going to call Alicia just to tell her how annoying he was.

"And she did seem to think you could make time for an old…friend."

"I'm not exactly sure that's what I would call us," Charlie said.

"No?"

"You tend to remember your friends, don't you?"

Silence stretched between them. Thick, uncomfortable silence. Charlie was going to choke on it. She had half a mind to bail on this whole volunteer gig. The only thing holding her to her promise was the fact that Gram had already started rounding up other residents to attend, and she didn't want to embarrass her. Or disappoint her.

"I should see if the piano is in tune," she murmured.

"Right." Julian stepped aside, but before she could reach the piano he said, "Ah, here we go!" Charlie turned as he waved a group of peppery-haired residents into the room.

"Welcome, welcome! Everyone please take a seat. I am so excited to formally introduce you to our newest music director, Charlie..." He hesitated.

"Ward," she supplied with a frown. Honestly! Had he forgotten that, too?

"Just making sure it hadn't changed in the last eight years," he said under his breath.

What? Did he think she was married? Almost as if he'd read her mind, his eyes flicked down to her left hand, then back up.

"Charlie Ward," he continued. "I'm sure some of you have already met Doris. Charlie is Doris's granddaughter, and she has graciously offered to volunteer her time with us today."

Charlie didn't know about *graciously*, but she plastered a smile on her face anyway. It was a beaming smile, all teeth—the kind that used to light up stages. The show must go on.

But how could it? The fact that she was even considering performing made her smile fall away. The last time she did this was with Tom and the Austin Symphony Orchestra. That was close to three years ago now. Her stomach soured at the thought.

There was solitary *whoop* that might have come from Gram and a general murmur of interest as the residents found their seats.

Julian turned to her. "Well, that's it for me. You're on."

"Wait!" She grabbed his hand, her pulse kicking up in her throat as his fingers twisted around hers briefly. It felt...good. How tightly he held her. And that was all wrong. She shook her head, eyebrows converging in the center of her forehead. Because with the good came the bad. She didn't get one without the other. "I don't... I'm not sure I can do this."

He chuckled. "Stage fright?"

Charlie opened her mouth to say something, but her heart was beating so uncomfortably fast she thought she might be sick, so she snapped it closed. She couldn't perform for these people. Not the way Gram wanted. Not without Tom. It wouldn't be right. Guilt tightened like a vice around her rib cage, and she struggled for her next breath.

"Hey," Julian said, placing both hands on her shoulders. He rubbed them up and down, leaving a trail of goose bumps in their wake. "Are you okay?"

"I—" She couldn't find the words to explain about losing Tom or about not performing since he'd passed. She'd hardly done much singing at all, avoiding the business, turning down jobs. She'd taught a bit of piano here and there to make ends meet, but it wasn't the same. This felt like she was about to stomp on Tom's memory. How did she wrap all that up into words that would make sense to Julian?

His thumbs turned circles against her arms, and Charlie felt heat creep up her neck. It was like reliving her youth, hands sliding over her, her body reacting to the touch. She wanted to lean into the comfort. *No, no, no!* She needed to lock the feelings back up in that box, bolt it closed and toss it into the deepest part of the ocean.

"No one here has any big expectations of you," Julian said, leaning close enough that he could look her in the eye. His whispered words caressed her cheek. "You know what I was thinking about?"

"What?" Her gaze followed his as he dropped his hands.

"The way you used to talk to people. Anyone. Everyone. You could start up a conversation with a stranger at the store or someone walking past your grandmother's house while we sat on the porch."

"You remember that?"

He nodded. "You have a way of engaging with people. Of making them feel comfortable and welcomed into any space. I always marveled at how you did that. And I figured you couldn't possibly have a shy bone in your body."

Listening to him talk made her breath catch, the fondness threatening to give her whiplash. One second he acted like he barely knew her, like he *wished* he didn't know her, and the next he was recounting details of that summer. She didn't understand him. Confusion bled through her, quickly replaced by frustration which ate away at her panic, burning it from her veins.

"Look, if you really don't think you—"

"No," Charlie said, stepping away. "It's fine."

"You're sure?"

She looked at him, trying to peer past his concerned exterior to figure out which Julian Guerrero stood before her: the boy who'd always made her feel seen or the man who seemed to prefer to forget her. She couldn't tell, so she gritted her teeth and nodded. "I'm sure."

"You're gonna do great," Julian said, backing away. "I've gotta go track down a bus driver. But if you have any issues, you know where my office is."

"Sure." He had a job to do, and so did she. Because she'd agreed to this.

Charlie turned to face the roomful of elderly residents. Well, roomful might be too optimistic. There were about eleven of them, one of which included her grandmother.

In truth, the population wasn't that different from the crowds that used to turn up at the concerts she and Tom performed. When you sang a lot of arias and classics from the Golden Age of theater, most of the audience tended to be over sixty-five.

She took a deep, steadying breath. *Focus*. The voice was like a muscle. All she had to do was get those first notes out, and then time and hours of practice would hopefully take over and do the rest.

"Well," Charlie said, addressing her little crowd as she tried to ignore the way her hands were shaking. "I guess it's just us today. I am very happy to be here with you. Unfortunately, I came upon this role somewhat unexpectedly." She glanced at Gram across the room, raising a brow, earning herself a few chuckles. "So I don't have anything grand planned for our first class together. Instead, I thought I might sing a little for you."

Charlie crossed to the piano and hit middle C. Her entire body reacted to the note that rang out. It felt a little like crawling out of her skin. "That's very out of tune," she said, and the group laughed again. "A capella it is."

She grabbed the old mic stand and dragged it back to the center of the room just to give her hands something familiar to hold, something to ground her.

"Okay," she said, easing herself into performance mode. "This first number is one some of you might recognize. It's from a little musical that came on the scene in 1964. *My Fair Lady*."

There were smiles of appreciation and laughter as she glanced at the group.

"Kidding. It's not that little. I'm sure most of us have

seen this show. If not onstage, then perhaps the movie with the ever-charming Audrey Hepburn as Eliza Doolittle."

"Charlie and her brother spent a good many summers twirling around my living room to that movie," Gram said to the group.

"We certainly did," Charlie said quietly, anxiously, feeling like she might be sick. *The show must go on.* "Ladies and gentlemen." She forced a smile, the words almost catching in her throat. "This is 'I Could Have Danced All Night.'"

Four

Charlie

Charlie never wanted to see another piece of dishware ever again.

Gram had squirreled away dishes in every room of the old Victorian, and only now that Charlie was trying to organize the house did she realize just how extensive the collection really was. There were flower-patterned dinnerware sets and tea sets and crystal wineglasses and champagne flutes and…too much. It was just too much crap for one person.

Charlie carried an empty box through the foyer, cutting into the dining room and groaned at the massive china hutch. There were sets upon sets of dessert plates and soup bowls and silver ladles and salt and pepper shakers shaped as random animals winking at her from behind the glass. Suddenly the freshly prepped cardboard box in her hand felt entirely inadequate.

She'd already spent the early morning avoiding the second floor by tackling Gram's bookshelves.

Gram had put sticky notes on everything, noting which books had been slated for donation and which were to be kept in the family. Charlie had recognized an adventure series she and Tom had been obsessed with when they were teens. She remembered lining up in town for the midnight summer release of the last book. Gram had indulged them both with a copy, mostly to stop them from fighting over who would get to read it first.

The memory had come out of nowhere, slipping past her defenses, as clear as the day it happened. Remembering that night had almost winded her, and Charlie had spent an hour on the floor in front of the bookshelf, flipping through the yellowing pages, blinking away the weight behind her eyes. She wouldn't cry. Not in this house. If she did, she might never stop.

Her phone buzzed, and she slipped it out of her pocket to find a text from Alicia. **You around?**

Yes, she replied.

Wanted to make sure you hadn't gotten trapped under a piece of furniture.

I haven't even ventured into the basement yet, so who knows what horrors might befall me there.

Oh God, came the reply followed by a crying laughing emoji.

Charlie smiled briefly at the message. Somehow Alicia always knew when she was in need of company or a pick-me-up or just the sound of someone else's voice. Sure, she may have been Charlie's agent, but she was her friend first—her best friend—and since Tom's passing, Alicia had not once failed to pick up her phone.

Some people would say that it was a bad idea to mix business with pleasure, but Charlie had never been more grateful to have Alicia in her corner. A person who cared not only about her career but about her as a person. Another agent might have gotten fed up with her indecisiveness after Tom's death and dropped her, but Alicia had promised to be there for Charlie when she was ready to perform again. Until then, she was simply her friend.

Honestly, I don't think I realized just how long sorting through this house would take.

Well, you're not in any rush, right?

Besides needing to get the hell out of here before Elm Springs could leave her a mess that no one was equipped to deal with, least of all her? Yeah, sure. No rush. But something inside Charlie was racing against some unseen hourglass. The longer she was here, the more the past would creep in. She could already feel it pressing on her— the house, the town, Julian— and she knew she needed to escape before the threads holding her closed snapped.

The desire to flee from these feelings had been her one and only goal these past two years, and despite wanting to make sure Gram was settled at Glendale, that cloying thought beat like a drum at the back of her head.

Charlie wandered into the living room and took a beat to absorb it. The walls were a light pink, the chunky carpet patterned with roses. In one corner of the room stood

Gram's record player and her collection of vinyl. In the other, by the bay window, was the empty space that used to house Gram's piano. This room had been Charlie's first stage. She'd spent countless hours bouncing on the sofa cushions next to Tom, an empty water bottle in hand, as they belted ballads at the tops of their lungs.

But this place was no longer a stage.

Soon it wouldn't belong to them at all.

Charlie made her way across the room to a small glass cabinet. Inside were commemorative plates celebrating anniversaries to husbands Charlie never knew. In some ways, Gram's house had always felt like a museum. A trove of treasures she got to pick through every summer. Now, with Tom's face immortalized in pictures on the walls—gap-toothed smiles looking back at her, cheeks sun-kissed and freckled from hours spent down by the river—it was starting to feel like a tomb.

Charlie placed the cardboard box on the floor as she hunted down the Bubble Wrap she'd bought earlier in the week. The last thing she needed was for her mother to sift through the boxes to find everything broken.

She found the Bubble Wrap in the front hall, where she'd dropped her keys and her purse upon returning from Glendale yesterday.

There were pictures there, too, in thin gold frames, set out on the entryway table. They were displayed to visitors like an offering—her, Mom, Dad and Tom at Christmas. Her and Tom as kids, Gram's feather boas wrapped around their necks, pearl necklaces strung around their wrists like bracelets. Her and Tom, basically babies, in a wagon, so young and blond they'd almost looked like twins. Her and Tom with Gram on her birthday, fighting over who would blow out the candles. Her and Tom in their respective caps and gowns. It seemed like every moment of their lives had been captured on this table.

Except the one that changed everything.

The photos stopped abruptly, each frame like a headstone dedicated to what had come and gone. Charlie had the sudden urge to flip them all face down. To tear the photos from the walls. *Soon enough*, she thought, carrying the Bubble Wrap back down the hall.

She loved this house. But she also hated it now, too.

Her phone buzzed as she reached the living room, this time with a call. Charlie picked up, and Alicia's voice poured through.

"You never answered my question," she said without even a hello.

Something in Charlie unraveled at the sound, the ache inside her lessening. Alicia had a short, choppy way of speaking, her words always tumbling from her mouth faster than Charlie could keep up with them. And her laugh! Her laugh could be heard in the next building, so loud and infectious and filled with joy. Alicia was the type of person who could make your day better just by the sheer force of her presence.

"Which question?"

"I said you're not in any rush, and you ignored me."

"I wasn't ignoring you," Charlie said.

"How are things going at the retirement home?" Alicia asked.

Awful, horrible, terrible. Charlie didn't even know where to begin. She'd walked right into an unexpectedly frigid winter storm named Julian who had the audacity to say he hardly remembered her. And then—*and then*—

ask her to give up her already limited time to some non-existent music program. Her pulse sped up just thinking about the smug satisfaction in his eyes as Gram roped her into the job.

Charlie flopped down on the nearest sofa, a hand pressed to her forehead as she stared at the ceiling and sighed.

Alicia made a sound. "Uh-oh, everything okay with Doris? Is she having moving reservations?"

"Oh, Gram's fine," Charlie said. "Frankly, I'm surprised she isn't complaining more about having to leave her house. But she's taking it in stride."

"Did that fall scare her more than she's letting on?"

"Maybe," Charlie agreed. "I'm just glad she didn't actually break her hip. I think it would have made the move that much worse."

"It's a big shift either way," Alicia agreed. "Going from that massive house to a tiny apartment."

"Going from being completely independent to…" Charlie hummed. "I mean, she's still very independent, and there's plenty to explore at Glendale."

"But she's recovering okay?"

"Yeah. Apparently they have some yoga class they like to take the residents to, so knowing Gram, she'll be more flexible than I am in a month."

Alicia laughed, the sound making Charlie smile. "I wouldn't put it past her. You got everything moved over?"

"The piano made it."

"Priority number one," Alicia said. "The rest of it?"

Charlie rubbed her hand over her face. "God, there's so much. Every time I put something in a box, a new stack of crap appears."

"Take it one section at a time," Alicia suggested. "And take breaks so you don't get overwhelmed."

The corner of Charlie's mouth quirked.

"So, what's the actual problem then?"

"Hmm?"

"That was an awfully heavy sigh."

"Okay, listen to this," Charlie said.

Alicia chuckled. "I like when your stories start like that."

"Gram is giving me a tour of Glendale a couple days ago, right? Because the movers have to do their thing."

"Sure."

"And there's this really lovely woman showing us around and introducing Gram to all these people, and so she wants to introduce us to the activities director as we pass his office."

"That's great."

"That's what I thought, too. Especially because I scoped out the website, and I realized that I *know* this activities director from my college days. So my first thought is oh, Gram'll have a familiar face around."

"Know him how?" Alicia asked.

"We dated about eight years ago. No, er, not dated. We flinged."

"Flung?" Alicia snorted.

"Sure. We had a fling-thing for the summer."

Charlie could tell Alicia was grinning as she asked, "How awkward was that?"

"The epitome of awkwardness!" Charlie all but yelled. "Mostly because he acted like he barely remembered me!"

"Oh."

"Like I know it's been a solid few years or whatever, but I very clearly remembered him. And he straight up said that maybe he had a vague recollection of me. Vague, Alicia! He used the word *vague*."

Alicia cackled.

"I had to remind him how we met. How *he* asked *me* out." Charlie shook her head. "I don't even know why I'm still so mad about it."

"Because the hot guy from your past is ignoring you?" Alicia offered, and Charlie could practically hear the smirk crawling across her face.

"I never said he was hot."

"He's hot in my mind until you say otherwise," Alicia said. "Like all ripped and muscled, with forearms that are very toned from using them between your—"

"Okay," Charlie cried. Alicia knew she had a thing for arms, and she didn't need to give any more mental space to Julian's. "Thank you for that very unwanted image." Her stomach dipped, the sensation unexpected. She hadn't felt anything like that for a while now, and the fact that Julian had jump-started those desires was infuriating.

Alicia cackled some more. "I'm envisioning those Fabio book covers. You know the ones where he's busting out of his clothes?"

"Long silky locks blowing in the breeze?" Charlie finished. "Yeah. That's definitely not what's happening here."

"You didn't say he wasn't hot."

Charlie wanted to tell Alicia that Julian was a toad that had never turned into a prince, but that was a lie. Julian had deliciously filled out in the years since she'd seen him last—maybe he'd been hitting the gym?—but no. *No!* She would not give an ounce of her energy to acknowledging his hotness.

"He was just so insistent that he didn't remember me

or Gram. But then he'd mention something about that summer, and I don't know... Trying to figure him out is driving me nuts."

"Maybe seeing him again after all this time brought up old feelings," Alicia suggested.

"Yeah," Charlie muttered. "Irritation and discontent."

"I mean *real* feelings. It's been a while, right? Since you've actively dated anyone." Alicia diplomatically avoided mentioning how losing her brother had derailed everything in Charlie's life. Dating really was on the bottom of her priority list.

"I'm not really interested in dating." Especially right now. Especially him.

"You don't have to date him. But if there's already history there, you could just...you know," Alicia teased, "reminisce a little. Get cozy and—"

"I'm also not interested in *that*," Charlie said, cutting her off. Especially that. "The man can't decide if he wants to be hot or cold with me." And yet she'd still agreed to a music gig she never wanted.

Alicia hummed. "Bad sign."

Charlie snorted. "I obviously wronged him in a past life. Or he just really didn't think very highly of me that summer we spent together." Sure, they'd been young. But Charlie sort of thought she might have made a similar impression on him. He obviously remembered something of their summer together. That much was obvious. But why was he working so hard to deny it?

"Maybe you broke his heart," Alicia said.

"Or maybe I was just one of many summer flings he entertained back then and he really did forget who I was."

She scowled at the thought, and at how much that bothered her.

"Ah, the good old days," Alicia said, chuckling. "Now everything is so serious."

The good old days indeed. Back before Charlie had learned what it was to say goodbye to her brother. Back when her biggest stress in life was figuring out which piece of music she was going to perform at her senior recital.

"Okay, let's shift gears for a minute then," Alicia said. "I know you've got a lot on your plate right now, but I did have an audition come across my desk that might actually be perfect for you."

Charlie wallowed in the beat of silence that followed. It sat uncomfortably in her stomach.

"Have I lost you?"

"I'm here." She'd gotten used to turning down auditions without ever giving them a second thought. She appreciated that Alicia kept that door open despite how many times Charlie kicked it shut. But now Gram's concerns echoed in her head. *Life goes on… You have to move with it, or you'll get swept away.*

"No pressure," Alicia assured her. "I can pass on it."

Charlie didn't want to get swept away, but she didn't want to have to face it, either. Everything was easier when she didn't let herself think about music and Tom and what she'd lost. Easier when she boxed her feelings up like the stupid china hutch.

Before everything happened, she'd been traveling around the country with Tom. Charlie had always enjoyed working with him, watching him guest conduct orchestras in different cities and pull together a show from scratch. Sure, she sang the tunes, but it was Tom who really made the magic happen. He had a special way of bringing together a group of musicians that she'd always admired. His dream had been to one day perform with one of the big five symphony orchestras: Boston, Chicago, Philadelphia, Cleveland. Or even the New York Philharmonic. But as far as what Charlie wanted... The thought of taking a proper stage without Tom there to guide her made her want to shrug out of her skin.

She tried to imagine it: standing before a crowd of hundreds, bowing to applause, all while knowing that Tom never would again. How could she do that to him? Pressure swirled behind her eyes. Gram's words echoed in her head. What was the right answer? What would plug the hole in her chest?

"Send me the audition," she found herself saying.

"Okay!" Alicia said, her tone filled with surprise. "Great. Let's see if it sparks your interest, and we'll go from there. No pressure."

No pressure. Right. Then why did it feel like she was going to explode? "Thanks," Charlie managed. She glanced at the time on her phone. "I gotta run and host a music class for a bunch of geriatrics."

"Come again?"

"Long story for next time. But just know that's reason number two that Julian is on my shit list. Talk soon?" she said, knowing they would.

"You bet. I need to know all about this music class with horribly hot Julian."

"Just horrible," Charlie muttered. "We're leaving it at that." They hung up, the sound of Alicia's laughter fading.

Five

Julian

There had to be some sort of cheat code to properly filling out government grants. Julian was certain of it as he stared at the blank document on his computer. He scrolled through miles of unanswered questions until he reached the end of the application and slumped back in his chair with a defeated sigh.

He'd already been at this for the better part of an hour and still no end in sight. Despite the seven years he'd been doing this, submitting applications in the hopes of receiving additional government funding, he still hadn't figured out the winning combination. And every year, he had to admit defeat and relegate the music program to a work in progress.

If only he could figure out what the reviewers sitting in their fancy government offices wanted to hear. Was it statistics on the positive effect of music on the elderly? Or maybe they wanted to be entertained? He could give them any number of funny or heartwarming personal anecdotes from his time at Glendale. The problem was Julian never knew which way to lean with these applications, and he was obviously doing something wrong because for years he'd heard nothing but radio silence. He wasn't foolish enough to think that he was the only person trying to squeeze more money out of a broken system, but he figured after this many tries, he might have struck it lucky at least once.

Julian minimized the application, giving his eyes a break from the screen as he checked the big calendar on his desk. There was less than a month until the end of December. Until another year came and went. It had been a good year, he supposed, though he couldn't shake the feeling that he wanted to be able to do more for the residents.

Maybe he should consider hiring a grant writer. There were people that made a living perfecting these types of applications. But what would that cost him in the end besides precious funds from his already taxed budget? If the application still amounted to nothing, then he'd be eating into his meager funds for no reason, which would mean fewer trips to the community center, less programming and fewer supplies to run those programs. Julian already knew that if he let the paint run out in the art room or failed to provide gardening supplies in the spring there would be hell to pay.

He snorted under his breath at the mental image of being hunted down the halls of Glendale by an angry mob of cane-wielding residents.

Okay, a grant writer was probably not the right choice.

Still, he had to try something to keep this music program going once Charlie left. Charlie, who didn't even want to be here. Charlie, who'd been occupying his mind for days now. Charlie, whom he needed to stop thinking about because she was only a temporary fix to a long-term problem. And as far as he and Charlie were concerned, that was for the best.

But he still needed an action plan for the new year. Julian opened another document on his computer screen, finding the Volunteers Wanted poster he'd been working on earlier. After a quick spelling-and-grammar check, he hit Print. There was no guarantee that he'd scrounge up another volunteer in the community, a market he'd already tapped, but he needed to try something. Maybe he should have titled the poster Christmas Miracle Wanted.

Julian rolled across his office on his desk chair to reach the printer when a familiar squeak issued from the hall. He looked up in time to see a small cart appear in the doorway, followed by a beaming smile.

"Morning!" Warren chirped as he followed the cart into the room. He kicked on the brakes and leaned against the cart in his scrubs, his ID badge hanging from one of his pockets and a stethoscope poking out of another. Though most of the residents at Glendale were independent, there were a few that needed additional care, requiring a small team of medical professionals.

"You're making the rounds early," Julian said, grabbing his printed posters.

"The staff have CPR recertification after lunch."

"Oh right. You told me that."

Warren was both a colleague and a friend, and one of the most dedicated nurses Julian had ever met. He'd been working at Glendale even longer than Julian and was the kind of guy who would sit down after his shift for a coffee with a lonely resident. Julian had always admired that. Actually, he aspired to be a little bit like Warren.

Glendale was lucky to have him. *Julian* was lucky to have him.

Warren cocked his head and frowned. "You got a headache?"

"No," Julian said. "Why are you asking?"

"Because you've got that pinched look you get right before you start complaining about the headache the budget is giving you."

Julian smirked. "I'm fine."

Warren gave him a pointed look.

"Really, I swear."

Warren tapped the top of his cart. "Tylenol and applesauce is my special of the day. Just saying."

"Isn't that the special every day?"

Warren's lips turned up at the corner. "Pretty sure it's the sixth food group when you hit a certain age." He stretched. "I'm almost there myself. Everything's starting to ache."

"Yeah, right. You're going to outlast both me and Diane. What I really need you to get me is something that will help me write a winning grant application."

Warren hummed, sitting down in the chair across from Julian's desk. "Fresh out of that, I'm afraid."

"Figured."

"But I'm serious," Warren said. "You look stressed. What's up?"

"Nothing. Just the usual music program blues."

Warren leaned against the desk, his eyebrows lifting. "What are you talking about? That volunteer you found—Charlie? She's fantastic."

"You met her?"

He nodded. "I couldn't find some of the residents in their usual hangouts. Then I heard all this commotion coming from the end of the hall. So I popped by the music room. I swear I've never seen it so full. Residents were literally hanging out the door, trying to get in on the action." He barked a laugh. "Felt like some sort of exclusive club I hadn't been invited to."

"Really?" Julian frowned. He hadn't had time to pop down to the music room the last few times Charlie had been here. Or more like, he'd been avoiding it. The less he put himself in her direct path, the less he had to worry about owning up to the fact that his pulse quickened every time they were in the same room together. Out of sight, out of mind.

"What do you mean, *really*?" Warren scoffed. "You gave her the position. Didn't you know she could sing like that?"

Julian shrugged a bit. "Yeah, I guess. I mean, she attended Juilliard. I've just been a little busy up here." He held up his Volunteers Wanted posters. His time was much better spent figuring out what to do when Charlie left. Plus, he really hadn't wanted to deal with more of those warring sparks of annoyance and exasperation and…wistfulness? Every time the past surfaced, he was forced to remember how amazing it felt to be wanted the way Charlie had wanted him that summer. And then he'd remember how wretched it felt being left behind.

Tossed aside.

Abandoned.

When summer ended, she'd gone back to Juilliard, and he'd returned to college, but the feelings had lingered, and for a while they'd made it work. Phone calls between classes. Late night texts. Links to funny articles and memes and things that reminded them of each other.

Then it all fell off. It was slow at first, with distracted conversations and missed calls and unanswered texts. Then all at once she disappeared from his life without ever telling him why, and Julian had promised himself never again.

"Well, I'd make time to check it out if I were you," Warren said. "Tons of residents in attendance. I could barely get through the door to check the blood sugars. Standing room only," he joked. "If Charlie keeps this up, you could start selling tickets. Then you wouldn't need Diane's budget."

"Now there's an idea," Julian muttered. But the fact that this would all disappear the moment Charlie left irritated him. She couldn't just waltz back here, make this kind of impression and then ditch them. Well, she *could*. She could do whatever she wanted.

And that bothered him. The fact that she could come back and make him feel like this, tugging on some invisible something inside him... Julian grumbled under his breath. He wasn't twenty-one anymore, tripping over himself because some pretty girl blinked twice at him. He needed to remember that. In fact, the sooner Charlie was out of here, the better.

His attention drifted back to his computer as an email notification pinged. It was the monthly community center newsletter. He often browsed it for activities that might interest the residents. This month an unfamiliar banner took up the top portion of the newsletter. It was an advertisement for the Elm Springs Twentieth Annual Christmas Choir Competition.

"Have you seen this?" Julian asked, clicking on it.

Warren leaned across the desk. "Every year if I'm not working. It gives the family something to do on Christmas Eve. Usually a fun time. Why?"

"No, this," Julian said, using the mouse to direct Warren's attention to the fine print. He read it off. "This year, the Christmas Eve event is being sponsored by the Elm Springs Arts Council, with a grand prize of twenty thousand dollars for the winning choir." There was a website link for more information.

"Well, that's new. I didn't even know the Arts Council had twenty grand for that kind of thing." Warren laughed. "Not since they commissioned that weird fountain in the town square. You know the one with all the metal dog statues?"

"I think this is a sign," Julian said. This was the Christmas miracle he'd been hoping for!

"What is?"

"The competition! It's exactly the kind of lucky break we need." Julian followed the link to the website, reading even more fine print. "It's for amateur choirs only."

"Right," Warren said, sounding confused.

"Think about it. If we won, with that kind of money, I could actually afford to hire a music director to keep the program going while I work out additional funding."

"Okay, yeah," Warren said. "But here's the first problem. Unless I'm mistaken, Glendale doesn't have a choir."

"The word you're missing is *yet*."

"Yet?"

The plan came together faster than Julian could explain it. He was on his feet suddenly, envisioning a stage and applause and a giant check made out to Glendale Retirement Village. "I'm gonna need Charlie's help."

"And what if Charlie doesn't want to help?" Warren said. "Sounds like a lot of work, and I don't know if you've forgotten, but you don't actually have any money to pay her."

The image in Julian's head cracked but didn't completely

shatter. Charlie could say no to his proposal, abandoning him and his great idea. It wasn't like she didn't already have a track record for that. But what if he could convince her?

Never mind *what if.* He had to convince her!

"I just won't give her the chance to turn me down." Even if he had to get down on his knees and beg, he'd do it. This opportunity was too important.

Warren made a face, following Julian into the hall. "Why do I feel like there's some sort of evil mastermind plot spinning around in your head?"

"Because there might be," Julian said with a grin. "I'll keep you posted."

He parted ways with Warren at the elevator, hurrying into the stairwell. When he popped out on the first floor, he could already hear the rhythmic clapping and the soaring notes that bled from the music room as the door opened and closed, admitting more residents. Julian picked up his pace.

He squeezed through the door once he reached it, inching through the crowd that had gathered at the back of the room. There were more residents than chairs, and he made a mental note to track some down if this sort of participation was going to continue. He spotted Doris in the crowd and lifted his hand in hello.

She nodded, coming to stand beside him.

"Wow," he muttered to her as Charlie's voice filled the room. "Like big wow." Her voice was warm honey smoothed over the notes, rich and golden and impossibly light. She stood at the front of the room, commanding attention, and Julian felt his mouth go dry as Charlie's magnetic energy filled the room like smoke. It seeped beneath his skin, filling his lungs, infiltrating his veins, both unsettling and electric as his very bones were drawn toward her.

Snap out of it!

"Told you she could carry a tune," Doris said, nudging his arm, breaking whatever spell Charlie had cast over him.

"I guess I just never expected her to be this good," Julian said. "That feels like a ridiculous thought now. I mean, Juilliard. Of course she would be this good."

"I've been saying that her whole life, but it does make me feel good as a grandmother to hear other people acknowledge it."

"You must be very proud of her," he said.

Doris's gaze grew distant for a moment. "Always."

Julian quieted to really take in Charlie's performance. He watched every movement of her hands and every twitch of her brow, captivated by the shapes of her mouth. Her presence grew as she sank into the music, letting it envelope her. This was Charlie's world, and Julian's heart raced as he glimpsed it.

Fate had an odd sense of humor, he thought, bringing Charlie crashing back into his life. That summer had been so long ago, and yet here she was, exactly when he needed her.

No, not when he needed her, when the residents needed her. Julian had learned better than to rely on people who'd walked out on him. His parents had shown him again and again that he wasn't a priority, and though he'd mistakenly thought things with Charlie were different, he'd walked away knowing better than to invest in relationships he couldn't trust.

Instead he got good at figuring things out on his own, relying on himself, trusting himself. Because carrying around the weight of heartbreak was worse than going it alone.

But listening to Charlie now, feeling the way her voice moved around him, it tangled his emotions, confusing before with now. He couldn't afford the confusion, and the rational part of him knew that relying on Charlie was a bad call—experience had shown him that much.

But Glendale needed her, so somehow he needed to convince her to see them through this competition.

Because the residents deserved that. Her grandmother deserved that.

And maybe he would never understand what happened between them. Maybe he'd never understand why the people he cared about never stuck around. But even if no one ever chose him, he could still choose to make the residents' lives better. And wasn't a little hurt and heartache worth that?

Charlie finished the song, the last notes lingering in the echo of the room. They were quickly eclipsed by rousing applause and jaunty whistles. Julian raised his hands, clapping until his palms ached.

Charlie ducked her head demurely, tucking her blond hair behind her ears. It was practiced nonchalance. Somehow, she avoided acknowledging her own talent. Her own greatness. And she did it well. Because there was no way she didn't know how truly wonderful she was.

"You're going to need a bigger room if this keeps up," Doris said, leaning in close enough for him to hear over the clapping. "Maybe an entire auditorium."

Julian grinned at the image that conjured. "I sure hope so."

Charlie thanked the group for listening and wished them

all a great rest of their day. Before the crowd could disperse, Julian inched his way to the front of the room.

"Can I get everyone's attention, please?" he called. The murmurs quieted as the residents turned to face him. "I'd like to thank everyone for attending today, and Charlie for being such a wonderful volunteer." Her eyes cut toward him, suspicion written into her features, but Julian plowed on before he lost his nerve. "We are beyond grateful to have someone of her talent among us. And I know I keep saying that I'm going to find a way to keep the music program going…"

Charlie's brows arched with interest. "Did you find a permanent solution?"

"I…definitely have an idea," Julian offered. "The Twentieth Annual Christmas Choir Competition. This year there's a prize being awarded by the Elm Springs Arts Council to an amateur choir to support musical development. A twenty thousand dollar prize."

"Oh my," Maggie said, giggling as she laid a hand against her chest. "Imagine winning that."

The murmurs in the room picked up again. Julian looked at Charlie, gauging her reaction. At first there was nothing, and then his hidden request seemed to dawn on her, and she shook her head hard, her cheeks flooding with color that reminded him of sunset. "No. Absolutely not."

Julian folded his hands together, pressing his fingers to his lips, trying to hide the smile that threatened to overtake his face as Charlie glared at him. He failed. Grinning, he addressed the room again. "I think Glendale should give it a shot. So what we need to do is put together a choir. And we could really use an experienced music volunteer to help with that."

He could practically hear Charlie's teeth grinding together. "I know what you're trying to do, and the answer is still no," she muttered under her breath.

"You wouldn't run off on Doris so soon?" he whispered, using the best card he could. Charlie had no reason to do it for him, but for her grandmother—that was a different story. She'd always been so devoted to Doris. Julian could understand that love. He could *use* that love. "She only just moved in. Don't you want to make sure she's comfortable?"

A muscle in Charlie's cheek twitched. "That's not going to work."

"I know you want her to settle in and feel connected here. You know what could be a really great bonding experience for her? A choir."

"Julian—"

"I'm just saying… Feels like a really great opportunity. I would hate for Doris to miss out."

Charlie crossed her arms, her shoulders hunched up by her ears. He was a spider weaving his web, and he knew she was almost caught. Almost his.

Glendale's, he corrected himself.

"Do you really think we could be a choir?" Maggie asked, looking astonished at the idea. "That we have the talent?"

"Of course," Harriet cut in. "How hard could it be? We just slap a group of people together and sing."

"Sure, Julian," Charlie said, tilting her head, regarding him through narrowed eyes. "How hard could it be?"

"I mean," he said with a laugh, "according to Harriet, not very."

"What do you even know about putting together a choir?" Charlie demanded.

"I've got the basics down," Julian said, lying through his teeth. "I know you need people. We've got people."

Charlie scowled at him.

"And!" he said. "You need music." He walked toward the piano and hit the keys. "Do. That's Do, right? Rei. Mi. Fa. So. La... La... La..." He frowned, hitting the key repeatedly. "That doesn't sound very La-ish."

"The piano is out of tune," Charlie said, uncrossing her arms to put her hands on her hips. Those perfectly curvy hips. "Thanks for noticing."

Julian licked his lips, getting back to the music, plucking another discordant note. "Okay, so that's a hurdle we'll have to overcome." He gestured to the residents. "But we like a challenge, don't we? We rise to a challenge. Perseverance is our middle name."

"I've got a piano in my place," Doris said. "We could have it moved down here. And I'd be happy to accompany whatever music we choose."

Charlie glared at her, too.

Maggie clapped her hands together. "This is so exciting!" she trilled. "I can get started on wardrobe. We'll want to coordinate outfits, I assume?"

"Oh my God," Charlie muttered, pinching the bridge of her nose as the excitement in the room kicked off.

"See?" Julian said, catching Charlie's eye. "Solutions. This is what I like to hear. All we need now is one very brave choir director."

"I'm not a choir director," she insisted.

Harriet snorted. "Well, not with that attitude."

"I'm no choir director, either," Julian said. "But I'm willing to give this a shot." He knew he didn't have one ounce of musical talent. He also knew he'd sprung the idea on Charlie. It wasn't fair of him to get the residents fired up about the idea before she'd had time to consider it. And in doing so, he'd made it almost impossible for her to say no. But he didn't come down here to play fair, because she'd come crashing back into his life, and that was unfair.

Charlie looked around at the residents, her gaze landing on her grandmother who'd been pulled into a boisterous conversation with Maggie and Harriet. He knew the last thing Charlie wanted to do was disappoint Doris. Charlie's frown softened the tiniest amount, and Julian could tell she was considering the idea.

"Think of it this way," he said, stepping a little closer, suddenly overwhelmed by the scent of her—strawberries and vanilla and something flowery. Something that reminded him of summer. *Focus, dammit!* "Without you, I'm liable to get us laughed offstage. Do you really want to subject these lovely people to that kind of embarrassment?"

"Yes, do you want us to suffer that shame and ridicule?" Harriet cut in, smirking. "To be forever known as the retirees that butchered *Silent Night*?"

"Or to be the choir whose Bells didn't Jingle," Julian added.

"Is that the legacy you want us to leave behind?" Harriet said.

"I, for one, am not prepared to be part of that cautionary tale," Doris said.

Charlie huffed. "Okay. *Okay.* Fine."

"What was that?" Julian asked, grinning from ear to ear.

She glared at him so hard it should have hurt. "I said fine. I'll do it."

"Hear that, folks?" Julian lifted his arms in success. "We officially have a choir director!"

"Codirector," Charlie told him. "I'm not doing all the work here. This is your big idea."

"Codirector," he amended. He could handle that. "And she has agreed to help us turn some of Glendale's very own into a choir before the competition."

The residents started talking all at once.

"So dust off those vocal chords!" he called over the voices. "Auditions start tomorrow bright and early."

"Auditions start at ten," Charlie clarified. She glanced at Julian. "I'm not going to be here any earlier."

"You heard the lady. Auditions at ten. Prepare to wow us tomorrow!"

The group filed through the doorway, chatting song choices and music, the conversation brimming with excitement. It had been a while since Julian had heard them this pumped about something. He sighed, feeling hopeful as he turned to Charlie. "I think this is gonna be really great for them."

Charlie simply rolled her eyes. "You have no idea what you're doing, do you?"

"I have a good feeling."

Charlie huffed, gathering her things. "Hope it's a twenty thousand dollar feeling."

"Maybe it is," Julian called after her. "I'm full of winning ideas."

Charlie looked him up and down as she reached the door. "You're definitely full of something."

Six

Charlie

It's honestly a nightmare, Charlie texted Alicia. What the hell do either of us know about directing a choir?

You know about singing. That's a good start.

You sound like Gram. And you both know it's not the same thing. The only person Charlie had ever known who would be remotely interested in this turn of events was Tom. And even he might have questioned how to turn a random group of elderly residents into a passable choir before Christmas.

But your experience is not nothing. Plus it's not like they know any better. I say, trust your instincts and see what comes of it.

My instincts were too slow to realize Julian was roping me into disaster. I'm not sure I can trust them. Also, you're being unhelpfully optimistic.

I just like the fact that I'll get more updates on how you hate the ridiculously handsome activities director.

Charlie frowned at her phone.

He's just ridiculous. This idea is ridiculous! And he's a scheming cheat for using a bunch of cute old people and Gram against me

Mm-hmm. Maybe he just wants to spend more time with you. Ever think of that?

Huffing, Charlie flipped her phone over even as her stomach fluttered. It was like a dusty, dormant moth had been startled in a corner. Choosing to ignore the feeling, she glanced around the common room.

She was seated next to the fireplace, in one of the wingback armchairs across from Gram. Two great bookcases framed the far wall, well-worn tomes lined up in a colorful display. Around the room, an array of small tables boasted half-completed chess games and abandoned solitaire. The room was suspiciously devoid of garland and twinkle lights, but outside a winter wind battered at the windows, leaving snowflakes to melt down the panes. It was the kind of day that made Charlie want to pull one of the books from the shelves and tuck herself beneath a blanket.

Instead, she had her laptop open on her knees, scrolling through her old set lists with Gram as they prepared for today's auditions. Charlie had shown up bright and early at Gram's request so they could go over her song selection. She'd made a point of telling Gram she didn't have to try so hard. The whole reason she'd agreed to this with Julian was to allow Gram to make connections, so her being part of the choir was sort of nonnegotiable. But Gram was nothing if not dedicated to the shtick, and she was taking this audition very seriously.

"How about that one?" Gram said, pointing to the screen.

"'Ten Minutes Ago'? From *Cinderella*?" Charlie frowned. "That's usually a duet." She considered her previous performances and the occasional tune that Tom would join her for while onstage. She remembered him turning from the orchestra and grabbing a mic, smiling at her as they performed duets the way they had as children in Gram's living room. "I suppose you could just sing a few bars."

Gram hummed the song, and Charlie mentally batted at the memories that were conjured with the first few notes.

"You really don't have to audition," she said again, making sure that was clear. "Besides the fact you've volunteered to play piano, I already know you can sing. Plus I'm confident Julian really wants you in the choir."

She hadn't actually seen Julian yet this morning. Perhaps she should have dropped by his office to figure out the logistics of how this audition process was going to work, but truthfully she was still annoyed with him for forcing her into yet another thing she wanted no part of. How was she supposed to turn him down in front of a room full of elderly people, all looking at her, their faces creased with excitement? She was becoming far too entrenched in the happenings at Glendale for her liking.

"What about you?" Gram asked.

"What about me?"

"Do you want me in this choir?"

"Obviously."

"You don't seem too thrilled by the idea."

"It's not that," Charlie said, feeling a little bad that Gram would think so. She sighed. "I'm just not sure I'm thrilled in general. It has nothing to do with not wanting you to be a part of it." This was Gram's chance to really build community here. If Charlie couldn't shake her annoyance, she was going to ruin it for her. "I guess I'm just nervous."

"You, nervous?" Gram said with a smile. She patted Charlie's knee. When she was young and worried about performing, Gram would pat her arms or her shoulders, telling her she was getting all the butterflies out.

"I've never done something like this before. And there's a big prize on the line that Julian is really eager to win so he can support the music program. That's a lot of pressure when I'm not even sure we'll be able to cobble together a choir, never mind thinking about the actual performance."

Gram reached for her hand and squeezed. "I have no doubt you'll do wonderfully."

Charlie shook her head. "You say that about everything."

"I have to. Until you prove me otherwise."

Charlie smiled a little. Gram had always had far too much faith in her talent—maybe more than she deserved. She just didn't want to ruin this opportunity for Glendale. Part of her also didn't want to fall short of Julian's expectations. Though why she cared what he thought was beyond her. This was the man who couldn't be bothered to remember her name. She didn't owe him anything. Not her time or her mental energy or the space in her dreams where he'd annoyingly been cropping up each night.

"It's been a long time since I've gotten to properly audition for anything," Gram mused.

"I wouldn't say this is a proper audition."

"Still, it's kind of exciting. Takes me back to my youth."

Charlie scrolled down her song list. "Speaking of things from your youth. Something from *The Sound of Music* could be a good option." Gram needled her side, and Charlie chuckled. "I'm sure most of this crowd is going to go with the classics."

"Because we have excellent taste at our age."

"Of course. Also, you never told me if you wanted to keep the old bookshelves in the sitting room or if you wanted me to donate them."

"That's real wood, you know."

"You've said."

"They just don't make furniture like they used to."

"You've also said that."

"I wonder if your parents could make room for them in their place. I'd hate to let them go."

Charlie doubted it. After Tom passed, they'd accumulated a lot of his things. "Maybe. I'll leave a note for them to think about it."

"All right, I've decided," Gram said. "I'll sing 'My Favorite Things.'"

"Good choice." Charlie brought up the lyrics and handed her laptop to Gram so she could review them, though she doubted she needed it. Charlie had worn out Gram's VHS copy of *The Sound of Music* when she was eleven. She imagined those songs were permanently etched into both their brains.

"I think this volunteer gig has been really good for you so far," Gram noted.

Charlie gave a noncommittal grunt. Sure, there'd been a few moments when she'd actually caught herself enjoying her music room performances, but the guilt that ate at her afterward had burned raw in her chest. So they would have to agree to disagree about that. Falling for this music program and for old flames and for the world she used to share with Tom was never going to work. She would always be drowning in the memories.

"I received an email from Alicia," Charlie said, trying to shift the subject away from Glendale.

"About a job?"

"An audition."

"Well, that's good," Gram said. "That's something."

Charlie avoided her eye. Because even though Alicia had done exactly what Charlie had asked and sent through some potential work opportunities, she hadn't even bothered to look at them. Each email remained in her inbox, unread.

"Anything of interest?" Gram asked.

"A few I might explore," she lied. "Maybe I'll look at going out for a tour audition."

"Oh, your parents and I could fly out somewhere fun to come see you."

Charlie swallowed hard. She felt guilty for performing. She felt bad for not performing. She didn't know what the right answer was anymore. Goose bumps prickled on her arms, and she willed away the sensation. She just needed to lock it all away until she was finished with Gram and Glendale and Elm Springs. Hold it together until she didn't have to walk into this building anymore, stare Julian in the face and have to fend off a tidal wave of memories from before.

From a time brimming with things she'd carved out of her life in Tom's absence.

"I should probably get down to the music room and prepare before everyone starts showing up."

"I'll see you down there in a bit," Gram said. "I think I'll pop upstairs and run through the song a couple times."

"Sounds good."

They parted ways, and Charlie worked her way down to the music room where she organized the chairs, moving them aside to give the residents more space for their auditions. Then she set up two chairs near the front of the room. One for her and one for Julian. With plenty of space in between.

"You're here early," Julian said, appearing in the doorway a few moments later. He had a folding table under his arm. He carried it into the room and set it up in front of the two chairs Charlie had just placed. He moved the chairs closer together.

"So are you."

"Wanted to make sure we were set up before we got rushed by choir hopefuls." Julian jostled the table to make sure it was steady, then pulled a small notebook and pen from his pocket and set it down. "So, how does this work?"

Charlie scoffed, already exasperated with him. "I should be asking you that, codirector. This was your big idea."

"You're right." His green eyes were bright as he pressed his hands against the table, leaning toward her. "I was just giving you the opportunity to contribute."

"Oh, is that what you were doing?" What did he think he was, charming? Charlie crossed her arms, regarding Julian and his cheeky grin. She watched as it softened into something more deliberate, and a fluttery weight landed in her gut.

"Of course. I'm happy to take your ideas on board. I

want to make sure you feel like a valued member of this team."

Charlie's face flushed. "Valued? Without me, you'd have no idea what you're doing."

Julian's eyes dropped briefly to her lips. "Guess we'll never know."

Charlie's entire body flushed. "I shouldn't even have come."

"And yet you did," he said, gaze flicking back up, forcing Charlie to tear her eyes away.

Truth was, she felt out of her depth. She'd attended Juilliard and taught piano, but she was a performer, not a choir director. She really should have just said no to him yesterday, ending this farce.

"When I asked Google how to start a choir last night," Julian continued, "it said to start by defining its purpose and target audience."

"You Googled?"

He winked. "I'm full of great ideas. So, purpose, win twenty grand. Target audience. The lovely residents of Elm Springs. I'm crushing these codirector responsibilities."

"If you think that's all you need to do to win this thing, you're way out of your league."

His smile wavered a bit as he slumped down in his chair, and she annoyingly felt a nagging pang in her chest. She remembered how disappointed he'd been that day in the elevator, when he'd revealed there wasn't a budget for the music program. For years, music was all Charlie had lived and breathed. How could she not support that now?

"I suppose," she began, some ridiculous part of her not wanting him to look so dejected, "that we should hear the auditions and separate the residents into voice types for a start."

Julian picked up his notebook and pen. "Voice types. Got it. And then we go and win this competition."

"Probably need to squeeze some rehearsal in there first," Charlie said.

"Ah, yes, rehearsal." Julian flipped his notebook around. "Here's the game plan. Voice types. Rehearsal. Win. Three steps. I think we can manage that."

Charlie sat down beside him. "That easy, huh?"

"I mean, there will probably be some obstacles along the way. But I think we can sort them out. Together." He held her gaze, his eyes softly creased at the corners.

Warmth surged through her. No, not just warmth. Heat. Spiraling, tumbling, dizzying heat. She remembered falling into those eyes. Falling into him. Over and over again. Even now—

Nope! Now nothing.

Charlie looked away as the door opened, glad for a distraction from the torrent of feelings that spread through her. They were like a spark on kindling, and she was going to stomp them out, one stubborn flame at a time.

Another staff member poked her head into the room. "Hey, Julian! I brought Frank like you asked."

"Perfect. Thanks, Sherri." Julian hopped up to greet an older man in a wheelchair. After shaking his hand, Julian poked his head out into the hallway before closing the door behind him and Frank. "We've got quite the crowd gathering out here."

Charlie sighed. She supposed there was no more avoiding it.

"Charlie, this is Frank," Julian said, introducing them

as Frank guided his wheelchair to the center of the room. "I thought he might enjoy auditioning."

"It's nice to meet you, Frank," she said.

"I explained to Frank that we're aiming to win a competition. You got your music picked out?" Julian asked him.

Frank produced a tiny speaker from his pocket and plugged his phone in. Charlie was impressed as he accessed Spotify.

"He's a bit of a tech guru," Julian muttered to her as he walked back around the table.

Charlie perked up as she heard familiar music start.

"This is 'Climb Ev'ry Mountain,'" Frank said, introducing his audition piece before he started singing.

Charlie gaped as a rich baritone voice filled the room.

Julian looked at her and held up his arm. "Goose bumps," he whispered.

The song was traditionally sung by sopranos, but Charlie appreciated how seamlessly Frank adapted to the music. It was beautiful. She could have listened to him all day.

When Frank stopped singing, she and Julian erupted into applause.

"Wow," Julian said. "Just wow, Frank. What are you doing hiding that voice?"

"What a treat," Charlie said. "That number is a particular favorite of mine."

"From 1959 to 1963," Frank said, *"The Sound of Music* ran for more than 1,443 performances at the Lunt-Fontanne Theatre."

Charlie grinned, impressed. "Frank, I did not realize you were such a Broadway fan. I am in excellent company today."

"Tech guru. Broadway aficionado. He is a man of many talents," Julian said.

Frank beamed at them both. "I will see you at rehearsal."

Charlie was pleasantly surprised by his confidence as Julian rolled him into the hallway, inviting in the next auditioner. When Julian plopped back down beside her, she leaned in. "You don't really expect me to tell any of the residents that they haven't made the choir, right? Because it sounds like Frank is coming to rehearsals regardless."

"Is he not good enough?" Julian asked, confused.

The woman in the room started to warble through her audition.

"No, he's great. I just meant… I don't think I have the heart to make cuts."

"I didn't really think we would," Julian admitted. "Thank you, Elaine," he called. "That was excellent. Can you send in the next person?"

"Then what's all this audition nonsense for?" Charlie asked.

"Because holding auditions gets them fired up. And if they're fired up, they'll be excited and eager to win." Julian added Elaine's name next to Frank's in his notebook. "Plus this is what choir codirectors do, don't they?"

Charlie huffed and settled into her chair, but she couldn't deny that a small part of her was entertained.

Over the next hour, they watched over a dozen auditions. Gram was a soprano. Maggie, more of a mezzo soprano. Harriet was an alto while Jim Henshaw was a tenor. There was no one quite like Frank, but Charlie was impressed with the natural talent she saw, and she stole Julian's notebook to make her own lists. Because now she wasn't just entertained by the auditions, she was laughing at Julian's little asides—why did laughing feel so much easier with him?—and scribbling notes on how the voices complemented each other.

"All right," Julian said as the last resident left the room. "I think that's it."

He took Charlie's finalized list, pinned it to a board at the back of the room, then swung open the door. "We would like to thank everyone for auditioning today," he announced in a booming voice. "Unfortunately, we can only take the very best."

Charlie smirked, knowing no one had been cut.

"Please check to see if your name is on the list and then take a seat."

The residents piled through the door. Charlie was reminded of flooding the hall after high school auditions to see who'd made the school play.

There were gasps and squeals as the residents spotted their names. Maggie clapped her hands together, her cheeks so rosy it made Charlie's chest ache. She hadn't realized quite how much this would mean to some of them. And as she watched their joy, a flicker of warmth washed through her.

Once the residents were seated, Julian looked to her.

Charlie stood, clearing her throat. "I just want to say that I am truly impressed with the talent we saw here today. And I can't believe you've been letting me stand up here this whole time doing all the work."

That earned her a few chuckles.

"First thing I'd like to do is get everyone arranged by voice type," Charlie continued. She walked over to Frank, placing her hand on his shoulder. "Do you mind if I reposition your chair?"

"Not at all," he said, lifting his hands into his lap.

Charlie took the back of his wheelchair, moving him to the middle of the group. "Okay, Frank and his lovely baritone voice should be here. Where are my other baritones?"

A few of the men stood up, carrying their chairs toward Frank.

"And what about my tenors?" Charlie asked.

The group looked around in confusion. That was expected. Not everyone knew their voice type. She consulted her list. "That's Jim, Earl, Leroy and Nelson." Her tenors joined the baritones in the middle of the group.

"Now can I get the sopranos to the left," Charlie said. "That's Gram, Maggie, Leane and Dot. And finally, my altos to the right."

More chairs squeaked as Harriet, Elaine and Patrice repositioned themselves.

"Okay," Charlie said, looking at her reorganized group. She suddenly had flashbacks to the first few classes at Juilliard. "I guess we should start with some vocal warmups. How does that sound?"

She'd started to take warmups more seriously recently. That first class she'd hosted had been a bit of a shock to the system after two years, so Charlie had gotten back into good habits. Hydration. Vocal care. Her voice was an instrument, and she still needed to look after it to perform her best. And so did the residents. "I'll have my codirector demonstrate."

"Umm..." Julian began.

She smirked, waving him up beside her. "I told you I'm not going to do all the work, didn't I?"

Julian stood, looking sheepishly at the crowd. "Just take it easy on me."

"Afraid you can't handle it?"

There was something playful in his gaze. "I guess we'll see what I can handle."

Charlie swallowed hard. "Stand up straight."

"I am."

She pressed on the middle of his back, feeling the hard muscle flex along his spine. His chest puffed up, his broad shoulders rounding. She suppressed a shiver. "Straighter. Like this."

Charlie made minor adjustments to his posture, hands placed against thick forearms or along the ropy muscles of his biceps, doing her best to fend off Alicia's comments. But she failed, imagining one of Julian's hands disappearing between—

Charlie almost gasped at the intensity of her thoughts. What was wrong with her? She reached up and tilted his jaw. "I'd like you to hum along with me."

She demonstrated, and Julian copied. Poorly.

"Why are you making that face?" he asked.

"I didn't know you could screw up humming."

He tried again, much to the amusement of the residents.

"No, like this," she said, chuckling. She clutched his face between her hands, gently, and with her thumbs, formed the correct shape with his mouth.

"For everyone's reference, this is a demonstration of what not to do," Julian said. The group laughed as Julian gave the warm up another shot.

"Something easier, then," Charlie said. "Try some lip buzzing." She performed a couple trills and waited for him to repeat the motion.

Julian's lips puckered.

Charlie arched an eyebrow. "Can you take this seriously, please?"

"Lip buzzing? I didn't know it was possible to *not* take that seriously." He tried again.

"Okay, now you're just beatboxing or something."

"Can we add that in?" Harriet asked. "I think I'm actually quite good at that." She raised her hand to her mouth as she and Julian started some odd, terrible beatboxing battle.

"Moving on," Charlie said loudly.

Julian leaned toward her and buzzed his lips by her ear.

She shoved him away, grateful no one could hear the way her pulse spiked. "Okay, that's enough warmup demonstrations."

"Why? Are you not impressed by my vocal talents?" Julian asked.

"Actually, I'm a little concerned about your inability to carry a tune."

"What are you talking about?" He sang out some notes for the group.

"Give me advanced warning next time if I should turn off my hearing aid," Harriet said.

Charlie laughed, the sound exploding out of her, loud and bold and so full of glee that she caught herself. Was she actually having…fun?

The moment she realized that, panic set in, flooding her entire body with a cold chill. She couldn't afford to feel this way. It was more than she'd allowed herself to feel in months. This was for Gram. To build her a community. Not a space for Charlie to lose herself or enjoy herself. Guilt gnawed at her. She had to take this more seriously, the way Tom would have. This wasn't fun and games. This was a job. The results of this competition could mean the continuation of the music program. So she had to get in and get out without getting attached, because she couldn't afford for the wrong emotions to show up and ruin everything.

"Okay," Charlie said with renewed focus. "I think we just need to dive right in and get the group singing together."

"Hold on a second," someone called. Charlie looked up to see Warren standing in the doorway. He pushed his medication cart to the side. "If you're gonna be a choir, you're gonna need a name."

"A name!" Julian said. "Of course. We'll need something to put on the application form. Okay, people. What are we working with?"

"The Glendales?" Maggie suggested off the bat.

Gram and Harriet both wrinkled their noses.

"The Oldies," Jim suggested.

"No!"

"The Classics," Patrice said, shrugging. "That's better than oldies."

"The Classics has a nice ring to it," Maggie said.

Charlie didn't love any of these options. Neither did she love the Elm Springers, the Glendale Choir or Glendapella.

"How about the Glendale Shakers?" Julian said. "Because we like to shake it to the beat?"

"At this age, I shake whether I want to or not," Harriet said with a grin.

"Oh! Maybe we can work in some coordinated dance moves," Maggie said.

"And we're not too old to shake other things," Harriet

added. "Are the kids still twerking, or has that gone out of fashion?"

Oh God, Charlie thought.

"Let's try to keep it PG," Julian said, shaking his head. "The first thing we need to do is get an audition video filmed to submit with our application. If the council likes us, we're in. So let's not try to scare them off with our racy moves."

Harriet smirked.

"Audition video?" Charlie said. She hadn't realized they needed to film something. That meant they needed to be a functioning choir long before Christmas. "When's that due?"

"About a week and a half," Julian said. "Or else we risk missing our chance at the competition altogether."

She lowered her voice. "You need to tell me these sorts of things."

"I sort of thought I'd handle the logistics, and you'd handle the music."

"The music is affected by the logistics," Charlie said.

"Is it?"

"Isn't it?" God, she wanted to shake him.

"Don't stress. It's all coming together."

Charlie didn't know what exactly he thought was coming together, but if he—

"All right," Julian said, breaking Charlie from her train of thought. "All in favor of calling ourselves the Glendale Shakers?"

Hands shot into the air. "Aye!"

Seven

Julian

"Whoa, whoa, whoa," Charlie called, shaking her hands from the front of the music room to get the group's attention. The choir broke off mid *rockin'*. They didn't even get around the Christmas tree. "Let's pause there for a second. This isn't working."

Julian sighed and stopped the recording on his phone. He glanced up, watching the choir exchange confused looks. This was the third time Charlie had interrupted the filming since they'd started rehearsal this morning. At this rate, they weren't going to have time to get something filmed before the competition application was due.

Julian deleted the draft, sending it off with all the others he'd trashed in the past hour. "What's the problem now?"

"Maggie needs to switch places with one of the other sopranos." Charlie gestured for the residents to change positions. "Her voice is coming through too heavily. She's all I can hear during the chorus."

Julian pursed his lips. *Really?* "Things sounded fine to me."

Charlie shot him a daggered look that told him he should probably stop talking. She'd been doing that all morning, too. "Well, if all you want is fine—"

"Look," Julian said, taking a step closer to her and lowering his voice. "That's not what I meant. But don't you think you're being a little too—"

"Too what?" she demanded loudly, crossing her arms.

Julian's eyes flickered to the residents and back. He could tell he'd waded into dangerous territory. He'd forgotten how fiery Charlie could be when she was passionate about something. He remembered the harmless arguments she used to have with her brother on Doris's porch. Julian would sit there, amused as they debated the minutiae of theatrical performances long into the night. But this wasn't some good-natured debating, and he hated that they were arguing in front of the residents. It didn't really instill a whole lot of confidence as codirectors.

"Look, I'm just saying…"

Her hazel eyes seemed to blaze with heat, daring him to keep going. He lost himself momentarily in their depth, in the rosy color of her lips, in the soft blush on her cheeks.

What was he trying to say?

"Weren't you the one who said that I should handle the music and you should handle the logistics?"

"Yes," Julian said. "But I think in this case—"

"Then let me worry about the music."

"I would argue there's an element of logistics here. You know…" he tapped his phone "…like getting this little performance on film."

"Maybe if you weren't hovering so much," Charlie said.

"I don't think me hovering is the problem," he replied.

Charlie crossed her arms, her nostrils flaring, and he found himself drawn to her intensity, leaning in, thinking about—

"Why don't we take five?" Doris said, stepping forward. She eyed them both with a raised brow. "Give everyone a chance to hydrate?"

"Sure," Julian said. "Good idea."

The moment the group dispersed, Charlie swept him off to the side of the room.

"You okay?" he asked.

"Too what?" she said, ignoring the question.

"Huh?"

"Before. You said, 'Don't you think you're being a little too...'" Charlie said. "What were you going to say?"

Julian lifted his shoulder. "I don't know. It just feels like you're being a little critical of the choir. I think they're doing really well considering all we had last week was a name."

"I'm giving them notes," Charlie said. "That's how they're going to improve."

"Yes. Notes are good. But I think we should remember that most of them are in their seventies and hard of hearing. You could dial it back a little. That's all."

"Dial it back?" Charlie looked at him like he'd sprouted a third eye. "Do you want to make it into this competition or not?"

"Of course I do." He let out a heavy breath. "They're doing the best they can. And for like a week of rehearsals, I think they're sounding pretty good."

"Pretty good does not win you twenty thousand dollars." Charlie prodded him in the chest with her finger. "That's what we're doing here, aren't we?"

Julian batted her finger away before he could do something ridiculous, like take her hand. "Ideally—"

"Then let's take it from the top!" Charlie called, stomping back over to the front of the room.

"Okay then," Julian muttered under his breath. "Good conversation." Apparently they weren't really taking five.

The residents scrambled back to their places, exchanging looks of uncertainty. Doris's lips were pulled into a tight line as she settled back on the piano bench.

Julian opened his camera app on his phone again. None of this was going the way he'd expected or hoped. He couldn't put a pin in why Charlie was so out of sorts today, but it almost felt like she was deliberately trying to make this process more difficult. All they needed to do was film a nice little video so the Elm Springs Arts Council could decide whether they would be performing on Christmas Eve. He wasn't asking for perfection, just for Charlie to let the choir actually get through the song.

"Gentlemen in the back!" Charlie snapped. "Straighten up, please. Eyes forward."

Julian got into position, just off to the side of Charlie. He lifted his phone. "Are we ready?"

"Yes," Charlie said. "Here we go. And one…and two…and…"

Julian hit Record, zooming in, taking in the residents and their smiles. There were fewer of them now.

"Stop! Stop!" Charlie called.

Julian deleted the recording and whirled around. "Now what?"

"The altos came in too late."

She couldn't be serious. "Who could even tell?"

Charlie's eyes narrowed. "Oh sorry, do you have a master's degree in music?"

"No, and neither does most of the Arts Council, I bet."

Julian watched Charlie's whole face shift from frustration to anger, her brows knitting together. Okay, maybe he shouldn't be antagonizing the one person who might actually be able to help him pull this off, but honestly this was getting out of hand.

Charlie needed to relax and deal with whatever was really bothering her, because how could she be this impatient with a bunch of seventysomethings trying their best? He was starting to feel a little irritated with her himself, remembering how hard he'd tried to get her to open up before she ghosted him eight years ago. He'd realized she was pulling away, but despite how often he asked her if something was wrong, she denied it, and then it was just over. And here he was again, asking if she was okay while she avoided his question.

Doris turned around on the piano bench, her hands pressed against her knees as she regarded Charlie. "Now we really do need to take five," she said, fiddling with her watch. "I'm starting a timer."

"Fine," Charlie huffed.

"Fine," Julian said. What was another five minutes?

Charlie stormed away to the table where she kept a book full of notes and started writing furiously. Julian went to brood on the other side of the room just as Diane popped her head in.

"Hey! How's everything going?"

"Oh," he said, caught off guard by her appearance. "Er… good. Great!" He looked around at the choir, mingling in tiny groups, throwing nervous glances in Charlie's direction. "They've been working really hard this morning, so we're taking a bit of a break. We're trying to get our audition video recorded."

"Yes, right. I remember you telling me that. Well, they're sounding better and better every time I pass by the room."

"You think?" Julian glanced over his shoulder to see if Charlie was listening. *See*, he wanted to say to her, but that probably wouldn't help his case.

"Absolutely. I've heard nothing but good things from the staff for days. Everyone's really excited about Glendale possibly performing on Christmas Eve. We've all got our fingers crossed for you. I just wanted to tell you that I'm really impressed with your out-of-the-box thinking here."

"Thanks," Julian said. "I appreciate that." It was a long shot, perhaps, but it was better than sitting around for the rest of the year, wishing for money to appear. "I figured this beat writing up another proposal that'll probably end up in some shredder."

Diane nodded. "I have a positive feeling about this."

Julian grinned. "You sure that isn't all the candy canes and caffeine?"

"Might be." She laughed. "Either way I just wanted you to know that all your hard work isn't going unnoticed. And if I had the budget, it'd be yours."

"I know," Julian said. He knew that if Diane could offer the support, she would. But he also understood that other things took priority, and she had to make tough decisions every day. Sort of the way he was going to have to make the tough decision to poke the grumpy Charlie-bear and attempt to film this video again.

"I'll let you get back to it," Diane said. "But can I throw my hat in the ring for 'Deck the Halls' for the final performance? Feels like all those fa-la-la-la-las would be a crowd-pleaser."

"I'll have the board take it under advisement," he joked. When she was gone, Julian turned around, bracing himself for round three…four? He'd lost count. All he could do was hope his out-of-the-box idea didn't crash and burn with the making of this video. He walked over to Charlie. "I think the choir's ready to give this another shot."

Charlie looked up at him from beneath her fluttery lashes. He couldn't tell what she was thinking, but boy, could he still sense the frustration that burned between them in her stiff posture and in the tight set of her mouth. Not that he was looking at it.

He cleared his throat. "If you're ready, that is."

"I'm ready." She breezed past him and called the choir back to their positions. Doris nodded from the piano. "Here we go," Charlie said. "And one…and two…and…"

Julian pulled out his phone and started recording. He stood perfectly still, afraid that an errant breeze might cause Charlie to halt the choir, but to his surprise, they reached the end of the song without any mishaps. He let out a relieved breath. Maybe Doris had made a good call. All they needed was a proper break to reset things.

Julian played the video back, his grin falling away the longer he watched. Now that he was really examining the choir, he couldn't ignore how rigid they appeared. They actually looked like they were afraid to move a muscle or crack a smile or do anything that would attract Charlie's scrutiny. It was all so serious, and not in a let's-win-this-competition way. It was more of a we-are-being-forced-to-stand-up-here-and-sing way. He couldn't send this to the Arts Council. They'd be rejected for sure.

"Charlie?" he called, worrying his lip. She'd already gotten so aggravated with him when he'd mentioned that she was being critical. What would she say about this? "Can you come take a look at this with me?"

She neared, leaning around his arm to watch the video. When it was done, she gave a curt nod. "Looks like we got it."

"Uh-huh, you don't see anything wrong?"

"I mean, the audio quality isn't the greatest," she said, "but that's more a problem with your phone."

Julian swallowed his grumble. "I'm talking about the way the choir looks."

"What about them?"

"Well…they're not really having any fun."

"What do you want?" Charlie snapped. "Them dressed in clown costumes, twirling balloon animals?"

Julian rolled his eyes. "That's not what I meant."

"And what did you mean?"

"Only that you've been sort of tough on them today."

"By asking them to be professional?"

"All I'm saying is that maybe if you lightened up a bit they would, too. They take their cues from you."

That had been entirely the wrong thing to say. He could see it now. Charlie coiled like a snake about to strike.

"If you think you can do a better job conducting this choir, then have at it, Julian!" She gathered up her things from the table and stormed out.

"Charlie!" he called after her. *Bahhhh!* He glanced back over his shoulder at the choir. "Uh, take five. No, twenty.

Actually, let's just call it for today. Good job, team!" He fist pumped the air, then dashed into the hallway.

Charlie was motoring, already turning into the lobby, shrugging into her winter coat.

"Charlie!" he called again, rushing after her. He ran past the front desk and out into a bitter, gray December day. It had been snowing all morning, more than Julian had expected. Charlie's car was buried under half a foot of snow. The parking lot hadn't even been cleared yet, and neither had the roads from what he could see.

"Where are you going?" he called after her.

"Home. To Gram's." She waved off his question. "Whatever. I have a house to organize. I don't need to be wasting my time here."

Julian groaned, his breath fogging in front of his face. "You weren't wasting your time. Just come back inside," he called. "The roads aren't clear yet."

Charlie stomped around her car, brushing at the snow with her coat sleeve. When she'd cleared enough to get the back door open, she reached inside for a snowbrush.

"Don't do something stupid just because you're annoyed with me," he called. "At least wait until the plows come out to clear the streets."

She ignored him.

The last thing he wanted was Charlie trying to drive in this. Best case she'd get stuck before she left the parking lot. Worst case she'd skid off the road and get into an accident. Julian picked up a handful of snow from the walkway, packed it together and hurled it in Charlie's direction. The snowball hit the windshield, releasing a spray of powder into the air.

Charlie squinted as the cloud of snow hit her face. She dropped the snowbrush. "Did you just throw snow at me?"

"Not at you," he clarified. "Just in your general direction."

"Knock it off!"

Julian ignored that request and threw another snowball. "Come back inside!"

Charlie picked up a handful of snow and threw it back. "Why? So you can tell me to lighten up some more?"

Julian dodged. "I didn't mean it, okay?"

"Yes, you did!"

A snowball exploded against the wall beside him. Hard. *Holy!* She had damn good aim.

"Everyone could see what you were thinking," she continued.

"Just...come inside. We can talk about it."

"I don't want to talk about it. I want to go home."

A snowball hit him square in the chest, and he groaned. *Dammit!* "Did that have a rock in it?"

Charlie froze with her arm up, glancing at the snowball in her hand.

"Don't make me come out there to get you," Julian warned, hands already up, ready to fend off another projectile.

Perhaps it was the challenge. Perhaps it was a desire to pummel him in the face, but Charlie let the snowball fly. Her aim was true again, and though Julian managed to bat it away, the spray of dust still left him shivering.

"All right, that's enough." He surged into the parking lot.

Charlie gave a little yelp and dove behind her car. "You started it!"

Julian chased after her, darting around the car. He twitched in the cold. "I'm not kidding, Charlie. I'm not letting you drive in this."

"You can't tell me what to do. I'm not one of your residents."

"I don't tell them what to do, either."

Charlie whipped around the end of her car. Julian doubled back, and though she was quick, he was quicker thanks to his long legs. He reached for her coat, just missing her.

Charlie jumped back, brandishing the snowbrush like a weapon, keeping him at a distance. "Stop it!"

"You stop it!" Julian latched onto the end of the snowbrush, hauling her closer.

She let out a puff of air, the space between them suddenly heated.

Julian felt like he'd just stepped into a sauna as his blood raced in his ears. "Don't make me throw you over my shoulder and haul you inside."

Her eyes narrowed in challenge. "You wouldn't."

He tugged on the snowbrush again, catching her wrist. "Try me."

"Okay," she squealed. "Okay!" She looked him up and down. He could feel the snow seeping into his socks. Feel Charlie's pulse skip under his fingers. "You're so dramatic."

"Well, I wouldn't have to be if you'd just cooperate," he said. Her cheeks were pink, the tip of her nose closer to cherry. He was tempted to brush his finger against her skin. To shift the blond hairs by her cheeks behind her ear. To tuck her into his arms, fending off the cold. He was tempted by delusion. "Truce?" he breathed.

"Truce."

He released the snowbrush and his wild desires, and she left it, leaning up against the car.

"Come have a coffee," he said, heading for the building. "As soon as the roads are clear, you can go."

"Fine," she muttered. He tried not to grin at the sight of her stomping along beside him. He didn't know why, but this felt like some kind of victory.

Charlie followed him back through the lobby. Erin frowned in his direction, but Julian shook his head. The universal sign for *don't ask*. He led Charlie to the dining room, blessedly empty between meals, and secured them two cups of piping hot coffee from the kitchen. They sat at a tiny table in the corner of the room.

"Did you really think the video was that bad?" Charlie asked after her first sip.

Julian shrugged. "Not bad. But you *were* being hard on them."

Charlie hummed. "Maybe."

"Maybe?"

She leaned her head on her hand, pouting. It was so adorable he almost reached for her hand.

"Look, it was still better than anything I could have done on my own. You're the best volunteer we've ever had." He wanted her to understand how amazing she'd been for Glendale. "I almost can't believe we lucked out with the opportunity to have someone of your caliber helping with the program."

Charlie turned away, a bit of a flush running up her neck.

"I mean it," he said. "You're really, really good at what you do."

"Thanks," she said softly. "All the schooling helps."

"Don't downplay your talent," Julian said. "I mean it. I'm sure Juilliard helped you hone it, but you have a gift, and I'm really glad you chose a career where you get to share it with the world."

She didn't look at him. Or maybe she wouldn't. He meant every word, though. She was born to perform.

"I was being a little tough," she admitted.

Julian smirked. "Was that so hard?"

Her eyes flickered to his, then back down to her coffee. "I realize that this is important to you. I'm not trying to ruin it."

"You haven't ruined anything."

She nodded slowly. "Can I ask… Why is the music program that important to you? You never really struck me as a musical guy. I thought you studied health sciences in school?"

"I did," Julian said. "A lot of my studies were actually in health and aging. Even took a couple of really interesting courses in cognitive neurosciences. But there was one that specifically looked at the role of music and the aging brain. I loved that course, and I think it partly inspired my desire to establish a successful music program here."

"And what was the other part?"

A muscle in Julian's cheek twitched as his thoughts turned to Grandma Sofia. "Actually, uh…it's mostly because my grandmother had dementia."

"I never knew that," Charlie said softly. She frowned, looking somewhat perplexed, like she was racking her brain for the information.

Julian smiled a bit. He couldn't remember if he'd ever mentioned his grandmother the summer they spent together. It had still been a sore spot for him, and maybe part of what he'd loved about the time he had with Charlie was the distraction and how easy it was to forget about the rest of the world. "I'm not sure if you remember that my parents are divorced?"

Charlie nodded.

"Well, after the divorce, things at home were pretty unstable for me as my parents figured out what their new lives looked like."

Charlie tipped her head, staring at him like she might be able to see straight past his bones, to the place his heart raced.

"Anyway, I started spending most of my time with my grandmother. She cleared out space for me in her home and in her life full-time."

"That's really sweet," Charlie said.

"She was an amazing lady," Julian agreed. "But when I got older… When I realized the disease was taking her from me and I couldn't return the favor of looking after her on my own, it was sort of devastating." Somehow even Grandma Sofia had left him behind, through no fault of her own. Julian swallowed down the weight of those feelings. "But the nursing home she ended up in had this amazing music therapy program, and on the days I visited, it provided a way for me to still connect with her. Even when she couldn't remember people or places or how to hold a fork, there was a place in her brain that music could reach. A place that brought her back to me. So I think for me, music is really all about connection. It unites people. I know that sounds silly."

"No," Charlie said softly, staring at him in a way that made Julian flush. "It sounds really nice. Glendale is lucky to have someone like you looking out for the residents."

Julian waved her off, slightly anxious about how personal he'd gotten.

"I mean it. I was so worried about how Gram would adjust to living at Glendale, but knowing how much you care about the residents and the programming here…" She shrugged. "I just want her to be happy, you know? I've been packing up her house and every room I tackle makes me think about everything she's given up. I never really thought about that before. About what it would be like to spend decades building a life only to slowly lose it to time." She shook her head. "Maybe that doesn't make any sense."

"I get it," Julian insisted. He did understand. "That's why I want this music program to work so badly. I want it to be a comfort as people make the transition to assisted living."

"I think that's partly why I let Gram talk me into this," she admitted. "I wanted her to feel comfortable and settled here before I left. And I really want her to find that sense of community and connection you talked about."

Partly, he thought. What other reason would she have had to say yes? He shoved those thoughts aside before he could dwell too long.

"I think Gram's been lonely lately," Charlie admitted, staring off across the dining room.

He studied the soft line of her jaw, remembering what it was like to kiss her there. "You don't get back to visit her as much?"

Charlie's face pinched all over and he had a sudden desire to smooth the harsh creases away, to be the person to comfort her, but he couldn't. There were lines here. Boundaries they both needed. "I, uh…" she started to say.

"I've found it easier not to be here. And my parents have been doing a lot of traveling lately. So Gram doesn't really have anyone."

Julian didn't understand. From what he remembered of their time together, Charlie had always loved spending time in Elm Springs. Her and her brother. "And Tom... He doesn't get back very often, either?"

Charlie clutched her elbows to her chest like she was preparing for a blow. "Tom actually passed away a couple years ago," she said, the words tumbling from her lips so quickly he thought he must have heard her wrong.

Julian blinked. It felt like a bomb had gone off in his head. He hadn't misheard, had he? Charlie didn't look at him, but it didn't matter. The words finally registered fully, and Julian felt them settle in his gut like acid, burning through his insides. He wished he could rewind the conversation or burn it from existence altogether. "Charlie, I'm so... I'm so sorry. I had no idea or I wouldn't have—"

"It's okay," she interrupted, hugging herself even tighter, her knuckles blanching around her elbows.

He was at a loss for words. He hadn't heard anything about Tom in town. Not that he would have. Doris was the only one of the family that had lived in Elm Springs, and it wasn't like they'd stayed in each other's lives these past eight years.

"You couldn't have known," Charlie said, continuing like she was compelled to fill the space. "But no, to answer your earlier question, Gram hasn't had all that much support in the wake of everything. Tom and I were traveling together and performing before it all happened, so we were away a lot. And since then, I've barely been able to stay in one place long enough to hold down a job, and

I certainly haven't been performing. Anyway, I guess I just mean that it'll be reassuring to know that Gram enjoys living at Glendale. That she has people to look out for her."

Julian wasn't sure what else to say. Suddenly all Charlie's panic from that first music class made sense. When she'd stood at the front of the room and told him she couldn't do the class, he hadn't understood her hesitation, but now he did. Maybe this even explained why she'd been so uptight with the choir today—she was still grieving the loss of her music partner.

"You know, Tom was always really kind to me," Julian said. "I remember that about him. He always made me feel welcome, even when I was crashing family time or stealing you away."

Charlie frowned, and Julian understood that she didn't want to talk about it anymore. He wanted to hug her, to drag her into his arms and squeeze until the pain she held so tightly ebbed away. Julian knew grief wasn't like that. It didn't just disappear. But he was still overwhelmed with the desire to hold her until it did.

He shifted the subject before he could do something foolish. "Just so you know, you don't have to worry about Doris. If you're not around for a while, I'll look out for her."

Charlie stared at him, her eyes wide and glassy, and she was suddenly so close. She reached for his face, her fingertips soft against his cheek.

He tilted his head a bit, pressing into her palm, memory flooding through him. Heat swelled in his chest, and he was overwhelmed with the urge to close the distance. The familiarity was like pulling on a favorite sweater. Comfortable. Right. And then, as if all the rational thought had bled from his body, Julian leaned in and caught her lips.

They were soft and supple, and so still, as if her body was responding to the shock. In a rush of panic, he thought about pulling away and apologizing, but then Charlie moved, tilting her head. Her lips parted as his hands wrapped around her upper arms, holding her close.

She tasted like burned coffee and strawberry chapstick. Julian kissed Charlie like he'd never stopped kissing her, and for a split second, it felt like he existed in a world where no time had passed. A world where Tom was still alive and they had endless summers ahead of them. Julian made a sound against her mouth, and Charlie fell into him further. His hands left her arms and wrapped around her back, smoothing over the grooves of her spine. She placed her hands on his chest, her fingers tightening in his shirt as his tongue swept across her lower lip.

The squeak of a cart cut through the fog in his brain, and Julian wrenched away suddenly. He couldn't be doing this with her. He couldn't let the emotion of the past cloud his judgment, messing with the present. Charlie was confused and upset and grieving, and he was opening himself up to the pain of rejection, to the reality of being left behind. He looked up to see Warren poke his head into the room. "Plows have come by," he called. "In case anyone's been stranded."

"Thanks," Julian called back, struggling to keep his voice even. His heart pounded, and all he wanted to do was drag Charlie back into his arms. But he couldn't.

"I should go," Charlie said, jumping to her feet. "Thanks for the coffee."

Julian opened his mouth to say something, but nothing

came out. He'd tried to make something work between them once already. He knew how this would end, so this time when she ran off, he didn't try to chase her. He didn't need to sign up to be her collateral damage.

Eight

Charlie

"Okay, everybody on the bus!" Julian called, his breath fogging in the cold. "We are leaving now. Not in ten minutes. Not after you've tried to fix the bingo numbers. Not after you've stopped to discuss this morning's episode of *The Price Is Right*."

"Terrible episode," Gram muttered as they wandered toward the bus. "How do you lose out on a car twice?"

Charlie rubbed her hands together, trying to get the feeling back in her fingers. "I think the woman panicked." She caught Julian's eye as she neared, glancing away quickly. Speaking of sweat-inducing, heart-thumping, lip-gloss-smeared panic…

"Maggie, Harriet, don't think I won't leave you here!" Julian continued.

Charlie glanced over her shoulder. Maggie and Harriet dawdled by the front entrance, whispering with an elderly gentleman before dashing toward the bus which was destined for the community center this morning. Charlie should have been back at Gram's house, sorting or packing or doing any number of moving-related things, but Gram had insisted on her company today.

After the way she stormed off yesterday during rehearsal, Charlie felt like she owed it to her. So she did her best to ignore the flutter in her gut as she raced past Julian and ducked into an empty seat near the back of the bus.

"We're here, we're here!" Maggie sang, climbing the stairs with Harriet right behind her. They squeezed past Julian.

"Way to rush a lady trying to organize her gingerbread team," Harriet complained.

What the hell was a gingerbread team? Charlie didn't want to know.

"If my hip acts up, I'm blaming you," Harriet told Julian.

"I'll get Warren on standby," Julian joked. "All right, Walt, let's hit the road." He clapped the bus driver on the shoulder.

The bus rumbled to life and pulled away from the curb slowly. Julian stood at the front, hanging onto a seat with one hand, the other holding a clipboard. "Thank you to all those who have braved the cold to join us today. We have two exciting events on the agenda. A showing of *Miracle on 34th Street* and the annual community Christmas Market."

"Which version?" Jim called.

"Of what?"

"The movie. Better be the 1947 version," he said.

Julian smirked. "Probably the superior 1994 version."

"Oh, absolutely not!" Jim complained. That was all it took. Suddenly the bus erupted into a spirited debate about black-and-white versus color and the pros and cons of the

Santas. Charlie was partial to the original herself, probably because that was the one she'd watched with Tom and Gram growing up.

"I'll tell you where you can stuff your Santa," Harriet said.

"Keep it clean," Julian warned. "Or I will turn this bus around."

"No, you won't!" came a chorus of voices.

Charlie used the distraction to spy down the aisle, taking in Julian as he laughed and gave Jim some good-natured ribbing. She hadn't been eager to trap herself in an enclosed space with him so soon. Not after that kiss.

What had gotten into them?

Frankly, she'd been thinking too much about the entire thing since it happened: the softness of his lips, the warmth of him, the way her heart had raced.

All she could remember was how good he used to make her feel and how simple life once was. Summer had been so easy, and falling for Julian during those long days had been even easier. It hadn't grown complicated until they both went back to school. They'd given it a shot—the long-distance thing—but it had been too hard to hold onto with the demands of her future hurtling toward her. It was no one's fault, really, simply a case of not the right place at the right time.

Charlie had had a choice to make back then. A career performing was all about making the right impressions on the right people, and she'd had to prioritize Juilliard. Besides, it wasn't like she and Julian had ever put a label on anything. But even though it hadn't worked out between them back then, there was something intoxicating about already knowing how good he could make her feel. She wanted that.

Wanted *him*.

But Julian was from a time before Tom's loss, a time that she'd already packed away. She couldn't reopen herself to those desires. To constant reminders of what her life had been. It would be like picking at wounds she was barely managing to keep closed.

And that was dangerous.

The image of Julian wrapping his arms around her, drawing her deeper into the kiss, burned at the forefront of her mind even as she wished it away.

She couldn't be that version of herself. That Charlie—the driven optimist with her career plotted out perfectly—had been buried with her brother.

A blush prickled in her cheeks. The heat spread down her neck. She could feel it like a flame licking at her skin. Eager, demanding.

Consuming.

Pull yourself together. Julian didn't want her like that anyway; he hadn't even remembered her.

But he kissed you like he remembered you, her mind whispered.

Stop.

She wasn't playing this game. She was here for a reason. Get Gram settled, get the house sorted, get this choir to the Christmas Eve finish line. Get the hell out of town. There wasn't room in her life for anything else. Or anyone. Kisses be damned.

"You okay?" Gram asked, turning to her.

"Fine," Charlie squeaked.

"You look a little flushed. Not getting sick, are you?"

"It's just warm in here," she said. "They probably have the heat cranked."

Gram hummed. "I'm quite comfortable."

Charlie swallowed hard. She needed to stop thinking about Julian and focus on the emails from Alicia that were piling up in her inbox instead. She needed to commit to work. Or, at the very least, to an audition.

She mulled that over as they made their way down the slushy streets through town, passing familiar storefronts and the diner where she'd first met Julian. Elm Springs looked like something out of a holiday movie, with tourists flocked to the charming Christmas window displays, all of them dressed up with garlands and ribbons.

When they reached the community center, Julian hopped off the bus, welcoming the residents as they climbed down the stairs one by one. He offered a hand where necessary, though Charlie carefully kept hers tucked away in her coat pocket. She hurried off after Gram and into the center.

A cacophony of voices drifted from the large auditorium where a projector screen had been drawn across a stage. There was a cute little booth dishing out popcorn and a series of tables set up around the perimeter of the space with various Christmas Market displays. From the looks of it, vendors were selling everything from handmade clothing to ornaments to homemade honey and candles, crafts and desserts. Charlie took a deep breath, overwhelmed by an intoxicating mix of melted butter and cinnamon and gingerbread.

"Have you tried Merla's mincemeat tarts?" Maggie asked, coming up and looping her arm through Gram's. She pointed out a vendor table. "She only sells them at

Christmas. I've been trying to get the recipe for years, but she won't part with it."

"Because you can't bake," Harriet muttered.

Charlie chuckled under her breath.

"Says who?" Maggie complained.

"You made Jim that plate of cookies once, and he swears he got food poisoning."

Maggie waved her off. "That was totally unrelated." She toddled away with Gram in tow.

Charlie exchanged a look with Harriet, biting her lip to keep from laughing.

"I'd advise against eating any Christmas baking she tries to give you," Harriet said.

Charlie nodded. "Noted."

They followed after Maggie and Gram as they secured mincemeat tarts and then moved on to the popcorn stand.

"Mm-hmm," Maggie said. "Smells divine."

"Smells like I'm gonna have to double up on my cholesterol medication," Harriet said.

They joined the short line, waiting for buttery popcorn. Charlie spotted Julian near the front of the line, conversing with a young woman.

"That's Heather," Maggie said, leaning back to inform Charlie like it was a trade secret. "She's the event coordinator here. Married five years. Two adorable children."

"Just in case you were wondering," Harriet said, giving Charlie a sly smile.

"I wasn't." They all took a step forward. "You know what," Charlie said. "I think I'm going to wander around some of the vendor displays."

Gram snatched her arm. "You're supposed to be spending time with me."

"I don't think you need another escort to get popcorn. The three of you seem to have it under control."

"Any particular reason you're avoiding your codirector?" Harriet asked, inspecting her fingernails.

Charlie's pulse skipped. "What?"

"Just an observation."

"I'm not avoiding him," she spluttered. God, was she that obvious?

"No, of course not," Harriet said, taking Charlie's other arm. They steered her toward the front of the line.

"Welcome, ladies," Heather said, filling tiny red-and-white popcorn bags. "How are we liking things?"

"Excellent as always," Maggie said. "Though it would be better if Merla would sell me her mincemeat recipe."

Charlie stood there awkwardly, looking anywhere but at Julian, wondering how rude it would be if she simply slipped away. But suddenly they were all tipping to the side as Gram staggered. Her arms flailed, knocking Heather's giant bowl of popcorn clear off the table. It tumbled to the floor, kernels spilling free.

"Gram!" Charlie yelped as she and Julian simultaneously reached to steady her. "Are you okay?"

"Oh, fine. Fine!" Gram said a little breathlessly. "It's just this buggered hip. Has a mind of its own." She apologized to Heather. "Let me tell you, never get old."

"No one ever cried over spilled popcorn," Heather said with a smile. "There's more in the kitchen."

"You didn't mention that your hip was bothering you," Charlie murmured, trying to get Gram's attention.

"Didn't I?"

Behind Gram, Maggie and Harriet were suddenly very preoccupied shoving mincemeat tarts in their mouths.

Charlie frowned. Gram hadn't mentioned her hip since before the move to Glendale. When had it started acting up again?

"I'm old," Gram said, patting Charlie's arm. "Things hurt unexpectedly at my age. But again, I'm so sorry, Heather. I'm sure Charlie would be more than happy to help you make some more popcorn. I'd do it, but you know..." She winced as she flexed her leg. "These old bones. Probably best I have a seat. Yes, definitely from the fall. You go be a doll and help Heather out with her popcorn. Perhaps Julian can show you to the kitchen. He seems to know his way around."

"Oh, that would be a big help," Heather said, looking between them.

"You're sure you're okay, Doris?" Julian asked.

Gram waved him off. "I've got Maggie and Harriet. They'll help me putter into a chair."

Maggie and Harriet scrambled to Gram's sides, making a show of helping her limp away.

"We've got this," Maggie called. "You two get popping or whatever it is you have to do."

Get popping? Charlie grimaced.

"You're sure I'm not putting you out?" Heather asked, drawing Charlie's attention.

"Oh no," Charlie said. "Happy to help." She smiled despite herself. Gram was getting very good at offering her up for things.

"Okay, great," Heather said. "I had a few volunteers on it, but they've been gone for ages. Julian, you know your way to the kitchen, don't you?"

"Sure do," he said, sounding less than enthusiastic. "Just this way."

Charlie followed him back across the auditorium, wondering what she was supposed to say. "Sorry about her. Gram can be—"

"A handful?" he suggested.

She snorted. "As much as Maggie and Harriet apparently."

"It's okay. Glendale's full of characters. I'm used to it. Though I do think those three together are going to spell trouble."

He walked beside her, and the awkwardness seeped in along with something else. Something that threatened to strangle her. Damn that kiss! Charlie knew she should have pulled away the moment it happened, that she should have ended things right then and there. But he'd tugged her closer, wrapping his arms around her, holding her to him like a memory. And she'd tried to understand why it felt so right when everything else about the past now felt so wretched. Why did she want to kiss him again?

They turned down a hall, revealing a bank of offices. "I never realized this place was so big."

"They won a grant about five years back," Julian said, "and did a major expansion. Added a gym for sports. The industrial kitchen. Classrooms. Workspaces. It's really become the hub of the town."

When they entered the kitchen, they found the two other volunteers bent over in front of the microwave. They looked about five years younger than Gram.

"We've been sent to help," Julian explained.

"Perfect timing!" one of the women said. "This contraption has dials instead of buttons. I don't know what's going on. Could you just put these bags through the microwave for Heather?"

"Sure," Charlie said. The volunteers hurried off, leaving her and Julian alone. She occupied herself taking the plastic off one of the popcorn bags and shoved it in the microwave. She frowned at the dials, cranking one.

The microwave turned on. Charlie eyed it suspiciously.

"I don't think it's going to spontaneously come to life," Julian joked lightly.

"We'll see." She leaned back against the metal counter and took him in. He looked...confused. A line appeared between his brows. Maybe he was wondering how he'd gotten roped into Gram's schemes. "Everything okay?"

"Good, you?"

"Yep."

"Great," he said again, leaning over to look into the microwave. "I don't think this is working."

Charlie leaned over, too, accidentally brushing his arm, her skin flushing with goose bumps at the contact.

This was getting them nowhere. But where exactly did she want to be? A couple weeks ago he'd acted as if he didn't even remember who she was. Now though, things felt different. No, not different exactly. Familiar. He was still Julian. Still that sweet guy she'd fallen so hard for. If she was being honest with herself, she was the one who changed. She'd become a different person since losing Tom. Could she really blame him for not recognizing her?

He didn't know her anymore.

But I want you to, she caught herself thinking before she could stop herself. She wanted someone to see how hard she was trying to hold herself together and tell her that it was okay if she slipped. That if she let in a little light, the darkness wouldn't come flooding back with it. The popcorn bag jumped, the kernels exploding, and they both startled, glancing over at each other with awkward laughter.

Charlie cleared her throat, straightening up. "I'm sorry."

Julian rose slowly. "For what?"

"Kissing you the other day." She couldn't find any other way around the tension but to cut right through it. "Encouraging it the way I did. Especially at your place of employment. I don't know what came over me. That was a boundary I shouldn't have crossed."

"Do you really not know what came over you?" he asked quietly.

She shrugged, a blush creeping up her neck. "The past maybe. Being back in Elm Springs. Seeing you again. And I guess…it felt like the right thing to do in the moment."

He laughed as the microwave beeped. They both ignored it. "The right thing to do?"

"Yes." Because despite how hard she'd worked to keep from feeling anything, he'd made her feel something. And as terrifying as that still was, as much as she wanted to bolt, she couldn't deny that the laughter and the flutters in her stomach and the music had felt so, so good. Julian was making her unearth those things again. But he was also making her unearth Tom.

She usually held Tom close to her chest, but she'd told Julian because she'd felt safe. She was sinking back into him like sinking into the melody of a favorite song, and with everything else around her changing—losing Tom, moving Gram into Glendale—something easy was very tempting.

"Do you regret it?" he asked.

"No," she said, the truth of the word catching in her throat. "Do you?"

"It was unexpected," he admitted. "But not…unwanted."

She sighed. "I don't understand you."

"What do you mean?"

"You go out of your way to assure me you don't remember our summer together, but then you mention something and I know you have more than vague memories of that time." She huffed, blowing her blond hair from her eyes. "So which is it? Did you really not remember me? Or did you not want to remember?"

"I remembered," Julian admitted. "The moment I saw you in that hall, I remembered."

"You did?"

He nodded, staring at the wall. "I remember the way your hair had these almost copper strands in the sun. And I remember Tom teasing you the first couple of times I showed up to pick you up. And I remember Doris's coffee cake. The way it crumbled if you didn't eat it quickly enough. And I remember lying out next to the river with you, hearing nothing but bees and the rush of water."

Charlie swallowed the bubble of emotion in her throat. He remembered so many details. So many of the things she'd packed away. "Then why did you lie that first day?"

"I don't know," he said, his gaze falling briefly. "I guess I sort of panicked. It had been a long time since we'd seen each other and…"

"What?" Charlie asked. What wasn't he saying?

"Maybe I was a little surprised, too."

"At how much we immediately irritated each other?" she said, giving him a coy smile, trying to lighten the mood.

He shook his head; the tension ebbed. "At how good it felt seeing you again."

Charlie gasped as he pressed closer. "Julian—"

"You'd think something from that long ago wouldn't

linger," he said, brows drawn together. "You'd think the feelings would...go away."

"I think it's a choice," Charlie said, hugging her arms to her chest even as her body gravitated toward him. "To put the feelings away, to stamp them out."

"Are you saying you don't..." He trailed off. "Is this all..." He clutched his forehead. "I mean, dammit, Charlie, you've gotta say something!"

"Say what? What are you wanting me to say?"

He gestured awkwardly between them. "You kissed me back, and you don't regret it, so I'm asking if there's... *any*thing here?"

Charlie's breathing grew heavy. Ragged. Anything of what? The spark...the irritation...the desire? There was everything between them still, and it was dangerous. It was going to unravel her.

But maybe she wanted to be unraveled.

Charlie surged forward, wrapping her arms around Julian's neck, sinking into the softness of him, caving to the pressure of his lips. Everything would be fine, she told herself as he cupped her jaw, nipping at her bottom lip.

This was fine.

The pull between them... It was only because it had been so long since she'd had someone in her bed. It had nothing to do with her heart getting tangled up in something complicated. She'd had enough complicated to last her a lifetime. She didn't need any more.

They bumped against the metal counter and then the microwave. It beeped in response, demanding to be opened. Neither of them reacted to the noise. Instead, Julian's hands glided down her arms, and then to the small of her back before dropping to cup her ass.

He squeezed, and she groaned. "Is there somewhere a little more out of the way?"

"Popcorn not doing it for you?" he rasped.

"It's great," she teased. "Just hoping for something—"

"Private?" he suggested, nipping at her lips. He took her hand, tugging her out the door and back down the hall to that bank of offices. Charlie had no idea where they were going, but Julian seemed to know the way. He grabbed a doorknob, twisted and dragged her through, closing the door behind them.

The flick of the lock started her heart racing.

Julian twisted the blinds over the door. The room was dim, almost too dark to see anything but the hazy shape of furniture. He collapsed onto a small sofa, pulling Charlie down with him.

She wasted no time climbing into his lap and kissed her way down his throat.

He let his hands wander across her back and over hips, kneading her thighs. Charlie gasped into his mouth, the motion familiar. She ground down against him, and that was familiar, too. She pulled back a bit, breathing hard.

"You don't have to stop," Julian said.

He took her hips, guiding her movements more purposefully, and Charlie's eyes fluttered closed. She remembered this. She burned for this.

"Let me make you feel good," he whispered in her ear.

He'd been so wonderful at it. She bet he still was.

Charlie's hands fell to his shoulders, anchoring herself. Her lips grazed his jaw lazily. Julian repositioned, getting his thigh between her legs. She rocked against him, and he flexed, putting pressure on all the right places.

A moan bled between her lips.

"That's it," he whispered.

She trembled in anticipation, imagining all the ways in which he might make her come undone. She wanted him so badly he might not even need to touch her, but she wanted him to. His fingers. His tongue. She wanted everything.

His hands inched beneath her shirt, counting her ribs with his fingertips, grazing the underside of her bra. Charlie's head grew fuzzy. The haze was pleasantly warm.

But then there were voices in the hall, muttering about popcorn and the beeping microwave.

"Shit," Charlie said, her eyes flying open. "We didn't finish."

Julian smirked at her.

"I meant the popcorn," she muttered, almost breathless.

"I think they've already figured that out."

"We should stop," she said.

"We should."

He dropped his hands, and she stilled her hips, feeling wholly unsatisfied. She grumbled, climbing out of his lap.

"Wait," he said, dragging her back down. "Do you want to come?"

Her breath escaped her. She nodded, so close to him she could feel the stubble on his cheek.

"Okay," he said simply, sliding his hand down the front of her pants, inching his fingers past her underwear and the wet heat that gathered there.

Charlie cried out as he dragged his fingers against her clit.

"Shh," he whispered against her lips. "Hush."

She nodded, biting down on her lip as he found a rhythm

that worked, pressing his fingers against her. It was fast and frenzied, and Charlie came, shuddering in his arms.

"Yes, yes, *yes*," she hissed.

"Good," he said as her hips jumped. "Gentle now. I remember how sensitive you are after." He pulled his hand out of her pants slowly.

Charlie came back to her senses, holding him close. She could feel his eyelashes against her cheek.

"We should probably get back out there before Maggie and Harriet send the patrols," Julian whispered.

Charlie nodded, climbing out of his lap and gesturing to the door. "I'm gonna…"

"Yeah," he said, leaning his head back on the couch. "I'll be there in a second. Once everything is behaving."

Charlie fought off a tiny smile as she slipped through the door and smoothed her hands down her shirt, making her way back to the auditorium. It felt like everyone knew what they'd just done, but that was impossible. Right? She tucked her hair behind her ears.

The projector was on, the big screen filled with an error message.

She spotted Gram sitting front and center with Maggie and Harriet. She hurried over and did her best not to acknowledge the moment Julian entered the room.

"Are you feeling okay?" Gram asked her, reaching for Charlie's forehead. "You're still looking a little flushed. You're sure you aren't coming down with a fever or something? It's flu season."

Charlie batted her hand away, sinking down in her seat. "I'm fine."

She glanced up as Heather hurried across the stage. "Hi, folks. Looks like we're having some technical difficulties," she said. "I've put our more tech-savvy volunteers on the job, so things should be fixed in no time." She laughed uncertainly. "Until then, has anyone got any stand-up they want to run by an already gathered crowd?"

A few people tittered in response.

Then Julian called, "How about a song?"

Charlie twisted around, looking at him in confusion. He just winked at her.

"Be my guest," Heather said, waving Julian up. "A joke, a song. I don't think I'm in a position to deny, either."

Julian hurried onto the stage. "Ladies and gentleman," he called out.

Charlie shook her head. *Please no.* They weren't ready for this kind of thing.

"I would like to invite you to enjoy the musical stylings of Glendale's very own choir."

Charlie glanced over her shoulder, taking stock of the room. The residents looked surprised but eager as Julian waved them up.

Gram elbowed Charlie out of her seat. "Go on. We need the choir director up there."

"I thought your hip was sore?"

"It's feeling much better."

Charlie narrowed her eyes but allowed herself to be pushed along by Gram and Maggie. Harriet cajoled some of the less eager members toward the stage before waving to the crowd, hamming it up. Julian popped down to help wheel Frank up the handicap ramp.

"What are you doing?" Charlie said when she was close enough to Julian. "We didn't rehearse for this!"

"I think this is called an impromptu performance."

"*Julian.*"

"Can't disappoint your fans." He shot her a cheeky, dimpled grin.

"You are so annoying."

"That's not what you were thinking a few minutes ago."

"Screw you," she grumbled.

"I sort of wish you had."

Charlie turned away before her entire body could light up like a Christmas tree. It was only one orgasm. *Get a hold of yourself.* But it was more than that. She knew it as she watched him rile up the crowd. She'd let herself feel something for him again, and some part of her knew it was too late to stuff it back in the box. She could try, but the truth was, she was falling, and she didn't know where she would land.

"Ladies and gentlemen," Julian called. "Give it up for the Glendale Shakers!"

There was an abrupt round of applause.

Charlie turned to the choir. "Okay then," she said, a finger pressed to either cheek, reminding them all to smile. "Let's give them a show. And one…and two…and…"

Nine

Julian

"Be careful with those!" Julian called to his crew of resident volunteers. "This is fragile merchandise we're dealing with."

"Please tell me that's what I think it is?" Warren said, rubbing his hands together as he came over to inspect the boxes in the dining room.

Julian grinned. Every year he coordinated with a local bakery to make them a couple dozen gingerbread house kits for a friendly little decorating contest. The residents and the staff had gotten surprisingly competitive with it over the years, forcing Julian to establish an entire judging panel and rules of conduct—mostly thanks to Harriet-led gingerbread sabotage. "Is your decorating team picked?"

"Oh, the nurses had that on lock mid-September," Warren said. "We're not messing around this year."

Julian smirked, gingerly laying a kit and decorating supplies in the center of one of the tables. He knew Warren was serious. For a few hours every year, friendships were tested over gumdrops and royal icing, rivalries were set aside in favor of a steady hand, and the dining room reached *The Great British Bake Off* levels of drama. "Been perfecting your piping techniques?"

"You know it," Warren said. "Nobody in this place can touch my string work."

"That's a bold statement," Harriet said, joining them in the room. She had Maggie and Doris in tow.

Julian glanced to the doorway, expecting, wishing, *wanting* Charlie to be right behind them. Disappointment flooded him when the doorway remained empty, but there was a quiet thrill there, too—the thrill of anticipation—and it made him a little hot around the collar. His thoughts whisked back to the community center, to asking Charlie if there was something here and her throwing herself at him. Kissing him. Grinding down on his lap in that office. Julian swallowed hard, wrenching away from those thoughts before all his blood could rush south, and placed another gingerbread kit.

"The nurses took second place last year," Warren said to Harriet. "And we've been putting the work in. This year we're definitely taking first."

Maggie tutted, a secret little smile curling up the side of her face. "Don't count your trophies yet. I think you'll be surprised to see what the art class has up their sleeve."

"Are you still good to be on our judging panel this year?" Julian asked her.

"Of course." Maggie laid a hand on her chest. "I'd like to think I can be impartial."

"Mm-hmm," Warren said, eyeing her up suspiciously. "Your close friendships have been noted."

Maggie waved off his comment as Doris said, "Is it really that serious?"

"Absolutely. Glendale gets very competitive over gingerbread houses," Julian explained. "There's sabotage and intrigue. People are disqualified and banned from future competitions. Bonbons are thrown. Icing is tampered with. Gingerbread walls are knocked down." He lifted his hand to whisper. "The real trick is to make sure your icing is tacky before you start positioning the walls."

"And the administration staff always cheat!" Harriet added.

"They do!" Warren agreed. "Remember when they sneaked in that hot glue gun?" The two of them exploded into conversation like a pair of birds squabbling over birdseed.

"What do you win?" Doris muttered from the corner of her mouth.

"Mostly bragging rights," Julian said. "And a tiny trophy."

"Speaking of the administration staff," Maggie said, interrupting Harriet and Warren. "I should inquire if they actually plan on entering this year. I didn't see their team on the sign-up sheet."

"They'll be here," Harriet muttered, eyes narrowing. "To defend their title."

"I feel like we need a truce," Warren said, nudging Harriet. "We join forces. Take down the admin team?"

"Bring that new nurse with you, and you've got a deal. I hear she's good at blood work. Has steady hands. She'll crush the roof lattice."

"Good idea," Warren said, the two of them shaking on the deal. He hurried out the door, and Harriet, Maggie and Doris rushed after him, their heads bent close together.

Julian should probably have been more worried about the amount of plotting that was already taking place, but he was distracted by a familiar head of blond hair. "Hey, Charlie!" he called, practically hurling himself across the dining room to get her attention. "Charlie!"

She whirled around in the hall, unwinding a scarf from her neck, a book of sheet music tucked under her arm. "Julian, hey!"

She sounded a little breathless, her cheeks a little flushed, and all Julian could think about were the sounds she'd made yesterday, her voice trembling next to his ear as he'd unraveled her. He'd spent all evening reliving that moment. He licked his lips as he took her in, her snow-damp hair curling at the ends. She was beautiful, and he knew he was in trouble.

"What's all this?" she asked, drawing closer.

Julian tapped a sign on the dining room door. "Glendale's annual gingerbread house decorating contest."

She laughed. "You really like the competitions here, huh?"

"What can I say? The residents enjoy their traditions and their petty rivalries." They grinned at each other, and Julian felt a wave of desire crash through him. "So, what do you think? Will you be joining said contest this year?"

"Not a huge fan of gingerbread," Charlie admitted.

Julian made a face. "Good thing you don't have to eat it. You just have to create a masterpiece."

"Oh, a masterpiece?" Charlie said. "Is that all?"

"You could enter on behalf of the choir."

The corners of her lips twitched. "The choir needs to practice on the off chance we make it into the competition. No one needs a gingerbread-shaped distraction."

"I'd argue there's time for both," he said, studying her teasing smirk, wondering what she was thinking about. Was it kissing him? His hand between her legs? The way she'd writhed?

Work, his mind practically screamed at him. Focus on the work. Because whatever was going on between him and Charlie was far more complicated than sneaking away for some secret community center sex.

"But speaking of the choir, I do have something to show you." He fumbled around in his pocket. "Damn, I left my phone upstairs. Do you have yours?"

"It's dead," she said. "I need to charge it."

"Okay, come with me." He started down the hall toward the elevator.

"Where are we going?"

"To my office." She glanced at him, perhaps a little amused. "What?"

She shook her head. "Nothing."

The elevator door opened, and Julian hit the third floor button as it closed again.

"You're in a good mood," she said without looking at him.

"It's gingerbread day. I'm stoked."

"Mm-hmm," Charlie said, her eyelashes fluttering. "Stop staring at me like that."

"Like what?"

"Nothing is going to happen," she said, like she was trying to assure them both. Her eyes were bright, twinkling under those damn elevator lights again.

"What *nothing* are we referring to?"

"You know," Charlie insisted.

"Do I?"

Her lips twisted. "I'm not going to remind you if that's what you're waiting for."

"Hey," Julian said, holding his hands up. "I thought we were riding the elevator."

"Yes," Charlie agreed. "That's all."

"What else would we be riding?" he said, knowing he was treading too close to a line he should avoid. But he couldn't help himself. Couldn't help the desire to touch her. He lifted his hand, stroking a finger down her cheek, along her jaw. Some sensible part of him knew it would be terrible to lose her twice, but with her looking at him like that, he remembered what it was to feel wanted and to want her in return. The memory was intoxicating.

She blinked up at him. "I told you not to stare at me like that."

"Well, you never answered my question. How am I supposed to stop staring at you if I don't know how I'm staring at you?"

"Like you've seen me naked," she clarified.

"Well, I have. It's been a long time, though." *Don't do it, Don't...* "I could use a refresher."

Her breath hitched, and he liked the sound. Liked how unnerved she was and that needy look in her eyes. "Shut up," she finally said, fighting a grin. He dropped his hand. "We need to focus on the choir."

"I'm good at multitasking." A lie. He was barely managing.

Charlie took a step toward him, forcing him back against the wall of the cab. Every muscle in his body tensed, his heart knocking against his ribs. Then the elevator door rolled open, and he was saved from doing something foolish. Julian surged out of the cab, sucking in a settling breath as he led Charlie down the hall to his office.

He knew getting tangled up with Charlie again was full of unknowns. She was still grieving Tom, dealing with Doris, reluctantly volunteering. That had *unpredictable* written all over it, and she'd ghosted him for what felt like less. There was nothing stopping her from doing it again despite how right things had felt at the community center yesterday. So how could he get involved with someone who had no idea what they wanted? This was exactly the kind of situation he'd spent the last eight years avoiding—the one where he'd end up alone.

But... his mind screamed.

But what? He was smarter than this. Julian walked around his desk and shook his mouse to wake up his computer screen. "I wanted to show you what Heather sent to me this morning." He twisted the monitor toward her.

"Heather from the community center?" Charlie clarified as he hit Play on a video.

He nodded, waiting for her reaction. "Apparently it's going viral."

Charlie leaned close to him, staring at the screen, and he could almost feel the heat of her skin. *Focus*, he told himself, and he did, watching her face to spot the exact moment she recognized the auditorium and the choir.

"Wait, is this—"

"The community center performance," Julian said, nodding. "Someone recorded the choir and uploaded it online. It only had a couple thousand views when I looked at it this morning. Now it's already climbing through the tens of thousands. If this continues, I wouldn't be surprised if it hit a hundred thousand by the end of the week."

"But...why would anyone want to watch that?"

"What are you talking about?" Julian exclaimed. "Look at you guys! You're adorable. You sound amazing."

"Pretty sure Harriet is attempting to twerk," Charlie said, laughing as she pointed it out on screen.

"Which the comment section is loving," Julian said, shaking his head. He started the video from the beginning. He'd never seen the residents so enthusiastic. They beamed, clearly having fun, and best of all, so was Charlie as she directed them through the song.

Charlie knuckled a spot on her chest. Julian caught the motion from the corner of his eye, and he wondered if she was thinking about Tom.

Charlie cleared her throat. "They do sound great."

He scrolled to some of the comments, trying to distract her. "Look at this. People really seem to love them. 'Oh my God! How adorable. Reminds me of my grandparents.' And this one... 'Does anyone know who this choir is? I'd love to show them my support.'"

"You were right," Charlie said.

"About what?"

Charlie scrolled up and paused the video. "That I needed to lighten up. Look how big those smiles are when I'm not ordering them around. This is how happy people always looked when working with Tom," she said softly, growing quiet and thoughtful for a moment. "He expected greatness but never at the expense of loving the music. Maybe I was trying too hard to emulate him and asking for the wrong things." Her finger brushed over Doris's face on screen, caught in a moment of joy. "They should be enjoying themselves like this all the time. Or else what's the point of any of it?"

"I'm glad to hear you say that," Julian said. "Because I think we've found our audition tape."

Charlie's eyes widened. "You don't think we can do better? I mean, maybe if we—"

"Charlie," he said, halting her before she could overthink it. "I think this perfectly captures the Glendale Shakers. A little imperfect but with a lot of heart. And!" He pulled the keyboard closer so he could open up his inbox.

"There's more?"

He stood aside to show Charlie an email. "The local news station got a hold of me," he explained. "They want to do a story on the choir."

"No way!" Charlie said, scanning the email. "All because of the video?"

"I don't know where else they would have heard of us. I'll have to run it by Diane first, to make sure they're cleared to film in Glendale, but this could be great press. Might even bolster our application to the Arts Council if we've got public support behind us."

Charlie chuckled.

"What?"

"Who'd have thought that little performance would spark all of this?"

"I don't think anyone really expects when things go viral. But this was all you."

Charlie flushed. "Pretty sure you're the one who had the impromptu performance idea."

"Yeah, but the choir never would have been ready for that if I was running this solo. We'd still be trying to get that lip buzzing thing right." He reached out and brushed a lock of her hair behind her ear. *Danger zone. Retreat!* "And I'm serious. None of this would be possible without you, Charlie."

"We'll agree it was a team effort. Because without your encouragement and support, none of us would have gotten up there," she said. Her eyes bored into his.

Julian's gaze flickered to her lips. He didn't know what was happening between them. All he knew was that he wanted to hold her again.

That was foolish. *Don't dive too deep too fast. Don't get whisked away into the danger zone.* This wasn't a sunny summer fling, no matter how warm his chest felt. *Retreat… Pull back…*

Oh, to hell with the danger!

He surged forward and pressed his lips to hers. Heat spread through him, consumed him, and he wanted to drown in her. Charlie met him, nudging at his chest until he stumbled against the desk. He sat down, shorter like this, and Charlie took advantage, standing between his legs to deepen the kiss.

"We shouldn't," she said, even as she tilted her head, fitting her lips to his more snugly. "Not here."

"I agree."

"Not like this."

"Anyone could see."

The open door. Julian could have laughed at how little he cared. Sparks went off in his mind and all he could think about was how he wanted to sink into the softness of Charlie.

She moaned against him as his lips found her neck, sucking gently. "*Fuck*, Julian," she hissed.

He hummed in agreement. "Yes, I think you should."

She laughed against him, the vibrations echoing through his chest.

His hands traveled down her back, pulling her closer. How had this not worked eight years ago?

They broke apart to breathe, and Charlie blinked dazedly, her lashes fluttering. "I need to get to the music room," she said. It sounded like she wanted to do anything but that.

"Okay." Julian's eyes skittered to the open door, then back to her. When he slackened his grip, she stepped away, and his head finally started to clear. "I'll run the news visit by Diane and let you know how that goes."

"Good," Charlie said. Her fingers brushed over her neck where his lips had been moments ago. "If she agrees, I can get started on a song selection in case they want a performance."

"I'll keep you posted."

Charlie nodded and headed for the door.

Julian sank back against his desk. *Fuck*. What the hell was he doing?

Julian spent the rest of the morning putting together an email proposal, including the link to the viral video that had prompted his entire conversation with Charlie. When he was satisfied with it, he sent it off to Diane, requesting a short meeting.

To his surprise, she responded almost immediately and told him to come down to her office.

As he made his way there, a bout of nerves rocketed through him. What if Diane didn't like the idea? He didn't know why she wouldn't, but if she shot down his proposal, then there went a great opportunity to get the choir noticed. And sure, it might not harm their application in the end, but it couldn't possibly hurt to have a little good press.

"Hey," he said, knocking on Diane's door.

"Hey." She removed a pair of earbuds from her ears. "I hear the gingerbread contest is going to be fierce this year."

"Warren's convinced your admin staff are full of cheaters."

"No comment. Also, this is the most adorable thing ever, right?" She referenced her computer screen which had the community center video pulled up.

"It'll definitely put Glendale on the map," Julian joked. "If that's cool?"

Diane leaned back in her chair. "I have no issues with you running with this."

"So, you're okay with me touching base with the news to make arrangements?"

"Absolutely. Can't wait to see them on the local channel."

"And they can film the choir?"

"As long as they promise not to interrupt business as usual elsewhere in the building, I don't see any problems."

"Great," Julian said, excitement bubbling up inside him. "That's really... I think the residents will be thrilled. And Charlie's already on board."

Diane nodded. "I might not have the funds to give you right now, but I want this program to succeed, Julian. You've done amazing work getting them this far. Of course I'm going to support you in whatever way I can."

"Well, that video was all Charlie. If she hadn't been there to direct them, it might never have happened."

"I don't know where you found her," Diane said. "But she's a keeper. Maybe try to hold onto her for a while."

"Yeah, sure," Julian said, a tight smile stretching across face. He hadn't known how to hold onto her last time. What made this time any different?

He'd never been good at keeping people in his life. For one reason or another, they all seemed to drift away. His mom. His dad. His grandmother. The old Charlie. Maybe he was the real problem here. And if he wasn't careful, he'd drive Charlie away again sooner than expected.

Julian headed back upstairs, feeling slightly overwhelmed. For the first time in a long time, he was actually making progress with the music program.

But having Charlie back in town, getting reacquainted with her, was complicated. At times it felt like they were picking up where they'd left off, and he didn't know how to feel about that. His grandmother had been moved into a nursing home the year before they met, and though Julian wouldn't have admitted it to anyone, he was lonely, watching the dementia take her. When he found Charlie, she'd made him feel excited about the world again. She'd made him feel less *alone*. Now here she was, taking up space in his life once more, filling the lonely parts, and he knew it was a bad idea to let her in. Because if he did, he had to be prepared to tear her out again when she left. And that was terrifying.

He wished it could be as easy as having some fun. He wished he could call it casual. But starting over with Charlie wasn't as simple as just starting up again. This time Julian knew how much he had to lose.

By the time he reached his office, he'd determined to set those thoughts aside as he typed up his response to the news station. Maybe it was a bit of Christmas cheer or the fact that he'd sneaked too many gingerbread samples this morning, but he sort of thought they had a genuine shot at winning this competition. Charlie had changed the odds.

She'd changed everything.

And he had no idea where that left his heart.

Ten

Julian

"There's an entire news crew unloading in the lobby," Warren said, popping his head into Julian's office. "Did you know?"

"Already?" Julian hadn't even had a chance to finish his coffee or pop down to the music room to see if Charlie and the choir were prepared. He'd spent the last half hour tallying votes from the gingerbread decorating contest. He checked his phone. "They're early."

Warren ran his hand through his short locks. "I sort of feel like I should have gelled my hair or something this morning."

Julian laughed. "They're not here for you."

"You never know. This face was made for TV."

"Mm-hmm," Julian said. "More like for behind the camera."

"Ouch. Shots fired." Warren hit him with the classic

eyes on you move. "I'm only letting you get away with that because you're holding the voting box."

"I'm not telling you anything," Julian said, hiding away his tally sheet. He didn't want Warren to realize that the admin team had started to pull ahead in the count. "Don't even ask."

"Oh, come on," Warren complained. "The nurses are gonna take it this year, right? Blink twice for yes."

"No comment."

Warren sniffed. "I see you've had your media training."

"They're not interviewing *me*," Julian said.

"Not with that attitude." Warren leaned across the desk, trying to spy into Julian's notebook.

He flipped it closed. "Plus I don't think this is the kind of thing that requires media training."

A cheeky smile stretched across Warren's face. "Why don't you hold that thought until you see what Harriet is wearing this morning?"

"What the hell does that mean?"

"I've been sworn to secrecy." Warren reached for the notebook.

Julian tugged it out of reach.

Warren rolled his eyes. "Come on. It's not like I'm gonna say anything."

"You absolutely will," Julian said. "You'll go shouting it through the halls. But there's nothing to get excited about yet. I'm only halfway through the votes."

Warren narrowed his eyes. "Just know that if the admin team wins again, Harriet and I are prepared to launch an internal investigation." He plopped down on the edge of Julian's desk. "But this is super cool, huh? Having the news out."

"I didn't think it'd be this quickly. I only connected with them at the end of last week, but they were super eager to get the segment filmed."

"Well, they probably want the segment to air before the choir competition. Still can't believe you managed to wrangle this. Glendale never gets cool opportunities to be in the spotlight."

"It's mostly thanks to Charlie. I'd be way out of my depth if it wasn't for her. But cross your fingers that this little news spotlight pushes our application to the front of the pack as far as the Arts Council is concerned."

"Still haven't heard back?"

Julian shook his head. The competition was less than two weeks away. He'd managed to get their application in before the deadline, but they'd have to hear back soon, right?

"No news is good news," Warren said. "Don't stress until there's something to stress about. Or else you're stressing twice." He clapped Julian on the shoulder. "I'm gonna go make my medication pass and then I'll try to swing by the music room. I want to see the choir in action with the news crew."

Julian nodded. "You just want to see if everyone behaves themselves."

Warren threw his head back and laughed. "You've got that Maggie, Harriet, Doris trifecta now. So the possibilities are endless."

Julian sighed. "I want to say how much damage could a couple of old ladies do? But I'm afraid I know better."

"Exactly. Let's not forget who suggested having those nude model art classes," Warren reminded him.

Julian dropped his head in his hands. "God, I forgot about that."

"Hey, at least it's not live TV. They can always edit stuff out."

"Now that is the real Christmas miracle."

As Warren set off with his medication cart, Julian hurried down the three flights of stairs to the main floor. He swung by the music room quickly, catching Charlie's eye at the front of the room. "You've probably got about fifteen minutes. They're just unloading their equipment now."

An excited murmur whisked through the room.

"We'll be ready," Charlie assured him. "Just waiting on a few stragglers. If you see Frank in the hall, send him my way."

"He's not here yet?"

Charlie shook her head.

Odd, Julian thought. He figured Frank would have been one of the first people here, if only to clock the setup. He adored anything remotely techy and a camera crew would be right up his alley. "If I see him, I'll send him over," Julian promised, knowing he'd already lingered too long. He set off down the hall to meet the Channel 7 News team.

He spotted them in the lobby, surrounded by half a dozen black trunks which he presumed held a selection of lighting and camera equipment.

A man was leaning against the counter, chatting with Erin.

"Hey there," Julian called.

The man turned and immediately reached for Julian's hand, flashing a brilliant smile. He was younger than Julian and chipper, grinning from ear to ear while oozing an unnerving amount of confidence.

"Julian Guerrero," Julian said. "I'm the activities director here at Glendale."

"Nate Finch. Good to meet you. I was copied on all the emails you were exchanging with our outreach manager." He gestured behind him. "This is Bobby and Tyler. Best camera operators in the business."

One of them, Bobby or Tyler, snorted. "Not before coffee." He inclined his head toward Julian in greeting.

"Thanks for coming out," Julian said. "I know we were invited down to the studio but getting travel sorted for this crowd takes a minute. We really do appreciate you coming to us."

"No worries," Nate said. "We like field trips."

"Not before coffee," Bobby or Tyler said again.

"Coffee, I can definitely help with," Julian said. "If there's time? I'm not sure how this normally works. Do you guys have time for a cup, or do you want to jump right in?"

"There's always time for coffee," Nate said. "And then we can go over the details."

The others nodded, moving their equipment off to the side of the lobby so it wouldn't become a trip hazard. Julian escorted the team to the dining room and secured the goods. "Probably not the best you've ever had, but the residents don't complain, so that's saying something."

"It's hot," Bobby said. "That's all that matters."

He drank his black. Tyler and Nate filled theirs with so much sugar, Julian didn't know if it qualified as coffee anymore.

"So," Nate began while perusing the display of gingerbread houses. "We're going to film a short interview. Do you have someone who can take point on that?"

"That should be our choir director, Charlie. She's probably best equipped to answer any music-related questions you have."

"Is she the woman from the video?" Nate asked.

"That would be the one."

"Okay, great. And do you think any of the residents would like to answer a few questions? It'd be great to hear directly from them, too. Nothing major. Just what being a part of the choir means to them. What they're looking forward to. Favorite Christmas carol. That sort of thing."

"Heartwarming," Bobby piped up.

Nate nodded. "Exactly."

"I'm sure some of them would love to participate." Julian spotted Frank rolling past on his way to the music room, a little slower than usual. "If I'm being honest, I'm more worried I'm gonna have a harder time keeping some of them *away* from the camera."

Bobby laughed. "We're used to it."

"Okay, great. Anything else you need from us?" Julian asked.

"A bit of footage of them singing a song or two," Nate said. "We don't have to worry about anything being perfect. Our editors will cut it together depending on how big of a TV spot they have to fill."

Good, Julian thought. They could edit out all the Doris, Harriet, Maggie shenanigans.

When the crew finished their coffee, Julian led them down to the music room where Charlie and the choir were rehearsing.

Julian was glad to see that Frank had finally made it. He introduced Nate and Bobby and Tyler to the group. Most of them had seen Nate Finch on TV at one time or another, and though he was only a local news anchor,

Julian could tell some of the residents were a little starstruck. Or maybe they were just working out the jitters. Julian watched Maggie fluff her hair until it was practically standing on end with static.

"No need to be nervous," Nate said as Bobby and Tyler unpacked their cameras and started wandering around, figuring out their angles. "We're just going to get some shots of you doing what you do every day. Pretend we're not here for the moment and resume rehearsals as you always do."

The group looked to Charlie for direction.

Charlie, who did not bat an eye with the addition of the small news crew. Charlie, who smiled at them encouragingly.

Julian supposed she was used to this kind of pressure. Having a camera on her was probably no different than having hundreds of eyes looking at her from an audience.

"I'm really glad you agreed to do this," he said to her as the crew sorted themselves out. "I mean specifically today. I'm always grateful for your help with the choir, but especially with this."

"I had nothing else going on this morning," she teased.

Julian smirked. He knew that wasn't true. She had a lot of work still to do on Doris's place, but he also knew that the choir was growing on her. Maybe she needed them just as much as they needed her.

His gaze lifted as Bobby walked behind the choir. Harriet wiggled her fingers at the camera, and Julian got a look at her attire. He'd almost forgotten what Warren had said. His face fell. She was wearing a holiday sweater that said This Shit Happens Earlier Every Year.

"Oh my God," he muttered.

Charlie frowned. "What?"

Julian darted to Harriet's side, leaning close. "You can't wear that on TV."

"Why not? It's my color," she said, holding out her sweater and looking down at it.

"The color isn't the problem."

Harriet gave him a wry grin. "I'm seventy-three. I think I can wear whatever I want."

"Someone's going to have a problem with it." And by someone, he meant Diane.

"I'm just spreading the holiday cheer."

Julian rubbed his face and fled back to Charlie's side before he could make a scene. "Try to make sure Harriet stands in the back."

Charlie frowned. "Why? Oh…" She started laughing. Laughing! She covered her mouth, but both her cheeks turned pink from trying to hold back.

"It's not funny," Julian all but hissed.

"It is. A little."

"Diane is going to kill me if that ends up on TV."

"Would she really be surprised?"

"God!" Forget murder, Diane was going to fire him.

Charlie covered her mouth again, her shoulders shaking.

Julian glared at her from the corner of his eye. "You're not helping."

"Me?"

"Yes, you! We need to be a united front."

"My job is to make them sound good. You're in charge of logistics. Why didn't you suggest matching outfits?"

"Because I…"

"Mm-hmm, I'm listening?"

Because he was too busy thinking about the way Charlie was slowly driving him to distraction. "I didn't think I had to police their outfits."

"And that was your first mistake. But I'm sure they'll block it out," Charlie said. "Or cut her all together. They're not about to put that on TV. Let her have her fun."

"Oh? Look who's all about the fun now."

Charlie shrugged. "Someone might have suggested I be less uptight."

"I can't imagine who." They grinned at each other and Julian felt the heady rush of desire sweep through him. "Again, thanks for this. I know it's for Doris—"

"Not just for her," Charlie said quickly.

Julian's heart throbbed in his chest.

"There's also Frank."

He snorted, shaking his head. He wanted to kiss her. Here. Now. With the cameras rolling. He didn't care who saw, and that was a wild thought.

"I think we're ready to start that interview!" Nate called.

Perfect timing. Charlie stepped away to answer questions about her music experience and the choir, which was just as well. It was easier for Julian not to think about certain activities when she wasn't standing right next to him.

Bobby had Charlie framed up with the piano in the background, and she looked into the camera confidently as Nate asked about her previous experience. Charlie mentioned Juilliard and Broadway. She was polite about it but quick to divert her answer back to the choir. Julian didn't know if that was because she was treading too close to Tom or because she was trying to shift the spotlight.

"And what do you hope to accomplish with the choir?" Nate asked.

"We're very excited to possibly have the opportunity to

perform at the Twentieth Annual Christmas Choir Competition. The residents are really looking forward to it." Charlie crossed her fingers. "So here's hoping everything pans out with our application."

She was a natural, making them all look good. She talked about the music program and mentioned Julian, and though he had no desire to be on TV, he was touched that she'd called him out by name, telling Nate that none of this would be possible without his dedication to the residents. Julian's heart warmed hearing Charlie talk about Glendale and bonding with the choir. Maybe she was a damn good actor, but he thought she looked happy.

Nate paused the interview and asked for a couple resident spotlights. Charlie pointed him toward Doris, as their piano player, and Frank. Harriet gave a sly grin but Charlie opted to add Maggie to the mix instead. Maggie fluffed her hair some more.

When Nate was done with the residents, he turned to Julian. "I think all we need now is a little performance, and we can wrap up."

"Anything in particular you'd like to hear?" Julian asked.

"You guys choose," Nate said. "But ideally something Christmasy."

"'Jingle Bells'?" Charlie suggested. "It's easy, quick. Should fit nicely into the segment."

"It's like she's done this before," Bobby said, grinning.

While Charlie gathered up the choir, Julian moved off to the side, stepping out of the way just as they started with a cheery, "Dashing through the snow..."

Warren snuck into the room as they were singing, standing next to Julian. "I can't believe we've been sitting on all this talent."

"I think Charlie's talent brings it out in other people."

Warren hummed in agreement. "She's a good fit for you."

Julian started to nod before the words actually registered. "Er, what?"

"Charlie," Warren whispered. "She's good for you."

Julian bit his tongue. The last thing he needed was for rumors about him and Charlie to start circulating around Glendale before he even knew how to feel about it. "I don't know what you're talking about."

"You mean you don't see the way you look at her?"

Julian rolled his eyes. "Give me a break."

"I'm serious, man. It's nice to finally see you just... I don't know, not trying to power through on your own. Trusting someone else to do right by the residents."

Julian's jaw tightened. He supposed he clung to this job, this role, a little tightly. He just never wanted the residents to feel left behind. He knew what it was to feel like that. And maybe part of him had kind of stagnated here—in this job, in life—afraid to let go of the things he did have, afraid he might get left behind again if he didn't cling with both hands.

Nate clapped as the choir finished singing, jumping back in front of the camera to close out the segment. Everyone held their positions as Tyler gave them a silent countdown on his fingers and finally lowered the camera. Once Julian had said goodbye to Nate and Bobby and Tyler, he and Charlie debriefed the choir—they wanted to know if there'd been any word on the application.

"No change," he said.

"Well, that's just not possible," Maggie huffed on her way out the door to Doris and Harriet. "We're excellent.

Maybe I should reach out to Graham Burbank to inquire. He's on the Arts Council. We used to be friendly."

"What kind of friendly?" Doris asked, clearly amused.

Maggie waggled her eyebrows. "The only kind that matters."

Julian hung back to help Charlie tidy up. He could hear Harriet cackling down the hall.

"So, I've been thinking," Charlie said.

Julian looked up from where he was stacking chairs. "That Maggie is going to try to buy our way into this competition?"

The corner of Charlie's mouth twitched. "No. I'll let you worry about that. I was thinking that if we actually get to perform, you should be onstage with us. The choir was your vision, after all. You should get to share in that moment."

Julian shook his head briefly. "I think we've already established that I can't carry a tune."

"I was counting on the rest of the voices to drown you out." She laughed at the look on his face.

"How about I just stand in the wings and clap the rhythm?"

"Can you even keep rhythm?"

He shot her a heated look. "I've been known to. On occasion."

Charlie held his gaze, a flush creeping up her neck. "Guess we could get you a little triangle to ding. In case the rhythm thing proves too difficult."

"Now that I could definitely handle. But this is your moment with the residents. I'm cool to wait offstage."

"I just think it would be nice if you were there," she said. "It's good to try new things once in a while."

"Is it?"
She nodded.
What about old new things? he wanted to ask. He thought about what Warren had said about not powering through on his own. Maybe if he stopped being afraid of being left behind for two seconds, he'd realize that Charlie made him want to let go. Made him want to see what else the world had to offer him. All he had to do was take a chance on investing in something new again.

"We started this together and we should finish it together."

"Yeah?" he said.

Finish it together. What did that mean? Was there a world where he convinced Charlie to stay long enough for them to figure out what this music program could be?

Long enough for them to figure out what they could be?

Eleven

Charlie

Charlie slumped down on the piano bench in the empty music room with a huff, her phone pressed to her ear. "I understand you're not a moving company. Yes, of course. I only wondered…" She frowned. "Right, no. I understand." She rubbed the aching space between her eyes. "No, I definitely still want you to come for pickup tomorrow. I'll figure out another way to get the furniture moved. I promise. It will be on the porch as promised." The ache shifted to the middle of her forehead. "You have a great day, too."

Charlie hung up.

"You don't really sound like you're having a great day."

Charlie twisted on the piano bench. She hadn't heard Julian arrive. She'd shown up early to tweak the songs for choir practice. She'd also almost forgotten that she'd arranged for some of Gram's furniture to be picked up tomorrow for donation. "Just a complication with some house stuff. No big deal."

Actually, it was probably going to be a big deal when she was standing in the basement later tonight trying to figure out how to move a sofa by herself.

"Anything I can help with?"

Charlie stood, gathering up the sheet music she'd been looking at. "It's all good. I just didn't realize that the charity Gram's donating her furniture to won't actually move said furniture out of the basement. And I get it, they're run by volunteers who are pushing sixty-five, and they don't want them having to trip through people's houses. I guess I only now realized that all this furniture is trapped in Gram's basement, and I am only one person—"

"Charlie?" he interrupted.

"What?"

"This sounds like exactly the kind of thing I can help with."

Her pulse skipped, the thought of having Julian around to help with all sorts of things, of being alone with him, a little too enticing. "No, no. I'll figure something out."

"By tonight? Who else do you know that's going to help you drag furniture out of Doris's basement?"

"Well, no one, but—"

"Exactly. So why don't you ask me?" he teased.

She let out a heavy sigh. Because she was still trying to keep a lid on her feelings, and the closer Julian got...the more she thought about his hands on her, his voice rumbling in her ear, the heat of his breath on her neck. Bad things. Complicated things. "I wasn't trying to trick you into offering up your help."

"I know that. I'm the one who crashed your phone call."

Charlie studied his expression. She really could use his muscles. Purely for furniture-moving purposes. Nothing more. Her gaze dropped to his hands, to his long fingers, to those ropy forearms, and heat surged through her veins.

Julian's lips twitched, and she wondered if he suspected exactly what she was thinking. "Ask me," he said.

"No."

"Charlie, just ask me."

She didn't want to be a burden. She didn't want to make Gram's house his problem. She didn't want to be alone with him in the house. Actually, she did. And that was the real problem.

"C'mon," Julian said. "I've been looking for a way to pay you back for getting roped into volunteering. You've surprisingly complained very little. Let me do this one thing for you."

Well, when he put it like that... Besides, what other option did she have? These things needed to get done. "Fine. Can you come over tonight and help me move Gram's really heavy furniture to the porch?"

"I'd be delighted."

Charlie snorted. "You might be less delighted when you see it. It's very old and very heavy."

"I think I can handle it."

"Just don't blame me if you hurt yourself."

"You mean if I pull one of my many muscles?" He flexed a bit.

"That's not what I said." Charlie's gaze drifted against her will. She was very interested in getting acquainted with those muscles again. The little taste she'd had at the community center had only been enough to awaken her desires, not to sate them.

Julian winked playfully. "But it's what you were thinking."

"You don't know what I was thinking."

"I bet it was that you should get me to sign a waiver before doing this very dangerous task."

"Hmm... That's actually a good idea. To release myself from all liability."

"I'm more interested in what the job pays."

Oh, now he wanted payment? "I thought you were doing this out of the goodness of your heart?"

"It's true. I am quite fond of Doris." Julian's eyes dropped to her lips, and for a long moment Charlie thought he might kiss her like he had the other day in his office.

"I can do pizza and beer," she said.

"That'll work. See you tonight."

Charlie trapped a sneeze behind her hand, rubbing at her watery eyes.

She needed to get out of this horrible basement and the avalanche of dust that had accumulated. Now she was almost glad the charity had refused to move the furniture out of the basement, because the last thing she needed was some poor old men tripping over antique rugs or choking on dust bunnies.

Charlie abandoned the basement for some fresh air, coughing as she sat down in the recliner in Gram's living room. She picked up her phone as it started buzzing in her pocket. "Hey."

"How goes the furniture situation?" Alicia asked.

"Currently locked in a stalemate. I've at least managed to unbury the couch, but that's as far as I'm getting on my own."

"Did you underestimate how heavy everything was?"

"That and how awkwardly shaped. I couldn't even get the side tables up the stairs on my own because I couldn't get my arms around them enough to get a grip."

"Have you abandoned that project for today then?"

"No, Julian actually offered to come over and help me. He's swinging by after work, and we're going to get the big stuff out of the basement. I'm just waiting on him now."

Alicia's tone shifted. "Horribly handsome Julian, huh?"

Charlie groaned. "Don't say it like that."

"Like what?"

"You know."

Alicia laughed.

"Stop. He's doing me a favor."

"Like the favor he did for you in the community center?" Alicia asked. She'd practically blown out the phone speakers when Charlie told her what they'd done.

"No, that is not the kind of favor I'm talking about." Charlie touched her cheek, glad Alicia couldn't see how red her face was turning. "As he pointed out, he actually owed me a favor since I'm such a gracious volunteer choir director."

"Speaking of the choir," Alicia said. "I watched that video you sent me of their performance at the community center."

"Cute, right? They're actually going to be on the news soon. We just did a little interview."

"I sent the video to some colleagues. A few of them had already seen it."

Charlie climbed to her feet. "I think it has something crazy like one hundred thousand views now." She cleared some boxes out of the hall to make space between the basement and the front door.

"Your name is starting to circulate," Alicia said. "People are interested in this little feel-good story, which could be very good career-wise."

Charlie frowned. "I'm not trying to capitalize for a career move."

"I know that," Alicia said. "I'm just saying, there's some buzz. Have you had a chance to look at any of the emails I sent you?"

"Er… I've glanced at a couple," Charlie said, biting down on the lie. The thought of taking on any kind of role made her more uncomfortable than usual, and not just because of Tom. She needed to see if this choir competition panned out so she could figure out when she could actually leave Elm Springs. Until she knew that, what was the point of looking at any of the emails?

"Okay, well, I've got to run to a meeting, but keep me posted. And I'll let you know if I come across anything that I think will intrigue you. Talk later?"

"Sure thing. Bye," Charlie said, getting back to work and trying not to feel guilty about blowing off Alicia's emails. The timing just wasn't right. But soon… Maybe.

She'd only just finished clearing out the hallway when the doorbell rang. Julian was early. She hurried to answer the door.

Julian stood there, wrapped in his coat and a scarf and a pair of hot-pink knitted mittens.

She raised an eyebrow.

"A present from the resident knitting club," he said, holding his hands up.

Charlie swung the door open farther. "You didn't dip out early, did you?"

"I was all caught up. No new emails in my inbox." Julian shrugged. "Figured I'd swing by now."

She stepped aside, letting him in. "You didn't have to do that."

"I've put in a lot of extra hours over the years. Diane was happy to let me sneak out."

"As long as I didn't pull you away from anything important."

"Just more complaints about the gingerbread contest being fixed."

"I really do think the nurses were slighted," Charlie said, chuckling as Julian rolled his eyes. "Come on, they made a gingerbread hospital!"

"They make one every year," he said, playfully exasperated. "The admin team is just more creative."

"I think I'm Team Harriet and Warren on this one. There clearly needs to be an internal investigation."

Julian tutted. "I come all the way over here to help you and get nothing but accusations." He pretended to leave.

Charlie grabbed him by the front of the coat and hauled him back inside, closing the door to the chill. "I'm kidding. But you can't deny those gingerbread men with the little icing casts were adorable."

"They took second place again. That's almost a win."

"Don't say the word *almost* near Harriet. Any word from the Arts Council?"

"Nothing." Julian sighed. "But I'm trying not to check my email every two minutes. Moving furniture might actually be a nice distraction."

"I'm sure they'll reach out soon," Charlie said. Though

as the days passed, she'd started to worry that maybe Glendale hadn't made the cut. She kept the choir rehearsing on the off chance they did, but the reality was she had no idea what kind of amateur competition Elm Springs might stir up.

"Fingers crossed," Julian said. He shed his coat and scarf and hung them on the coatrack like he'd done it a thousand times before.

For a beat, Charlie realized he had. Julian had stood in this hall, had eaten at Gram's table and had sat in her living room with Charlie cuddled next to him on the couch. Looking at him now, she was suddenly twenty-one again, Tom was alive and...*nothing. Don't drift away with those thoughts. Not now.* She cleared her throat. "I really appreciate this."

"Of course. I'm happy to help." They looked at each other for a long beat, then Julian glanced toward the basement door. "Put me to work?"

"Do you want a drink first? Gram has coffee, and there's beer in the fridge."

"Work first," he decided. "Then I'll take the beer you promised me as payment."

Charlie led him to the basement, pausing for a beat. "Before we go down, just remember, you were warned."

Julian snorted as they descended the stairs. By the time they got to the bottom, all he could do was mutter, "Wooooow."

"Told you," Charlie said, feeling slightly vindicated.

"I should have taken that warning seriously," Julian said. "Maybe asked for more than pizza."

"What could be better than pizza?"

He caught her eye, and for the next hour, Charlie tried

not to think about what his answer might have been as they hauled furniture out of the basement. When they were done, Julian heaved and collapsed on the dusty old couch that had been relocated to the porch. Beads of sweat dotted his forehead.

"I wouldn't do that if I were you," Charlie said. "Might get swarmed by the dust bunnies."

"They can have me," Julian wheezed. "That's the most labor I've done in a long time."

"Should have demanded your payment up front," Charlie teased. She nudged him out of the way so she could cover the couch with a tarp.

Julian perked up. He was probably ravenous now. "Time for sustenance."

"Pizza from Gordo's?" she suggested.

"Pepperoni with hot honey?"

"We'll get half hot honey, half something else."

Julian grinned. "Still have your aversion to spicy foods?"

"Unless you want me to have hiccups for the rest of the night."

"It's very cute."

Charlie headed inside to place their order and tried not to dwell on *cute*. By the time the pizza arrived, they'd cleared enough boxes from the living room to utilize the sofa. Charlie hadn't gotten around to canceling Gram's cable yet, and Julian quickly flipped it to the local news channel.

"Look!" he said excitedly. "There we are."

"I didn't know this was on tonight!" she said, settling down next to him.

"Hold on," he said, texting furiously. "I'm just letting

the admin team know. Hopefully someone can go put the news on in the common room for the residents."

He was quiet for a moment, then the corner of his mouth curled.

"All good?" she asked.

"They were already on it. Apparently Maggie saw a commercial break earlier and rallied the choir to the common room."

"Should have known she'd be on top of it," Charlie said, taking a sip from her beer before setting it down on the coffee table next to Julian's. She pointed at the TV as the footage played across the screen. "Frank looks so dapper with his bow tie and suspenders."

Watching the news bite, seeing the residents smile and laugh and clap their way through "Jingle Bells," Charlie knew she'd made the right decision letting go of the reins. Music was something to be enjoyed, and she was glad Julian had helped her remember that.

"I see they cut out any front-facing view of Harriet's sweater," Julian noted.

Charlie laughed. "I told you they would. You really think this'll improve our chances of getting into the competition?"

"I don't see how it can hurt."

Charlie sighed. "The choir will be so bummed if they don't get to perform."

Julian laid his head against the back of the couch. "I know."

"I won't be able to bear the looks on their faces." An uncomfortable feeling twisted in her gut as the news bite ended. She hadn't realized just how badly she wanted this for them.

"You okay?" Julian asked, putting down his plate.

"Just thinking," Charlie said.

"About?"

"I don't want Gram to be disappointed. Glendale should be a new chapter for her, and I want that to come with good memories."

Julian glanced around the room. "There's...a lot of pictures of Tom. More than I remember."

Charlie pulled her knees to her chest. "Gram had a lot of them framed after he passed. For the funeral. And the wake. And she just never put them away again."

"That must be...difficult," Julian said diplomatically. "Being surrounded by all of this."

"I think that's why I stayed away from Elm Springs for so long," Charlie said quietly. "It's easier to keep my emotions in check, to not let them overwhelm my life, when I'm not thinking about him constantly. But Tom's frozen in time here, and if I let my guard down, even for a moment, those memories flood in along with the grief, and... I haven't quite figured out how to deal with that yet."

Julian's eyes flickered to the hall, to the boxes she'd piled in front of the stairwell. "Why does it look like you've cordoned off the second floor?"

"Umm... Tom," she started. "When he was... They offered him really nice hospice facilities, but when it came time for that, he just wanted to be in the place that he loved most in the world. Outside of a stage, that is."

"And that was here," Julian finished, his soft words filled with realization.

Charlie nodded, feeling sick. Her heart crashed against her ribs. The pizza congealed in her stomach.

"Shit, Charlie," Julian said under his breath. "Sorry doesn't feel like enough, does it?"

"Honestly, after it happened, *sorry* started to feel like the most empty word in the English language."

"Do you mind me asking how it happened?"

"Cancer," Charlie said, forcing the word out. "You never think it'll be you, you know? It's something you expect to hear in your seventies, not your thirties."

Julian shook his head.

She put her plate on the coffee table next to his. "You know what still gets me to this day?"

"What?"

"That I didn't even notice when he got sick."

"I'm not sure anyone really does. Right? Not at first."

"But it seems so obvious now when I look back. He was suddenly tired all the time and losing weight. We were traveling for concert performances and doing back-to-back shows. Fatigue just sort of comes with the territory when you're touring. But I actually joked that we were working him too hard," Charlie said. She rubbed her brow. "That moment plays on repeat in my head sometimes. Like, what was wrong with me? Why didn't I see what was happening? Maybe if I'd figured it out sooner or if I'd asked the question—"

"Hey," Julian said, reaching for her hand, threading their fingers together. "Nothing about this situation was fair, Charlie. Wishing for hindsight when all you can do is look forward… Don't do that to yourself. Don't carry that around."

She swallowed hard, words turning to clay in her throat. She suspected she'd always feel like there was more she could have done.

"Is that why you stopped singing?" Julian asked.

"It's funny," Charlie said. "Music is all I know how to do, and yet I can't seem to find a place where it makes sense anymore. Tom always said to find a place where the music sings to you. But since he's been gone, nowhere feels right. And the moment it starts to feel wrong, it's just easier to pick up and leave. I keep thinking it can't go on like this, but it does... I'm fighting so hard to stay right now because I want Gram settled and secure. I don't want her to feel like I abandoned her, but some days it's—"

"Overwhelming?" he said, not looking at her.

She sighed. "Having to constantly fight off the feelings is exhausting."

"Grief doesn't follow any kind of time line," Julian said. "I don't think you need to be fighting those things."

"That's not the only thing I've been feeling, though," she said, catching his eye. She didn't want to read more into this than she should. Maybe they'd gotten caught up in the heat of the moment, sneaking around the community center. But if it did mean more... "You're caught up in there somewhere," she admitted. "When I look at you, I remember a time when Tom was still alive, and I'm worried that I'll never escape that. That I'll never be able to let myself enjoy something without opening myself up to all that pain." She shook her head. "I don't know if I'm making sense."

"It doesn't need to make sense," he said. "I think grief is ours to process however we need. And this hasn't exactly been easy for me, either. Seeing you again."

Charlie frowned. "What do you mean?"

"You meant a lot to me. Back then." Julian's hand tightened against his knee. "To this day, I'm not sure why you pulled away, but I took it pretty hard."

"Oh," she said, his words taking the wind out of her. "I sort of thought we just…drifted. Didn't we? Long distance was hard, and school was demanding, and life pulled us in different directions."

"Is that really how you saw it?"

She nodded. "How did you see it?"

He sat back, running a hand through his hair. "Honestly, it sort of felt like you ghosted me. Like you woke up one day and decided I wasn't worth your time and cut me out of your life."

Charlie sat up straighter, her heart flip-flopping at his honesty. "I didn't realize! God, if I'd known—"

"It's fine," he said, brushing her off.

"It's not fine." She reached for him. Squeezed his forearm. "I never meant to hurt you like that."

"You weren't the first." He huffed a humorless laugh. "Trust me. Seems to be par for the course with me."

She held him tighter. "What does that mean?"

Julian licked his lips. "When my parents divorced, I think they were both so eager to start new lives, that they kind of…left me behind. My mom got remarried, her attention shifting to the new family she was building. And my dad wanted freedom that didn't include being tied down with a kid every other weekend. It felt like I went from having a family to being wanted by neither of them. And then with my grandmother, well, she was amazing in all the ways that mattered, but then the dementia crept in. I know it wasn't in her control, but that didn't change how it felt to be left behind again. And then you… Sometimes it feels like I've spent my whole life chasing after relationships that keep slipping through my fingers. Seeing you that first day took me right back there, and it was easier to pretend like I didn't know you."

She stared at him, the moment heavy. "I'm sorry I did such a shit job of breaking things off with you. That I ever made you feel like I didn't want you, because that was never true. I just... There were too many things pulling at me. I wish I could go back and do it better, but maybe it was for the best. I'm not the same person I was back then. If we'd made it through the long distance, I might have ruined it when I lost Tom."

Julian's gaze softened, open and yearning. "I'm not the same person, either."

"So now what?" she asked.

"Maybe," he began, "we get to know these new versions of ourselves."

He leaned toward her, and Charlie's breath hitched. She'd changed since Tom's death, yes. But maybe it was okay for someone to know the new her. Maybe it was okay to sink into Julian the way she once had and trust him to make the world fall away.

His lips brushed hers, featherlight. He tasted like beer and hot honey, and Charlie opened her mouth, waiting for him to deepen the kiss.

He did, grazing his tongue along her lower lip, and she tipped into the sensations of him: his hand skirting down her arm, his palm on her hip, the stubble of his face against her cheek. If someone had told her all those weeks ago that returning to Elm Springs would mean returning to this, she wouldn't have believed them. She wouldn't have believed that any part of her heart could be open enough to let anyone in, but Julian had been there before, and he knew his way around. She didn't know what tomorrow would bring, but she felt sure of this moment and gave into the desire.

Julian crawled over her, nudging Charlie onto her back. She latched onto his arms, her hands curling round his biceps as he settled against her hips. She could feel him hard and straining between her thighs as she rolled her body against his.

"Christ, Charlie," he breathed against her neck.

She closed her eyes, humming in agreement, eager to forget everything. Tom's haunting memory and the choir competition and the auditions piling up in her inbox. Just for tonight, she wanted to push it all aside.

Julian's hands slipped up her shirt, palming her breasts as he sucked at her neck. She moaned, loud and long, no concerns about being discovered here.

Julian shifted slowly, shoving her shirt aside enough to kiss the space below her ribs, then her belly, before tugging on the drawstring of her sweats with his teeth.

"Is this okay?" he asked.

"Yes," she said, rolling her hips as he slid her pants down her thighs.

"And this?" he asked, hooking his finger in her underwear.

She looked at him, his smile a little sexy, a little smug. "Yes," she said, already trembling.

His fingers dipped below the elastic, tugging her underwear free, and he skimmed his fingers along her curves, barely touching.

"Julian, I swear if you don't—"

And then he touched her, not with his fingers, but with his tongue, and Charlie almost bucked right off the couch. He lapped at her clit with slow, concentrated strokes, building her up. He increased his pace, holding her hips steady to stop her squirming, before pulling away, his breath hot against her.

Charlie's chest heaved, and she reached for him, so breathless she couldn't even utter the words, *Don't stop*. Instead, she tugged at his hair.

Julian was unbothered, turning to kiss her palm instead. "Wasn't sure I'd remember how to do this," he said. "But that day in the community center—"

"If you say it's like riding a bike, I'm going to yell at you."

"I'd like you to be yelling for other reasons." He kissed her hip once before dragging his lips back to her clit.

This time he didn't stop, and Charlie rocked up against him, chasing the high she could feel churning inside her. It built and built until it finally peaked, exploding in a rush of giddy relief that surged through her, turning every limb to airy stone. She lay there, boneless, with Julian pressing soft kisses to her inner thigh, nibbling gently on her skin.

"Guess it *is* like riding a bike."

"Shut up," she huffed, laughing. She didn't even have the energy to swat him.

"We can give it another shot if you think I need more practice," he said, grinning.

Charlie lifted her head enough to look at him. "Practice does make perfect and all that."

"It does." He wiggled his eyebrows at hers. "Let's see how quickly I can improve."

"Not yet," she said, sitting up. "I need some practice, too."

She crawled toward him, pressing a hand to his chest, forcing him back against the arm of the couch. Charlie let her hand drag down his chest slowly, watching him, waiting to see if he would stop her. There was an obvious bulge in his pants now, one neither of them could ignore, but she paused. "Should I continue?"

Julian released a slow breath. "I really think you should."

She smiled at him, loving that she still affected him this way. Charlie cupped him through his pants, squeezing gently, and Julian dropped his head back. He was already worked up, but Charlie took her time unbuttoning his pants and sliding down the zipper before finally freeing his erection.

She stroked her fingers gently up the length of his cock, then curled her hand around it, lowering her lips to the head. She sucked, flicking her tongue against sensitive skin, waiting for Julian's reaction.

"Fuck," he said, pushing up on his elbows to watch her.

Charlie relaxed her jaw, taking more of him, using her mouth and her hand in tandem to drive him wild. Julian's hand slipped into her hair, curling the locks around his fingers. She imagined he was pleading with her silently: *don't stop, don't stop, don't stop.* And she didn't, not until he was groaning uncontrollably.

She released him with a pop, and he thrust into her palm, unraveling in her favorite way.

When he was spent, he reclined against the arm of the couch, eyes closed, and chuckled.

"I'll try not to be offended that you're laughing," Charlie teased.

"Sorry," he said. "It's a good laugh. A happy laugh. I promise. I just forgot how good this was with you."

Charlie's heart fluttered against her rib cage. "Another thing you forgot, huh?"

His chest shook as he reached for her. "But I've really enjoyed remembering."

Twelve

Julian

"Ow," Julian muttered, rubbing his nose. This was the second time he'd prodded himself in the face with an artificial Christmas tree branch.

"How's it going, Rudolph?" Harriet said, walking across the common room with the biggest ball of tangled Christmas lights Julian had ever seen.

Julian scowled and stopped rubbing his nose. "What the hell is that supposed to be?"

"The Christmas lights you asked for."

"Why do they look like that?"

"Do I look like Santa's elf to you? This is how they were handed to me by the admin team."

"Sure you're not just trying to sabotage their tree to make up for the gingerbread house situation?"

Harriet raised a long finger in his direction. "You said we were forbidden from discussing that further."

"Only because you and Warren were stirring up a protest in the dining room."

"You've managed to get away with it again this year, Guerrero. Next year you won't be so lucky. So enjoy whatever alliance you currently have with the admin staff. We're coming for you." She gave him the universal *I'm watching you* signal before slinking away to the other side of the common room where she'd conned Doris into making inappropriately shaped decorations for their tree.

Every year Glendale decorated ten trees. One for every floor of the building. The residents from each floor usually decided how they would decorate their allotted tree.

Julian always ended up decorating the one destined for the lobby. He glanced around to see if he could find some of his own help, but Maggie was busy micromanaging tinsel and Frank was trying to program a set of lights to blink in time with music.

Julian returned to his tree, wondering if he should attempt something more creative than the usual glass balls. Though if he was being honest, he was too exhausted to care. He'd spent most of last night getting reacquainted with Charlie in the best possible way. Leaving her asleep in bed this morning had been torture, but he also knew the residents needed some sort of supervision or else this tree situation was likely to run amuck. With Harriet left unchecked, he'd be plucking phallic-shaped ornaments off every tree in the building.

"I think you missed a spot."

Julian leaned around his tree, finding Charlie standing on the other side. The fact that she was still smiling at him must be a good sign.

He was tempted to lean over and kiss her. To wrap his

arms around her waist and feel the length of her body pressed against his. For a long moment it was all he could think about. A part of him knew he should be concerned about the speed of his deepening feelings, especially knowing that Charlie's feelings about him were mixed up with Tom and her fears and the grief that still plagued her, but the rest of him shoved that concern aside. And it was so easy to do when she was looking at him like that.

"Just there," she said, pointing out a huge gap in his decorations.

"I was actually waiting for someone of the shorter persuasion to come along and help fill the hole."

Charlie's lips puckered. "I'm not going to react to being called short purely because your ornament distribution is embarrassingly uneven. The bottom of your tree is practically naked."

Julian held her gaze, knowing she'd said that on purpose. "Good thing you're here then. I'd hate for someone to see the tree in such a revealing state."

Her lips curled into a smirk.

They hadn't talked about what last night meant. But the fact she was standing here, teasing him, was all the reassurance he needed this morning.

Charlie held her hand out for an ornament. "Put me to work."

"Actually," Julian said, stroking the center of her palm in a slow circle. Her eyes widened. "With hands like that, I might have a better use for you."

Charlie wiggled her fingers at him. "These old things? I wonder what better use you could have in mind."

They both knew exactly what she could do with those hands. And that mouth. And that body. But right now Julian wasn't thinking about that. Well, not only that. Instead, he picked up the giant tangle of lights Harriet had delivered him and dropped it into Charlie's waiting hands.

The weight of the tangle made Charlie grunt. "You've got to be kidding me."

"I wish I was."

"This should be illegal," she complained, pouting at him.

Those lips should be illegal, Julian thought, tearing his gaze away.

Charlie dropped into one of the wingback chairs, making herself comfortable. Her delicate hands tugged at the knotted light strand, carefully brushing over the tiny bulbs.

Julian needed to turn his focus elsewhere. Watching her make quick work of the tangle with her slim fingers was making his skin prickle with desire.

"Personally, I'd just buy new lights," Charlie said.

Julian cleared his throat. "So would I, but you know, trying to make the dollar stretch." He glanced over. Charlie had worked part of the strand between her teeth. He grumbled. That wasn't helping.

"I think you can find ten dollars in the budget for new lights," she said.

"But it's not only one set of new lights. If I get new lights for this tree, then everyone wants new lights and fancy ornaments and better decorations, which is definitely not in the budget. Plus I think it's kind of fun seeing what the residents come up with every year when they have to sort of improvise their decorations. They get very creative."

Charlie had grown distracted with something across the room. Julian spied over her chair. She was looking at the tree that Harriet and Doris were decorating.

"Not sure you want them getting *that* creative. Does that tin soldier have a—"

"I'm actively choosing to ignore it," Julian said, averting his eyes. "As I do most years."

Charlie burst into tinkling laughter. "Is that allowed?"

"I mean…we're all adults here."

"Except when someone's poor, unsuspecting great-grandchildren come to visit."

"I'll put a PSA out to keep the kids off the fourth floor," he teased. "And if that can't be avoided, I'll shove their tree into a storage closet."

Charlie grinned wickedly. "I can't wait to be old. Look at all the things you can get away with."

Julian laughed, but Charlie's grin faded quickly, a melancholy look replacing it. He knew immediately that her thoughts had strayed to Tom, and how much older she would get without him.

After talking to her last night, it was easier for him to read her. Julian knew his head was warning him for a reason, but his heart said that sometimes things worked out. They were called second chances for a reason.

Uncertainty coursed through him, catching in his chest. Was this their second chance or just an opportunity for him to be a fool?

"There!" Charlie exclaimed, getting the lights untangled. She held them up triumphantly. "I should be honored with a reward."

"Your reward is getting to help me string the lights on the tree," he said, taking one end of the strand and looping it around the very top branches. He continued winding the strand around the tree, until he reached the halfway point, then he passed it back to Charlie.

"I don't want to hear another short comment," she warned, walking around the tree with the lights looped over her arm.

"How about a little one?"

She glared at him as she rounded the tree.

"A petite one? A miniscule, teeny, wee little comment?"

"Wee?" she said. "Now you've gone too far." Charlie looped the light strand around him, getting him caught against the branches.

"Charlie," he muttered, trying to duck under the strand. But as he did he somehow got tangled in another.

"You're making a mess of things."

"I'm making a mess of things?" He stepped over a strand of lights, bumping into her. "Here, stop moving." He took hold of her shoulders and switched their positions. The strand ended up at the back of his knees, with him pressing Charlie up against the tree.

"Oh yes. This is much better," she said. "Sorta feels like you planned this."

"You're the one who came over to offer your help."

"Out of the goodness of my heart." Charlie tried to duck under his arm. "You're in my way."

"You've tied us together. Let me fix it."

Charlie stilled, and Julian snaked his arms around her briefly, sorting out the lights.

Her brows arched playfully as he worked. "You didn't have to arrange all this just to hold me again," she whispered.

Julian flushed, probably the same red as the decorations judging by how hot his cheeks were. His eyes darted around the room to make sure they didn't have an audience.

She patted his arm, chuckling a little, then stepped away once they were untangled.

Truth was, Julian wanted to be tangled up with her. He didn't want another whirlwind fling. And he definitely didn't want to give Charlie the chance to disappear from his life again.

Tread lightly. She was still figuring herself out. *Don't dive too deep too fast.*

Charlie finished stringing the lights just as Doris carried over a box of icicle-shaped ornaments to hang on their tree.

"Harriet said these got mixed up with our decorations," she said, handing them off to Julian.

"Yes," Charlie said, regarding her grandmother with amusement. "You two seem to be getting quite adventurous with your decorations."

"We've hardly scratched the surface," Doris said. "Just wait until you see the tree topper."

Charlie put her head in her hands. "Oh God. I don't even want to imagine. Harriet is a terrible influence on you."

"I'll have you know the tree topper was my idea." Doris winked and sauntered away.

"Well, on that terrifying note," Charlie said, "I should get down to the music room and prepare for rehearsal. You know, on the off chance we get good news from the Arts Council."

Julian was trying not to think about his inbox. He felt like the more he checked his email, the less likely he was to actually receive an answer.

"I keep envisioning a group of faceless men and women watching our audition video," Charlie continued, "and it's driving me a little wild not being able to read them, you know?"

Julian shook his head. "Not quite."

"Like I can't adjust in the moment the way I could at an in-person audition or change the program of a show based on the audience's reaction. We have to let the video speak for itself and hope the council recognizes how amazing the residents are."

Julian loved hearing her talk about the residents that way. "Whatever happens," he said, "you and I both know this choir deserves to be up there. And that's what really matters."

"Not winning?" she asked.

"I mean, the money could change so much," Julian said. "But please don't discount how much joy you've brought to the residents these past couple of weeks." He didn't want to have to let her go, not just for his sake, but for Glendale's. *How can I get you to stay?* "I've got a couple of emails to check, and then I'll be down for rehearsal."

"If you're busy with Christmas tree stuff, I can handle it," she said.

"I'm not too busy," he said. Not for the choir. *Or for you.* "You know I take my codirector duties very seriously, standing on the sidelines and clapping."

"You do more than that," Charlie said. "You keep everyone's spirits up when I'm demanding perfection."

"Do I keep your spirits up?" Julian asked, reaching out to stroke her cheek. He did it quickly, before anyone could see, liking the subtle color that spread beneath his touch.

"I think you know the answer to that."

"Do I?"

"That's one thing that hasn't changed in all these years,"

she said. She looked at him in a way that made his chest ache dangerously.

Charlie had stolen his heart before, and he couldn't hand it over again that easily. *Don't do this to yourself.* But the longer he looked at her, the more he wanted. He wanted her to forgive herself for the guilt she carried over Tom. He wanted her to be confident that Doris would thrive at Glendale. He wanted her to fall in love with music again. Mostly, he wanted to be the one to make her happy.

And that was a lot, because he knew that Charlie had to want those things, too. She had to believe she could be happy and that she deserved to live her life in Tom's absence. More than that, she had to want *him* the way he wanted her.

Julian's chest suddenly felt too small for all the emotion it contained.

"You okay?" she asked as they headed for the door.

"Of course," he said. "I'll see you in a bit."

She nodded and they turned, walking in opposite directions.

"Check it again!" Harriet said as Julian walked into the music room.

The entire choir was hunched around the piano, crowding in behind Charlie who frowned down at her laptop screen.

"I just looked," she insisted. "I promise nothing has changed in the last thirty seconds."

"You don't know that."

Charlie huffed, sounding exasperated. Doris put a hand on her shoulder. "It wouldn't hurt to check again," her grandmother said diplomatically.

"Do that thing," Maggie said. "What's it called, Frank?"

"Refresh."

"Yeah," Harriet said. "Refresh this business."

Charlie clicked her tongue. "The site's barely loading as it is."

"You might need to clear your browser history," Frank suggested. "The cache has probably reached its memory limit."

"See," Harriet said. "The cache thingy is full."

Charlie handed off her laptop to Frank.

He set it on his lap, and the choir shifted, crowding around Frank's wheelchair instead. Frank unfolded a pair of glasses from his pocket and perched them on the end of his nose.

"This doesn't look like a rehearsal," Julian said. "What am I missing?"

Charlie dropped one hand to her hip, the other gesturing in Frank's direction. "I was trying to check the competition website to see if there'd been any updates. But my laptop is not cooperating."

Doris popped her head up. "Maggie has it on good authority that today's the day we find out who'll be invited to perform at the competition."

"Whose authority?" Julian asked.

Maggie wiggled her brows in his direction. "I might know someone."

"That Graham Burbank guy you mentioned before?"

Maggie flicked her hand like Graham was old news. "Richard McDaniel actually. He sits on the board at the community center."

"Just how many people do you know?" Julian asked.

Maggie shrugged. "Enough."

"Status no change," Frank confirmed suddenly. "I've cleared the cache. The website hasn't been updated."

The residents groaned in unison.

"That's what I said," Charlie muttered.

"Right." Julian reached into his pocket for a piece of paper. "While the rest of you were busy not rehearsing, I was sent a very important email." Heads whipped in his direction, and Julian suddenly felt like an antelope that had stumbled into a lion pride. "From the Elm Springs Arts Council."

Charlie's eyes widened comically. "Oh my God!" she cried. "Why didn't you say something?"

"Way to bury the lede," Doris said, looking like she wanted to swat him on the nose with a rolled-up newspaper.

Julian unfolded the printed email very slowly, but Harriet launched across the room and snatched it from his hand.

"Read it!" Maggie said, dancing at Harriet's side, clinging to her arm. "Go on, read it!"

Silence fell over the room. Julian could have heard a snowflake hit the ground.

"We are pleased to inform you," Harriet began.

Doris threw her hands up. "They're pleased!"

Maggie squealed, and Harriet hushed her. "... That the Glendale Shakers are invited to perform at the Twentieth Annual Christmas Choir Competition!" Harriet's voice rose with every word. "Please see the below instructions for the day of the performance... Blah, blah, blah... Congratulations on your acceptance... We're freaking in, baby!"

The room erupted at once, voices overlapping, the celebration carrying on to an ear-piercing level. Julian shoved his way through the crowd.

Doris grabbed Charlie and squeezed.

"We made it?" Charlie said, sounding a little stunned.

"Did you really have any doubts?" Doris asked as she kissed her cheek.

"No. I mean..." Charlie laughed, then spotted him, and to Julian's surprise, dove right into his arms in front of everyone. "You were right about the audition video. It worked!" She pulled back, beaming at him with a smile bright enough to see from the very back of the balcony.

"But *we* did this," Julian clarified.

Charlie stepped away, and he reluctantly let her go as Frank reached for his hand, giving it a firm shake. Jim clapped him on the shoulder, and Maggie squeezed his arm excitedly.

Suddenly there was a sea of people between him and Charlie.

"Okay, okay," Charlie called, bringing some order to the room. She scanned the printed email. "The competition starts at 2:00 p.m. on Christmas Eve day. So that gives us almost eight days to polish up our performance. What we pulled off at the community center was great. I see no reason why we couldn't top that with some focus and hard work."

"Top it?" Maggie said. "Maybe we could actually win this thing!"

"That's what I'm talking about," Julian agreed.

"Why not?" Doris said. "We have the right codirectors behind us." She wrapped an arm around Julian, latching onto Charlie with the other, and pulled them close.

"And the talent," Maggie said, fluffing her hair.

"Don't forget the moves," Jim added, doing a little box step.

"Let's not get ahead of ourselves," Charlie said. "Let's focus on the music and having a good time—"

"If we want to win, we have to figure out who our competition is," Harriet interrupted.

The residents murmured in agreement.

Charlie caught Julian's eye. He shrugged. If the residents wanted to win, who was he to dissuade them?

"The list is up," Frank announced, staring down at Charlie's laptop. He wheeled into the middle of the group.

"These are the other choirs?" Doris asked, looking over his shoulder. "The Elm Springs Middles? I bet that's the middle school that's entered with a name like that."

"Oh well, that's us finished," Maggie said. "Game over. Who's more deserving of the win than a bunch of children?"

"When they've had two hip replacements, we'll talk about deserving," Harriet cut in.

"I think there's actually something else we need to worry about before we dissect the competition," Charlie said. "What song are we singing?"

"Something Christmasy," Doris said. "Obviously. I see no reason not to stay on theme."

"We could do one of those cool mash-ups," Jim suggested.

Charlie tapped her lips, nodding. "Take the best parts of songs we've already been working on."

"Song choice could shake up everything," Harriet said. "We want a crowd-pleaser. Something we can dance to. A tune that'll get the crowd on their feet."

"So maybe this is a little too on the nose, but I'm gonna

throw it out there," Julian said. "How about 'Grandma Got Runover by a Reindeer'?"

There was another one of those silent pauses. Julian glanced around, waiting for a reaction.

A booming laugh broke the silence. It was Frank, hunched over in his wheelchair, laughing so hard he was almost wheezing.

But above the laughter was a shocked outcry of voices. Julian had to duck a cane that was jabbed in his direction. He backed away from the crowd, envisioning a horde of Glendale's finest chasing him through the halls.

"Now you've done it," Charlie said, grinning.

"But just think of the audience reception!" Julian explained, getting the piano between him and the choir. "I'm thinking outside the box here."

"Don't think we won't vote you out of this choir," Harriet warned. "I'm still not over the gingerbread house results."

"Okay, I'm reading the room." Julian held his hands up in surrender. "There will be no grandmothers getting sacrificed to the reindeer at Glendale."

Thirteen

Charlie

"The harmony on that last chorus was gorgeous," Charlie said, her voice carrying across the room as *Last Christmas* drew to a close. "Really nice. Let's take five. Get some water. I want everybody to remember to stay hydrated."

"That's what my doctor keeps telling me, too," Harriet muttered. "Well, that and to stop sneaking éclairs in the middle of the night."

Charlie shook her head and laughed, the vibration settling deep in her chest. She knuckled the space between her ribs, wondering if that was the key, to let the feelings out in small doses, just a little at a time. "We don't have long until the competition, so protect your voices. Make sure you're doing your warmups and cooldowns. After the break, we'll run the mash-up one more time."

The residents dispersed, gathering their water bottles. Charlie watched Maggie and Harriet flit to Gram's side where she was seated at the piano. Her chest warmed, knowing Gram was slowly being enfolded into this little group, that she was finding her people and making connections that would hopefully last long after the choir competition had finished.

The door popped open, and Warren appeared. Charlie waved him over.

"Guess I just missed the performance?" he said.

"You can catch the second act after intermission," Charlie joked. "Hey, you haven't seen Frank yet today, have you? We're definitely missing his baritone. And it's not like him to skip out on rehearsal."

"Oh." Warren scratched at the back of his head, wincing. "Nobody told you?"

"Told me what?" Charlie said.

"Frank wasn't feeling too great yesterday evening. We ended up having to admit him to the hospital."

"What?" Charlie said. The words ricocheted around her head. No, that didn't make sense. "I just saw him yesterday. He came to rehearsal and was fine." He'd helped her out with her laptop. "We just got the official invite to the competition."

"I know," Warren said. "He's seemed a little rundown for a week now, and then... Well, it can come on hard and fast when you're older. I can't go into details, but he's being taken care of, and that's the most important part."

He was fine, Charlie thought again.

Just like Tom had been fine.

She didn't even know what to say. The shock of the news melted through her, burning as it went. She could feel bile inching up her throat as she glanced around the music room, looking from Gram to all the other residents she'd come to care about these past few weeks. Suddenly, it was all too overwhelming. All she could think about was Tom and hearing those horrible words for the first time: *I'm sick, Charlie.*

The force of the memory almost winded her. This was why she'd locked up her feelings in the first place. She couldn't do it again. She clutched at her throat. There was no air in the room.

She needed to be somewhere else, anywhere else. Somewhere she could breathe.

"Excuse me," she gasped out, crossing the room, desperate for escape. She stopped next to Gram, putting a shaky hand on her shoulder to interrupt her conversation with Harriet and Maggie. "I have to step out for a minute," she said, barely getting the words out. "Can you get rehearsal going again in about five minutes if I'm not back?"

"Of course," Gram said, squeezing her hand. As she looked up at Charlie, her smile fell away. "Is everything okay?"

Charlie swallowed down the sick feeling. "Yeah, all good."

Maggie and Harriet exchanged a nervous glance.

"Charlie," Gram said, getting to her feet. "You're very pale."

"Maybe you should sit down," Maggie suggested, gesturing to the piano bench.

"Everything's fine," Charlie said. *Fine. Fine. Fine!* Was the room starting to spin? "I just need to get some air." She turned on her heel and darted for the door, stumbling into the hall.

She didn't know where to go from here. It was frigidly cold outside, and she'd left her coat in the music room. The common room would likely be filled with other residents. Maybe Gram's suite? She headed in the direction of the elevator but turned into the dining room instead.

It was dimly lit and blessedly empty between meals, and she grasped the back of a chair, sucking in a sharp breath. She hadn't been gripped by anxiety this strong in a while. Not since the months immediately after Tom's passing. But that damn box inside her was splitting at the seams, all the unwanted emotion and memory leaking free.

"Hey, you okay?" Julian said, walking into the room. "Doris said you rushed off looking sick."

Charlie squeezed her eyes against the uneasy thrum of her heart. "I just needed a breather."

"Hey," Julian said again, softer this time. He came closer. So close Charlie thought she might burst into tears when he laid his hand on her arm. "Hey? What's going on? Did something happen? Talk to me."

"I…" She opened her eyes and smoothed her hair back from her face, hands trembling. "I don't know how you do this every day."

"Charlie, what are you talking—"

"Frank's sick!" she said. "Warren said he was admitted to the hospital last night. He couldn't tell me anything else. I don't know how serious it is. I don't know if he'll be back before the competition. I… It's so stupid. I *know* that." She fought the tremor in her voice. "But for a moment, it felt like finding out about Tom all over again."

"Okay," Julian said gently, rubbing slow circles into her shoulder. "That's okay. I get it."

"It's not okay!" she snapped. "I don't know how you spend so much time with the residents knowing that you're going to lose them one day. Maybe even one day soon."

His hand slid across her shoulder, wrapping around the back of her neck, bringing her forehead to his chest.

Charlie caved into the feeling, letting his steady breathing dull the sense of panic inside her.

"To answer your question, it was something I had to come to terms with. In this job, in any long-term care setting, illness and death walk alongside us. But I eventually realized that it was a disservice to myself and to the people I cared about not to enjoy every single minute of time I have with them." He stroked the fine hairs at the base of her neck. "And let me assure you that the beautiful moments make up for the sad ones. I haven't worked a day at Glendale when I haven't doubled over laughing or learned something amazing. It's those little things that make the inevitable loss bearable."

Charlie swallowed, the emotion jamming in her chest. That didn't make sense. "I don't... I don't know how you're okay with this."

Julian's eyebrows pulled together. "I guess I just try not to dwell on it."

"And that's what you think I'm doing? Dwelling?"

"That's not what I said."

She blinked up at him. "But it's what you meant."

"I just think... What good is worrying away the time I might have left with them? It won't stop life from carrying on."

And it wouldn't stop her from being swept away, Charlie realized. It didn't matter how hard she tried to keep her head above water, there was always a new storm, a new torrent, waiting to drown her. "This isn't working," she said, pressing a shaky hand to her chest.

"I think you're blaming yourself for something that wasn't ever in your control," Julian told her.

"Are we talking about Frank or Tom?" she said, a slight edge to her voice.

"Can't it be both?"

She gritted her teeth, feeling weight behind her eyes. She'd been silly to enjoy herself. She should have known it wouldn't last. How could it?

"These things just happen, Charlie."

"I don't know how to be okay with that," she said, stepping away from him. "I don't know if I can do this."

"And that's okay, too," Julian said. "I get that you're shaken. Why don't you take the afternoon, and I'll finish up with the choir?"

"No," Charlie said sadly. "I don't know if I can do this at all." And with that, she turned and headed for the parking lot.

Charlie puttered around Gram's house for most of the afternoon, not really sure where to focus her attention. She'd started wrapping Christmas presents in the living room, then ditched that to sort through Gram's mail, then tried to review some of the audition emails but ended up deleting most without reading them.

Her thoughts were still consumed by Frank's absence and her conversation with Julian. Logically, she knew grief wasn't linear and her reaction was valid—she'd paid for enough therapy to have learned that much. But that didn't stop her from feeling a little silly for running out on the choir.

Then again, she was so good at running. Part of her still believed that if she ran far enough and fast enough, these feelings and the consequences of those feelings might never catch her.

Even as a flush of embarrassment washed through her, she knew ditching rehearsal had been easier than facing the reminders of her grief or enduring Gram's looks of concern or Maggie's uncertain whispers to Harriet. Charlie hadn't realized just how fond she'd become of this little retirement community, and the thought of losing any of them turned her stomach.

She tried to put those thoughts out of her head, walking down the hall, peeking into rooms. It was time to start funneling the rest of Gram's possessions to a storage locker. Charlie sighed, seeing a lot of boxes and packing tape in her future. She wandered back to the living room with a sheet of Bubble Wrap. Already the house was looking emptier, and Charlie was unnerved by it. It felt like she was losing something all over again. Being alone in the old Victorian often felt like too much, but perhaps this was worse. Soon the house would be bare, and the memories, good or bad, would be gone. Packed away to live in a cold, damp storage unit.

Her eyes drifted to the second floor stairwell. Wasn't that what she'd tried to do with Tom? Lock him away in a place inside her that she never wanted to visit?

Charlie pressed her hand to her stomach. *Get it together.* It was only a house.

Her phone buzzed, and she grabbed it off the coffee table, eager for a distraction.

"Hey!" she said, wincing as Alicia squealed on the other end of the phone.

"Where are you? Are you sitting down?"

Charlie pursed her lips. "Um, should I be?"

"Yes, sit down. Right now!"

"Oh no," Charlie muttered. "What's happening?"

"Okay, so I've gotten a call from the New York Philharmonic. They saw your viral video with the choir, and they need a singer to fill a spot for a New Year's performance they're putting together. Well, I mean, they've been putting it together for a while, but the part we care about is that they've had someone drop out last minute, and they've invited you to take their place!"

"They've invited me to sing?" Charlie said, dumbfounded. "With the orchestra?"

"Yes," Alicia said.

"Holy shit."

"I know!"

"That's like...that's huge!"

"I know!"

The New York Philharmonic was one of the leading orchestras in the country. Tom would have drooled at the thought of being able to work with them.

"There's a bunch of well-known Broadway performers on the program," Alicia continued. "This could be an amazing way for you to return to the community."

"They asked for me?" Charlie said, still a little stunned by the news.

"Yes, you. Someone down at the Lincoln Center saw your little video and loved it. They inquired about your availability with me, and I said you're looking to get back into performing again. I think they're trying to embrace the social media thing. You know, attract new fans to the symphony, and as far as viral videos go, you're kinda famous."

"Ha!" Charlie said. She'd had exactly thirty seconds of

viral fame with the community center video. Then again, there was a reason they called it the power of social media.

"So?" Alicia said. "What do you think?"

"I think Tom would have gone absolutely wild over this news."

"He would have," Alicia agreed softly.

"Performing with an orchestra of this caliber was always his dream."

"Is that a yes?" Alicia asked.

"I think…." How could she possibly turn down this kind of offer? "I'd like to give it some serious consideration."

"Okay, great!" Alicia said, launching into the details. "You'll have to be in Manhattan for rehearsals by next week at the latest."

"Next week?" she said.

Alicia laughed. "Yes. It's a New Year's performance. Christmas is next week. The clock is sort of ticking on this."

"Right, of course." Charlie rubbed the space between her eyes. The choir! If she was in New York City over the holidays, she'd definitely miss the competition. But this could also be her chance to honor Tom and everything he'd hoped to accomplish in his life. She'd be a fool to say no. She *couldn't* say no.

Besides, hadn't she just told Julian she wasn't sure she could do this? Maybe this was a sign from the universe or, at the very least, a buoy to keep her afloat. "Okay. Send me everything."

"Are you sure?" Alicia said. "I don't want to pressure you, but I've got the contract sitting in my inbox already."

Charlie bit her lip. "Send it my way."

"On the way to your email now." Charlie could hear her typing away. "This is very cool, Charlie. And a big deal that they asked for you personally."

"I know."

"Call me back when you've had a chance to look at it. We should really aim to get it back to them by tomorrow morning if you're committed."

"I will."

"Talk to you later."

Charlie hung up and clutched her forehead. *What the hell just happened?* What horrible timing! Could she do both things—the performance at the Lincoln Center and the choir competition? No. But was one of those things significantly better for her career? Yes. Would Gram understand that? And Julian? And the rest of the choir? She thought so.

If they ultimately wanted what was best for her, they'd tell her to get to NYC tomorrow. Sure she was going to feel like garbage for ditching the choir this close to the competition, but they could squeeze in a couple more rehearsals before she left. And she would prepare Gram and Julian to be her stand-ins.

They'd probably be ecstatic for her.

And this was what she wanted—a new place to run where she could stop tripping over her memories every time she turned a damn corner.

Or did she want to stay?

She drummed her fingers against her lips. Her hand trembled. She didn't know the right answer. But maybe she was getting ahead of herself. She hadn't even had a chance to review the contract yet. There was still the possibility she wouldn't be able to commit.

The doorbell rang. Charlie glanced down the hall, frowning. She wasn't expecting anyone. She hurried to answer it, finding Julian standing on the porch, shivering in his coat.

"Hey," he said.

"Hi." Her eyes darted down to the takeout bag in his hand. Mackey's Diner.

"I thought..." He shrugged. "Have you eaten?"

"I actually haven't." The contract could wait, she supposed. She pulled the door open wider, feeling stress and desire and confusion swirl through her.

Julian passed her, slipping out of his coat. "How are you doing?"

"I'm..." Where the hell did she start? She was still upset about Frank, but now she was also worried about possibly leaving the choir before the competition. Charlie licked her lips. She shouldn't tell him that yet. Not until the contract was actually signed.

"I just wanted to make sure you were okay after the way rehearsal went," Julian said. "And the way our conversation went. Sorta feel like I dropped the ball."

"You didn't drop anything," she assured him. Warmth spread through her at his concern. She was touched that he'd cared enough to come and check on her. "I'm managing," she said finally. "What did you get for dinner?"

"Figured I couldn't go wrong with burgers. Hope you still like the double cheeseburger. That's what you were eating the day I asked you out."

She laughed. "Even I didn't remember that."

He gave her a cheeky smile. "There was also a vanilla shake on the order, but Mackey's stopped doing shakes."

"No! Why?"

He shrugged. "New management."

"Those shakes were amazing. So thick you had to eat them with a spoon until they melted a little."

He followed her into the kitchen, and they dished out burgers and chunky fries.

"They were amazing." Julian popped a fry into his mouth. "But they have a new line of smoothies now. Sometimes things change for the better."

Charlie coated her fries in malt vinegar and ketchup.

Julian eyeballed the concoction warily. "And sometimes they change for the worse. But I'll have to take you for a smoothie sometime."

Charlie's heart skipped. *Sometime.* "I'd like that," she said without knowing when sometime might be.

Julian grinned down at her. They ate standing in the kitchen, leaning up against the counter, dripping ketchup down their fingers.

"So, Doris kept the choir rehearsing for another hour after you left," Julian said. "And Warren brought some of the other nurses by the music room to have a listen."

"What'd they think?" Charlie asked.

"Standing ovation. Obviously. I really do think that adding 'Grandma Got Run Over by a Reindeer' into the mashup was the right call."

A smile tugged at her mouth. The choir had had a long debate about that one.

"You might even call it inspired," Julian continued.

Charlie rolled her eyes. "I wouldn't go that far."

Julian scoffed. "Don't knock my epic contribution."

"I do think there is something inherently funny about a choir of septuagenarians performing that song," Charlie admitted.

"Right! Sometimes I'm brilliant."

"Mm-hmm." Charlie ate the last few bites of her burger. "This was really good. Thank you. And thank you for coming to check on me."

"You're really okay? I know you said you weren't sure if you could do this choir thing but—"

"It was just such a shock earlier," she said.

"Right." He released a long breath like he'd been holding it since that moment. "As long as you're not making any rash decisions."

Rash decisions? No. Though there were decisions to make. Later, she told herself. When he wasn't bringing her dinner and looking at her with that dimpled smile. When the thought of his embrace wasn't so intoxicating. "I don't think it dawned on me how much the residents were starting to mean to me," she said. "So the news about Frank hit harder than I expected."

"You light up when you look at them," Julian said. "That's not a bad thing."

"You haven't heard anything else about Frank?" Charlie asked, trying not to dwell on his words.

"No updates yet. But sometimes no news is good news."

"Sometimes it is," she said, trying not to think about Tom. Because sometimes no news just meant the bad news had yet to break.

Julian cleaned up his plate and cleared his throat. "I should get going."

"You don't have to go," she said, catching his hand. With Julian here, she could ignore her inbox for a little while longer. She didn't need to read any contracts or make decisions about staying or going. Not right now. She could simply stand here while he smiled at her in a way that made her heart beat out of her chest. "You could stay," she offered, stroking her hand around the back of his neck.

"I could," he whispered.

She put gentle pressure on his neck, dragging him down into a kiss. "Then stay with me."

Fourteen

Julian

*S*tay *with me.*

Charlie's words surged through him, carried through his veins like liquid fire. Heat spread from the top of his head, coursing down through his limbs, and he knew the only thing that would quench the burn was to touch her. And he wanted to stay, wanted to reassure her that he was a steady presence in the storm of her complicated feelings.

Julian wrapped his hands around her waist, locking them behind her back as they pressed against the kitchen counter. He felt the pull of muscle as she stretched up on her toes, searching out his lips again. Julian lowered his head, making her search easy, and kissed her once, twice, three times.

Their plates rattled as they swayed, his hands shifting from the small of her back, down to squeeze her ass.

Charlie was all softness—the silk of her lips, the way she was draped in his arms—and he stroked his hands up, chasing the grooves of her spine like a ladder until he reached her neck. Then he sank his hands into her hair.

She groaned in response, her eyelids fluttering closed, and Julian grinned at the way her lips parted. At the color in her cheeks. And the way her chest heaved.

He kissed her again, flicking his tongue along her lower lip before catching her tongue and sucking it into his mouth, swallowing the sounds she made.

He liked all her little sounds.

It was a different kind of music.

One only he got to hear.

"I like it when you do that," she said, barely opening her eyes.

He liked it, too. He'd always liked kissing her. They'd been good at it from the very start. "You're really sure you want me to stay?"

"Very sure."

"Then maybe we should move this somewhere more comfortable?" Kitchens could be fun, but he knew there was a pillowy sofa in the next room, and he'd hate to waste it.

Charlie gripped his hand tightly and tugged him toward the living room.

His eyes widened as he took in the space, half a laugh tumbling from his mouth. It looked like a Christmas-themed hurricane had blown through. Shreds of wrapping paper littered the floor, strands of ribbon dangled from the arms of the sofa, while red and green and gold bows sparkled from every horizontal surface. "What the hell happened in here?"

Charlie let out an *oomph* of acknowledgment. "I started

wrapping presents for my parents and Gram when I got home, but then I got distracted and never got back to it."

"Hate to break it to you," Julian said, "but you might actually be really bad at gift wrapping."

Charlie gasped, nudging him playfully. "Take that back. I am a gift wrapping artist. You've never seen such fine work."

"There are shreds of paper everywhere. What gift wrapping artist shreds the paper?"

"I was making sure all my angles were right."

"What angles?"

"You know," she said, miming, "for folding in the end pieces."

"I'm not sure you should be set free with gift wrap." He leaned down to nuzzle her cheek.

"Take that back."

"It looks like Christmas threw up in here."

"It does not!" Charlie's lips twitched as she glanced around. "Okay, maybe you're right. Maybe I got a little carried away with things."

"This is a little carried away? We're gonna have to call in a professional cleaning service or else I'm worried you'll disappear under all of this mess."

Charlie rolled her eyes. "It's not that bad." She bent down, collecting a few scraps of silver wrapping paper.

Julian caught her hand and tugged her back up. "Leave it."

"You're the one complaining about the state of the room."

"I was simply impressed with your level of dedication."

"Felt a little judgmental," she said, poking his chest. "Don't mess with me or my gift wrapping."

"I wouldn't dare." He stroked his thumb across her cheek, and she caught his hand, guiding him toward the sofa. They plopped down in a sea of wrapping supplies. Paper crinkled under him, and he laughed as Charlie sank against his side.

"Sorry," she whispered.

He bussed her temple. "It's growing on me, actually."

"Is it?"

"Mm-hmm. It adds a certain pizzazz the living room was missing before." He reached down. A bow had stuck to the back of her shoulder. He peeled it off, and she huffed at his teasing.

"Point taken." She gestured across the living room to a stack of velvet-wrapped boxes with impeccably placed green bows. "But you have to admit, the end product is impressive. And that's what matters. How I got there isn't the point."

Julian grinned at her. He sort of felt like that about the music program. They may have been taking a messy, indirect route, but if he managed to make it work in the end, what did it matter? Because Charlie was still here. She still wanted to do this choir thing with him. Right? He swallowed hard, part of him wanting to ask again, wanting to be sure after today's hiccup.

Stay, he wanted to say to her. *For Doris. For the choir. For me*, he thought briefly, desperately. *Stay for us*.

"What did you get Doris anyway?" he asked instead.

Charlie smirked. "Wouldn't you like to know?"

"I would. I want to make sure we don't buy her the same thing." He nuzzled closer, his lips hovering against hers. He watched Charlie's eyelids close in anticipation, but at the last second he swerved and kissed her cheek.

She made a noise of discontent.

"Something the matter?"

She sighed. "No."

Julian plucked a piece of red ribbon from the couch, using the end to trace a pattern across Charlie's cheek. "I don't know why I was complaining to be honest. I actually really like wrapping things."

Her eyes opened. "Do you?"

"I'm particularly good at tying bows. Would you like to see?"

Now she was staring at him, curious. He took her wrists in his hands, pressing a kiss to each one, giving her a beat to pull away. When she didn't, he took the ribbon and looped it around her wrists, making his intentions clear.

Charlie let out a little gasp.

"Is this okay?" he asked, tying perfect loops.

"Yes," she breathed, tugging gently.

The ribbon was loose enough she could squirm free if she wanted. Hell, if she put enough force on it, the ribbon would snap. It was only flimsy gift wrap. But it wasn't really about how strong it was, it was what it represented.

Charlie was giving up a measure of control to him. She was trusting him to take care of her. To keep her safe.

She was trusting him with all the dark, cracked pieces of her heart.

And he would be so, *so* gentle.

Julian stroked his hand through her hair, shifting them so she was lying on her back and he was lying along her side. Then he pushed her bound hands back over her head, the ribbon dangling in pretty red curls over the arm of the couch. Charlie's chest heaved. She was like his own personal gift, and he intended to enjoy every inch of her.

He traced the lines of her face first, the arc of her brow, the straight bridge of her nose, the curve of her chin. When he was satisfied that he'd memorized each freckle, he let his hands drift down her neck, stopping at the hollow at the base of her throat. He angled his head, letting his tongue follow. Charlie's next breath stuttered, and he sucked gently at her skin.

She squirmed as his hand shifted, tracing the buttons along her shirt. With deft fingers, he popped one open, giving himself better access. He slipped another open, then another, tracing the valley between her breasts.

Charlie groaned.

He nuzzled at her, breathing in the fresh scent of her skin, while his hand traveled farther. She wore loose sweat pants and Julian tugged at the drawstring, searching her eyes for permission. "Is this okay?"

Charlie nodded, closing her eyes and swallowing hard enough for him to see her throat work.

Julian snapped the waistband gently. "Charlie?"

"Yes," she said. *"Yes, it's okay."*

He slipped his hand into the waistband of her pants, into the warmth there, and skimmed along her underwear. She was already wet for him, and he ran careful fingers over the place she wanted him most.

Charlie made a whiny, desperate noise, and Julian kissed her until they needed to part for air. Then he slipped his fingers into her underwear, sliding into wet heat, taking his time to explore just like the last time. Charlie's hips bucked, and her hands came up briefly. He saw the moment she registered that they were still bound with the ribbon. She sighed, pressing her head back into the sofa as he stroked her.

Charlie squirmed some more, brow furrowed in frustration.

He knew what she was desperate for. Julian removed his hand, and she complained loudly. "Hold on," he laughed, shifting down the couch. Charlie lifted her hips so he could drag her pants and underwear down her legs before burying his head between them.

"Mmm, yes," Charlie hissed as Julian flicked his tongue over her clit, drawing tight circles and sucking until she was arching off the sofa. Her body tensed, and he could tell she wanted to use her hands to touch him. To guide him. But she was at his mercy, and he set a deliberately slow pace that had her panting.

"Julian," she said, her voice raspy.

"Yes?" He grinned against her stomach. "Do you need something?"

She bucked her hips, and he lapped at her some more. "I need that." He dragged his tongue over her clit again, and her body twitched, looking for friction. "More. More, *please*!"

"Please will get you so far," he said, refocusing his efforts before working her into a panting, squirming frenzy.

Charlie cried out suddenly, rutting against his tongue as her orgasm took her. He stroked her trembling legs, letting her descend from the high, then crawled up the sofa to untie that pretty little bow around her wrists.

"God," she said, lifting her head to look at him. "That was new. You definitely didn't know how to do that the last time."

He snickered. "Maybe I've studied up in our years apart. Did you like it?"

"I think we both know I did." Charlie reached around

him, running her hands over his shoulders. "Maybe we should move to the bedroom?" She pressed a kiss to his chest. "More space."

"I like where this is going." Julian sat up, reaching for her hand.

Charlie led him down the hall to the spare room she was using and plopped down on the bed, watching him with a cheeky smile as he shrugged out of his shirt and unbuttoned his jeans. His pants hit the floor, and Julian leaned over, fishing his wallet out of his pocket to retrieve the condom he'd stashed there recently.

Charlie's eye flickered over him appreciatively, amusement etched into her features. "Did you think you were going to get lucky when you came over tonight?"

He flashed her a grin. "I think it's important to be prepared for all possibilities." He stepped closer and smoothed a piece of hair away from her face. "Did you not think this would happen again?"

She kissed his stomach, and the muscle twitched beneath her lips. "I hoped it would happen again," she admitted. "I've missed you."

She shifted back on the bed, reaching for him. Julian didn't need much convincing and climbed onto the bed as they wriggled out of the rest of their clothing. He let her pull him close, stroking his hands over her breasts, his touch gentle as he rolled her nipples between his fingers.

Charlie closed her eyes and hummed at the touch, then she tilted her head back and looked at him. "I hadn't realized how much until we were together again."

Julian's heart lobbed into his throat. She'd asked him to stay tonight, but was he a fool for wanting more? *Stay with me in Elm Springs. You could be happy here. We could try again*. He stared into her eyes, into the glassy reflection he saw, searching desperately for the answer to a question he'd been asking his whole life. *Am I enough?* Because for once in his damn life, he wanted someone to choose him.

"I've missed you," she said again, her voice thick. "You make things feel a little less heavy. And I like that."

To Julian, it sounded like a promise. Like she was invested in more than this choir. Like she wanted him for more than just tonight.

Charlie's hands kneaded the muscles in his back, and he sank into her embrace. He wanted to be held by her forever. He tipped his head and kissed her, slow and languid, stealing a moan from the back of her throat. "I've missed you, too, you know. You walked back into my life and turned it upside down—in the best possible way. I don't know if I can go back." He didn't want to.

Charlie pulled his focus as she shifted beneath him, rolling her hips, grinding against his erection. Julian sucked in a deep breath through his nose to keep his thoughts from spinning out of control.

He kissed her again. Lips, cheek, jaw. Then spent some time nibbling at her throat.

"Stop teasing," Charlie complained, shoving at his shoulder.

"I'm just being thorough."

"I don't see how it can be thorough when you're skipping over one very important part."

Julian lifted his head and laughed at the perturbed look on her face.

She reached over and snatched the condom he'd left on the bedside table, ripping it open with her teeth.

"That's hot," he said.

"Put this on."

"Bossy, too. I like it." Julian shifted to his knees, watching the way Charlie's eyes roamed the length of him. She looked like she wanted to devour him.

"Let me help," she said, sitting up and taking the condom from his hand, rolling it over his cock.

"Impatient?" Julian said, trying not to react to the feel of her hands on him.

"More like eager to see you perform."

"You know I might not be able to sing, but this is *my* stage."

Charlie snorted. "That was so corny."

Julian wrapped his arms around her, and she laughed, thumping back down on the bed. Charlie wormed her hand between their bodies, wrapping her delicate fingers around his cock. She squeezed, staring into his eyes.

"Would you like something?" he whispered.

"Yes."

"Tell me."

"You. Inside me." Her gaze filled with desire, her bottom lip trapped between her teeth, and he believed her. He believed how badly she wanted him. Julian let Charlie guide his cock between her thighs, and he braced himself on his forearms, nudging at her entrance. "Ready?" he asked.

"Yes," she whispered. "Please."

And with that, Julian slid inside, shuddering at the feeling. Charlie's mouth dropped open, her brow furrowing as breathy little "oh, oh, *ohs*!" filled the room.

Once he started moving, he didn't stop, chasing the climax that surged through his blood. He wanted to sink deeper into the heat, to give into the pressure that coiled at the base of his spine. His thoughts narrowed to the motion of his hips and the sound of their bodies coming together.

Charlie's breath faltered, and her hand disappeared between them again, rubbing her clit as her legs began to tremble.

Julian huffed, his head at her shoulder, and rocked into her again and again and again. He heard her cry out and felt the sudden jolt of a body flooded with pleasure. She stilled beneath him, and he gave a few final uncoordinated thrusts before his orgasm dragged him through the kind of pleasure that made him see stars.

Charlie stroked her hands over his back.

"The bed was a good idea," he whispered.

"Told you," she said, not quite laughing.

Julian rolled off her, and she snuggled into his side. Charlie wrapped her arm over his chest, indicating that he wasn't going anywhere.

Julian threaded his fingers through hers, content to bask in the bliss that still flooded his body. He didn't need any more than this—just the simple truth that he was wanted.

Fifteen

Julian

He woke to the sound of birdsong. He didn't know which of the birds had braved the winter, but they were twittering away outside the window. He popped his eyes open, taking in the thin streams of gray light that filtered between the blinds. He laughed under his breath. The house was simply filled with music. It was where Charlie had learned to sing. It was where Doris had taught her and Tom to play the piano. Where her love of theater was born. Even the birds seemed to recognize that.

Julian inhaled deeply, his senses overwhelmed by the smell of coffee. After the kind of long, physical night they'd just had, he wanted to bury his face in a mug. He rolled over and stretched contentedly. He'd forgotten how nice it was to hold someone into the night, to feel their weight at his side, to listen to the even sound of their breathing.

Charlie's side of the bed was abandoned, the sheets rumpled, but he could hear the clang of dishes as she puttered around in the kitchen. For a long, blissful moment, he considered what it would be like to wake up like this every morning. Things might not have worked out the last time, but now they could take their time figuring out how to be together. There was no schooling demanding their attention, no reason to rush off at the end of the holidays, no threat of long distance hanging over their heads.

Julian knew he could make her happy. And sure, Elm Springs might not be a Broadway stage, but after everything they'd talked about, it didn't really sound like that was what Charlie wanted anymore. At least not right now. She'd loved the stage because she loved performing with her brother. Now that Tom was gone, it seemed like she was hesitant to stand up there alone.

And if that wasn't what brought her joy anymore, then Julian would support her until she figured out what did.

He stood, slipped on his boxers and padded across the floor. It was an old, creaky house, and the moment he set foot in the hallway, Charlie's voice caught him. "I left you a new toothbrush in the bathroom," she called. "And towels if you want to shower."

"Thanks," he called back, heading for the bathroom. She had indeed left him a toothbrush next to the sink and fluffy white towels. He grinned down at them for no reason at all other than he liked the domesticity. He would still have to pop home for a change of clothes at some point, but this was a good start.

He fiddled with the shower and waited for the water to heat up, then stepped beneath the spray, groaning at how nice it felt. Doris had clearly splurged on an expensive showerhead. As the water kneaded the muscles in his neck, he considered what came next.

Charlie had obviously offered him the shower, and there was definitely coffee downstairs, so he doubted she was chasing him out. It was Saturday, and he actually kind of liked the idea of spending some of the weekend together... Or all of it. They could review the email for the day of the choir competition, just to make sure they were prepared, and then he could help her with whatever organizing she still had to do in the house for Doris. Maybe she'd even let him take her out for lunch or downtown to see the Christmas light display in the park. He could hold her hand as they walked between the evergreens. What a nice thought that was.

He finished up in the shower, brushed his teeth and put his clothes back on.

When he exited the bathroom, Charlie was humming along to the radio. Her voice drifted through the kitchen, soft and melodious. She sounded happy.

"Morning," he said, coming up behind her.

"Morning. How do you feel about bacon?" she asked, taking a package out of the fridge.

"A shower and breakfast? I didn't know this was a B&B type joint."

"I'm obviously hoping for a five star review."

"Well, you're definitely on your way." He inched closer to her. She leaned up against the counter, her tongue darting out to moisten her lips. "Hi," he said quietly.

"Hi," she said.

He lowered his head, making his intentions clear. Charlie smiled a bit, then pressed up on her toes so she could kiss him. It was a chaste thing by all standards, but it still filled his gut with butterflies.

"You didn't answer my question," she said, pecking

the corner of his mouth. "Bacon? What're your thoughts? Yes… No?"

"I feel very good about it."

Charlie hummed. Her hair was in slight disarray, her oversize shirt wrinkled, and he thought she'd never looked sexier. He found her hip, slipping his hand beneath her shirt to feel the soft skin beneath. His hand came to rest along the groove of her spine. He pulled her closer and kissed her for real, until he was light-headed in the best way.

"I can't feed you if you're going to keep doing that."

"I'm quite satisfied with this," Julian assured her.

Charlie chuckled against his lips. "Don't even try to pretend you're not starving."

As if on cue, his stomach growled.

She pulled back. "I can hear my five star rating crumbling."

"I don't know. This kissing thing is kind of nice, too. Might make up for the lack of food."

"Well, you've never had one of my bacon, egg, tomato breakfast sandwiches."

"You're telling me I'm going to prefer this sandwich to kissing you?"

"You just might."

"Now I'm curious." He gave her backside a pat, and Charlie smirked. "Can I help? I have been known to make some eggs in my day."

"You can help yourself to coffee," she said. "Or there's orange juice in the fridge. And then you can get out of my kitchen."

"Understood." Julian poured himself a cup of coffee and sat at the kitchen table where he could watch her move back and forth, dropping the bacon into a large frying pan. In another, she cracked eggs. While everything cooked, she took a cutting board from behind the toaster and diced up thick slices of tomato.

"You're not committed to a specific kind of bread, are you?"

"No," Julian said. "Should I be?"

Charlie popped a couple slices of bread into the toaster. "Gram only ever ate one brand of multigrain, and I feel like she ruined all other bread for me."

"It's funny the things that stick with us from childhood," Julian said. "Every time I see a woman with a giant purse, I swear I can still taste the caramel candies my grandmother used to keep in hers. I would sneak them on long car rides and spend twenty minutes trying to open the wrapper without getting caught."

Charlie laughed. "Gram used to keep a dish of sour candies on the coffee table in the living room. I can't tell you how many shops I've searched trying to find the same ones."

"No luck?"

"Never. It's like they only existed in my imagination."

"That's how I felt about my grandmother's gingerbread. She only ever bought it at Christmas, and I've tried so many places around town and can't seem to find anything remotely similar. The bakery I get the gingerbread house kits from is good but..." he sighed "...I miss that gingerbread."

Charlie tilted her head, regarding him. "Gram used to make these cookies with plum jam inside them around the holidays. They were dusted with powdered sugar and literally *so* good. She'd always know when Tom and I had been sneaking them, and I'm only now realizing that was because we probably had sugar all over our faces."

Julian waited for the mention of Tom to upset her, but she chuckled like she'd remembered it fondly.

He sat up, encouraged by her good memories. He wanted this for Charlie. He wanted her to be able to remember things without the weight of grief dragging her down. "Did you ever learn how to make the cookies?"

Charlie snorted, flipping the eggs and bacon as the toast popped. "If I ever mastered that plum jam, I'd eat it straight out of the jar. It's addicting."

"We'll have to ask Doris for the recipe."

Charlie added mayo to the toast and layered on a slice of tomato. "No chance. She hasn't even handed that trade secret down to my mom." She turned to him, blinking slowly.

"What?" he asked.

"Nothing, I...have all these Christmas memories flooding back."

"Tell me," he said softly.

She crossed her arms, leaning a hip against the counter, taking a moment to process. "I remember this one Christmas—I must have been about five or six, Tom just a bit older—Gram bought us recorders. They were under the tree, and we got them Christmas morning. Tom had been learning at school, so he was actually quite good, but I wanted to be good, too, and I just kept wailing on this instrument." She caught her lip between her teeth, shaking her head. "My poor parents sat there all morning enduring that."

"I'm surprised they didn't take it away."

"Oh, Tom took it from me and hurled it into the basement."

Julian laughed. "Is it still down there?"

"Probably. My dad went down to look for it but he couldn't find it in Gram's museum of junk. I cried for hours."

"So you're telling me there's a music thing you're horrible at?"

"*Horrible* is probably a strong word."

"Pretty sure you told me your brother had to ditch the instrument in the basement in order to save Christmas."

Charlie turned back to the counter, licking mayo off her finger. "I'd like to think that I picked up a thing or two at Juilliard. I think if I ever found that recorder, I'd be able to get a tune out without making anyone's ears bleed."

"Not sure I trust that," he teased.

"Speaking of instruments," she said.

Julian wrinkled his nose. "Uh-oh."

"What?"

"You have the same tone I use when I ask Diane for money."

Charlie grinned. "It might be a good idea to get some jingle bells for the competition. It'll make the performance a little more dynamic. Also adds a little sparkle and fun."

"Well, I'm all about fun," Julian said. "How much do jingle bells cost?"

"Probably not much. Now that I'm thinking about it," Charlie said, "the residents might be able to just make something themselves."

"I like that idea. DIY is always cheaper."

"And they do like their crafts." Charlie added fried eggs to the towering sandwiches she was making. Julian glanced to his left, to where Charlie's laptop was already open. He could probably Google the nearest craft store. Maybe that could be part of what they did this weekend—make a run for jingle bell supplies.

He shifted, pulling the laptop closer. When he touched the mouse pad, the laptop woke to Charlie's email. He went to open a new tab, but his eyes were drawn to the first message in the inbox. It had been starred as important.

He really didn't mean to pry. But his gaze locked on the word OFFER, and then he just…kept reading.

The New York Philharmonic? New York City? Rehearsals?

"Charlie," he said, feeling like someone had knocked him in the head with a rock-filled snowball.

"Yeah?"

"What is this?" His eyes locked on the dates. The proposed rehearsal times overlapped with the choir competition. That meant Charlie would be gone to New York City over Christmas.

She turned away from the stove. She had a piece of bacon on the end of a spatula. He frowned so hard the space between his brows started to ache. She hadn't mentioned anything about this job offer to him.

"What is what?" she asked. He flipped the laptop around, and her smile fell away. "Oh, that's something my agent sent over. I promise I haven't technically committed yet. I'm just reviewing the offer."

"Looks like you're pretty committed to me," Julian said, his pulse quickening. "There's a contract here."

Charlie grew quiet.

"Maybe I'm reading this all wrong, but from what I can see, this means you'd miss the competition. Right?"

A muscle in Charlie's jaw twitched. "Yes, that's what it would mean."

Julian scoffed, rubbing at his eyes. Nothing made sense. "Am I missing something here? You've just finished telling me about the damn jingle bells we need for the performance, but you don't actually intend to be here?"

"First," Charlie said. "I told you I hadn't decided yet. And second, it's not like I'm leaving you in the lurch. The choir has you and Gram for support, and as long as they keep rehearsing, they'll be ready. And if really necessary, I can video call to see how things are going."

"Video call?" Julian didn't know what to say. He'd been with her since last night, and she hadn't considered telling him any of this.

"Well, yeah," she said. "I think you and Gram can handle one little performance."

"It's not just one little performance." He shot to his feet, shocked that she would even say that. What happened to staying? What happened to doing this together? "You've built something here at Glendale. If you're giving it up for your dream, then go ahead, I'm happy for you. But if you're leaving right before the competition because—"

"Because this is an amazing opportunity," Charlie clarified. "Because Tom would have been so ecstatic to have an opportunity like this. He always wanted to perform with the New York—"

"Are you hearing yourself?" Julian said.

She jerked back from the force of his words. "What?"

"This doesn't sound like it's something *you* actually want to do. I think you're trying to prove something to yourself or to Tom's memory, but I don't think that's truly going to make you happy."

"Julian—"

"You just told me performing on that stage, with that orchestra, was your brother's dream. He's gone, Charlie."

Her eyes narrowed. "I know he's gone. Thank you very much for that. I wake up and realize that every day. That doesn't change the fact that it's something Tom would have wanted us to do together. And as you pointed out, he's not here." Her voice trembled. "So now I'm going to do it for him."

"Is this it then?"

"Is what it?"

Julian's heart throbbed, and he wondered if it would burst out between his ribs. "If you leave now, are you ever coming back?"

Charlie opened her mouth. Closed it. Looked away. "This was never supposed to be a long visit. And the music thing… It was always just a volunteer gig."

Just a volunteer gig. Anger pooled in his chest.

He should have known better than to get involved with Charlie again. In fact, he *had* known better. That was why his first instinct had been to pretend like he'd never known her at all. God, he wanted to scream. Old fears resurfaced, running through him like a cold chill. He'd made a stupid mistake opening his heart up to her again. Charlie was never committed to this place or to him or the choir, and he was an idiot for believing otherwise.

"Yeah, I get it," he said. "You don't do commitment. Of any kind."

Her eyes widened. "I can't believe that's what you think of me and that you don't see how important this opportunity is."

"No, I get it. I really do," he said, unable to keep the

hurt out of his voice. "It's an amazing opportunity. And if it's what you really want, then I want that for you, too."

"Really?" she snapped. "Because that's not how it sounds."

"Because last night you said you were okay with this. The choir. Frank." He lifted his hands, grasping at nothing. "You said you were staying."

"I never confirmed I was staying," Charlie said, tucking her arms against her chest. "I was careful not to say that for this exact reason. Because I wasn't sure what I was doing."

"Jesus, Charlie. I shouldn't need a codex to decipher your words." He couldn't wrap his head around the fact she'd been thinking all this through last night while he stupidly fell even deeper into his delusion. "And forgive me for thinking this was something you actually wanted! That I was something you wanted."

"Julian—"

He shook his head, the anger spilling out of him in waves. "What was last night, just a convenient comfort fuck? Was I a warm body on a night you needed one?"

"No, that's not what—"

"Is that all I am to you after everything?"

"God, Julian," she said, threading her hands through her hair. "When are you going to let go of the past? We were just kids having a good time."

"And what are we now, Charlie?" he snapped, staring at her hard. At her trembling jaw. "When are you going to accept that you can't outrun your grief?"

The acrid smell of burned bacon filled the air, and the smoke detector shrieked suddenly. Charlie snatched a towel from the counter, waving away the smoke. "You should go," she said, the hard edge of her voice carrying above the wail.

"Took the words right out of my mouth." Julian turned and headed for the door. He was ridiculous for thinking anything had changed.

Charlie didn't want him. She never had.

Sixteen

Charlie

Charlie attempted to close her suitcase, grumbling as the zipper snagged. She'd need to invest in a new one soon, though all it had to do was survive the car ride to New York City. Then maybe she'd stick around there for a while after the Lincoln Center performance. She had a lot of contacts in the city, and someone was always looking for a roommate or to sublet. Or maybe she'd finally take one of Alicia's many audition emails seriously. If she booked a national tour, she could keep traveling. A new city every week, a new state every month or so. The schedules were hectic, and she didn't love the idea of living out of a multitude of hotel rooms. But at least the chaos would keep her busy.

It would certainly keep her from thinking about Elm Springs and Glendale and Julian.

Charlie gritted her teeth, forcing the zipper past the snag. She'd pushed her departure to the very last minute, mulling over this decision. She knew accepting the offer to perform with the Philharmonic was the right choice. She'd known that even before Julian had put his two cents in. The only reason she hesitated now was because she'd let him get inside her head.

Maybe more than just her head. He'd started to worm his way back into her—

No! Close the lid. Lock it all away.

She was trying. But the way he'd looked at her the other morning—like she'd punched him square in the chest—wasn't fair. He shouldn't be allowed to make her feel this way.

What was he doing, looking at her private emails anyway? She knew he hadn't meant anything malicious by it, but still! This was her news to share when she was ready. It should have been happy news. He should have been congratulating her. He should have been absolutely ecstatic!

But instead he'd looked so…betrayed. She knew she was leaving the choir at a crucial time, but she was only ever volunteering in this role. And she hadn't even wanted to sign up for it in the first place. The choir, the competition, that was all Julian's idea. Charlie had done her best to set them up for success, so he wasn't allowed to look at her like that.

He wasn't allowed to make her feel worse than she already did.

This should have been the easy part—packing her things and leaving. She'd be a fool to turn down this opportunity for a little community choir competition. An invitation to perform onstage with some of Broadway's biggest stars? Charlie should pinch herself. Tom certainly would have.

Sure, maybe part of her felt a little guilty because if it

hadn't been for that viral video circulating, maybe Alicia never would have gotten that call. But it's not like she could blow off the Lincoln Center to stand onstage and ring some jingle bells.

This wasn't supposed to be a hard decision.

So, what was her hang-up? Her sense of obligation or her concern for Gram? The fact that her parents would be sad that she was skipping out on yet another Christmas? Yes, to all those things. But beneath that, in some dusty part of her heart, the worry that plagued her most was for Julian.

She had no idea where they stood or when she might see him again if she left. Would it be eight more years? Would she return to find him living a completely different life—happy with someone who wasn't her?

The thought made Charlie's insides twist uncomfortably. She fought off the panic that bubbled up her throat. They weren't...together. Not like that.

She liked him. A lot. But could she put her life on hold to stay here? *No...* She had to get back to performing, to be surrounded by applause at night and skyscrapers in the morning. She wanted an orchestra behind her. She wanted the Lincoln Center and whatever came after. And just like last time, Julian didn't quite fit into that picture.

What did it matter anyway? She was still furious with him as his words rang in her head.

I think you're trying to prove something to yourself or to Tom's memory, but I don't think that's truly going to make you happy.

He'd only been back in her life for a month. They'd been apart for eight years. He didn't know her well enough to say such things. He had no idea about her dreams.

What do you even know about your own dreams? some little voice in her head argued.

She dragged the suitcase off the bed in a huff. It thumped to the floor, narrowly missing her toes. Charlie was going to New York City regardless of what Julian said.

She knew what she wanted.

She wanted what Tom had wanted.

She hadn't intended for her goodbyes to be so rushed, but when she'd walked through the doors of Glendale, Alicia had messaged to say that there'd been a change in the rehearsal schedule, and the sooner Charlie could get down to the city, the better.

It was a three-and-a-half-hour drive into the city, and that was with good weather and traffic. Charlie had been keeping an eye on the snow. The last thing she wanted to do was get stuck on the freeway in some sort of blizzard, which meant she basically had to get on the road now. That didn't really leave time for her to round up the choir and say her goodbyes. Besides, it was getting closer to the holidays. Most of the residents were busy with visiting family or friends. The last thing Charlie wanted was to interrupt all that for some awkward farewell.

Was that a cop-out? Maybe.

But she couldn't bear for any of them to look at her the way Julian had—like she'd stomped on his heart. And that was why she should have left her feelings in that box, because caring this much about something—someone— only set her up for heartache when she had to say goodbye.

And right now she just needed someone to be happy for her, to understand why she had to do this.

"All packed?" Gram asked as they met in the lobby of Glendale.

"Yep. Ready to go," Charlie said. "The house is all locked

up." She handed Gram the spare set of keys she'd been using. "Most things have been packed up. Mom and Dad will have to arrange a storage unit when they get back."

Gram nodded. "It's been quiet here without you these past couple of days."

Charlie tilted her head. "The choir knows the performance forward and backward. I really think it's just a matter of having fun with it now."

"It's not quite the same," Gram said, "and you know that. You were a wonderful codirector. We're missing one half of the team."

Charlie tried to respond, but guilt ate at her. She sucked in a sharp breath, Julian's words echoing in her head. She wasn't running away from her grief. Not this time. So why wasn't Gram happier about all this? "I thought you'd be more excited for me."

"I am," Gram said, laying her hand against Charlie's cheek.

"You don't sound very enthused. This is a really big deal. I mean, it's the Lincoln Center."

Gram chuckled softly. "Yes, honey, I realize that."

Charlie frowned at her. "I thought you wanted me to get back out there, to get a job, to start singing and performing again. You told me to talk to Alicia. I did, and Alicia came through."

Gram looped her arm through Charlie's, and they started walking down the hall. "You're right, I did say all those things. I only ever wanted you to be happy, Charlie. And maybe I was mistaken, but I sort of thought you might have found some of that happiness here at Glendale with the choir. Maybe even with Julian." A sad smile flickered across her face.

Charlie blinked. She hadn't realized Gram had picked up on their rekindled feelings. They hadn't exactly been discreet, but they'd been careful. It wasn't like she'd waltzed up and kissed him in the middle of the music room during choir rehearsal.

"You can't hide the way you two look at each other," Gram said, almost as if she'd read her mind. "I may be old, but I've had my fair share of love stories, you know."

"I didn't come here to rekindle feelings." That was the last thing she'd wanted. "I came here for you, Gram. To make sure you found a home for yourself."

"I think I have." Gram patted her hand. "Or at least, I will. Don't you worry about me. Glendale has good people."

"It does," Charlie agreed. But her and Julian... She supposed they were only ever meant to orbit each other's worlds.

They reached the empty music room. Or what should have been the empty music room. Inside, Charlie spotted a man in a navy blue uniform setting up tiered platforms.

"What's this?"

"Julian meant it to be a surprise," Gram said. "He moved some things around in the budget and found a guy willing to build some risers for a bargain."

Charlie blinked at the sight. Risers would help elevate the singers, making sure everyone was seen while balancing the sound. There was even a space cut out in the center big enough to fit Frank's wheelchair.

"He wanted everyone to know we were a team worth showcasing." Gram squeezed her hand. "His words."

"They're perfect," Charlie said quietly, touched by the

gesture on behalf of the choir. "And you are a team worth showcasing. You'll be fabulous."

Gram caught Charlie by the face and kissed her forehead. "So will you. You'll call me when you get there and let me know how the first rehearsal goes? I expect tickets."

"I will," Charlie promised, even as bile rose in her throat. But she was committed to the New York Philharmonic. That was what she wanted. Not to drown in the weight of what might have been.

Seventeen

Julian

"I can help whoever's next!" a young woman called. She perched behind a long rectangular table in the lobby of the community center with a volunteer lanyard strung around her neck and a clipboard in her hand.

Julian darted toward her. "Um, hi. We're the Glendale Shakers. Signing in for our dress rehearsal slot."

"Oh!" she said, beaming at him. "I totally saw you guys online!"

"Yeah?" he said, hoping she was a fan.

"You guys are awesome. Like four different people tagged me in your video."

"Thanks," Julian said as she handed him a packet of paperwork. "That means a lot." He glanced down at the papers. "What do I do with all this?"

"Just fill out the details on the first page and the questionnaire, then return it to me before you leave the center." She scanned her clipboard. "Oh, you're on stage at 3:30 today. Make sure you're on deck ten minutes before to keep everything running smoothly. Heather said, 'Don't be late or else.' Not sure what 'or else' means, but she sounded serious."

"We'll be there," Julian promised, turning back to the choir. But as he went to gather up the residents, he spied Harriet already sneaking off. "Hey, hold on! Where are you going?"

Harriet wheeled around, her lips pursed. "Nowhere."

Julian folded his arms across his chest. "You have an I'm-about-to-get-up-to-no-good look on your face."

"We've got some time before our dress rehearsal slot." Harriet shot him an evil grin. "I figured it was time to properly scope out the competition."

Julian made a face. "Please don't do anything that'll get us disqualified before we perform tomorrow."

"Who's gonna know it was me?" Harriet joked. "No one ever suspects the little old lady."

"I would know," Julian said. "You are always suspect number one."

"You know what happens to snitches."

Julian blinked at her. Was he being threatened by a seventysomething-year-old right now?

Maggie hooked her arm through Harriet's. "Don't you worry, Julian. We're just going for a little stroll. We'll be back soon."

"Ladies," Julian warned. The last thing he needed was to be accused of cheating. He didn't know how you cheated at a choir competition, but if there was a way, Harriet would figure it out. Like locking the barber shop quartet in a closet. Oh God, why did that sound like something she might actually do?

"Don't look so alarmed," Maggie said, laughing. "We're just going to say hi to some of the other choirs. You know, introduce ourselves." She fluffed up her hair. "Wish them good luck for tomorrow."

"Intimidate," Harriet muttered. "We'll also do a bit of that."

Maggie brushed off her comment. "She's kidding, of course. We'll be nothing but charming." She tugged on Harriet's arm, and the two of them set off, snickering like schoolchildren that had toads in their pockets meant for the teacher.

Doris popped forward, giving him a sympathetic look. "I'll go with them to supervise. That way I can make sure they don't actually jeopardize our chance to perform."

"Thanks," Julian said, giving her a weak smile.

He wondered if she could see the hollow space in his chest Charlie had left after tearing out his heart. She was probably missing her just as badly. But it was different. Charlie would call. Heck, she'd probably have Doris and her parents out to see her perform. But he had nothing. No guarantees. No promises. Just the memory of them picking each other apart, prodding at their worst fears. Because this truly was his. He'd opened his heart again, he'd let Charlie take root inside, trusting that she'd stay, trusting that she wanted him, and then she'd turned around and left like he never meant anything to her at all.

Having to tell the choir that Charlie wasn't going to be here for the performance had been hard. But having to look them in the eyes as the fool who'd believed someone had actually chosen him had been worse.

And now he was forced to admit that he had no idea what he was doing without her.

Julian turned back to the rest of the choir as Doris wandered off. "Okay, we've got about thirty minutes before we have to be waiting in the wings," he said, glancing at his phone. "I guess now is a good time for water. Or vocal warmups. Right? We could do some..." He didn't even know what to start with. Lip buzzing? Some sort of humming? This was Charlie's area of expertise.

"We've got it covered," Jim said, taking pity on him. "We'll use one of the open classrooms to do our exercises."

"Sounds good." Julian pointed them down the hall. "You guys go do that, and I'll come gather everyone up in a bit." As they set off, he poked his head into the auditorium, feeling very out of place as a choir of schoolchildren were ushered off the stage by parents and teachers.

But it was only the dress rehearsal. What did it matter if they weren't perfect today? That was the whole point. To work out the bugs before tomorrow.

"Hey!" a voice called. Julian turned to find Diane hurrying across the lobby.

"You've left your desk in the middle of a work day?" he said, surprised to see her out. "Either the world must be ending, or you've been replaced by an alien."

"I can take a break every now and then," she said, frowning at something on her phone. Julian had no doubt it was an email.

"A break? Now I'm really worried," he teased.

Diane gave him a wane smile. "Chaos never ends. Not even for the holidays. But I figured I should pop down to get an early viewing. I've gotta do Christmas Eve shenanigans at my sister's, so we'll be heading off before the competition."

"I'm glad you're getting away," Julian said.

"I've allowed myself two days. I'll be back on Boxing Day if you need anything."

"We'll be fine," Julian told her. "You should take the week. I'll make sure Glendale is still standing when you're back." It wasn't like he had anywhere else to be. He hadn't celebrated the holidays with either of his parents in years.

Diane pretended to shiver. "Being away that long would give me anxiety. I'd start having panic dreams, and my husband would send me back to work."

Julian laughed. "Well, it was nice of you to stop by. I know the residents will appreciate it. We're on in about…" he checked his phone "…fifteen minutes." A barbershop quartet took the stage. "Speaking of, I should probably round the residents up. Make sure we don't derail the production." He also had to find Maggie and Harriet and Doris. If Doris wasn't on the piano, he really didn't know what he was going to do.

"I heard about Charlie leaving," Diane said suddenly. "That's unfortunate timing. But it sounds like she's got some big opportunities in New York City."

"Really big." The words soured in his mouth. He didn't begrudge Charlie stardom or fame. She was destined for bigger things than Glendale. And, he supposed, that meant bigger things than him, too. But hearing the words out loud stole his breath away.

"Next up!" he heard Heather call as she raced across the stage, waving a volunteer after her to fix the mic stand.

Julian's heart stuttered against his ribs, and he resisted the urge to rub his chest. "That's probably our cue," he told Diane. "I better get them onstage before Heather blacklists Glendale from our favorite workshops."

Diane nodded. "Break a leg or whatever they say."

"Yeah, thanks."

"Oh, I almost forgot. A little birdie told me that Frank's being discharged."

Julian's eyes widened, his mood soaring at the news. "He's getting out of the hospital?"

"Should be back at Glendale tonight. Charge nurse said there's no reason why he can't be onstage with the choir tomorrow."

"That's amazing news!" Exactly the kind of positive update he needed right now. He had to stop himself from looking around to tell Charlie. "Everyone will be stoked to have him back."

"I won't hold you much longer. I just wanted you to know that I am so impressed with what you've managed to accomplish here."

"Thanks, Diane."

"I know it's a long shot, but win or lose, you've done everything you could to make this music program a reality for the residents."

He nodded. Right now, he felt like a failure on a lot of fronts, so he appreciated her saying that. "I just really have to go and get the—"

"One more quick thing." Diane said. "There's an administrator role opening up at Glendale. Marlene is retiring unexpectedly."

"Marlene's been here forever," Julian said. She was the general manager. She also worked very closely with Diane.

"She has," Diane agreed. "But with her husband retiring last year and all the grandkids coming around, she's decided she wants to leave earlier than planned. By February, in fact. So it's time for someone new to step into her role. I've been mulling over who to hire, and I think I'd really like you to apply for the job, Julian."

His jaw dropped. "Me?"

"It's a different kind of role from the one you're currently doing—I know that—but I think you've proven how driven and adaptable you are. I need someone who's a go-getter. I also need someone who's dependable. Someone who genuinely cares about this community. And it's never been more obvious to me that that person is you."

"I, uh…" *Wow.* "I don't really know what to say." It would mean stepping away from his role as activities director and spending less hands-on time with the residents.

"It comes with a decent salary bump," Diane said with a cheeky grin. "And the residents are always telling me to give you a raise."

Julian laughed. "Let me guess. Maggie?"

"She's in my office at least once a week."

Julian ran his hand through his hair. "Can I take a bit to think about it?"

"Of course. I do need to put the job posting up soon, though. So, if you're leaning one way or the other, let me know."

"I will," he promised, already backing away to find the choir. "See you in a few days." He whirled around, running smack into Doris as he turned the corner.

"General manager?" she said. "Congratulations. That's a big step."

Julian rubbed the back of his neck awkwardly. He hadn't realized anyone had been there to overhear. "I, uh, yeah. Thanks. I'm not really sure about it yet."

"What do you mean?" Doris said as they set off down

the hall to collect the choir. "There could be no one better suited to the role."

"Because..." It was something he never would have considered in a million years. Because he was happy in his position. He was comfortable. He was...stuck. And he'd been stuck for a while now, latching on for fear of losing out. Or of somehow being left behind. "What if it doesn't work out?" he said softly.

"That's always a possibility. But in my experience," Doris said thoughtfully, "life is far more exciting when you ask yourself, 'What if it does?'"

Julian found himself at a loss for words. If he made the leap, he didn't know where he would land. But that didn't mean it wouldn't work out, right? And was he really going to stop himself from taking this opportunity out of fear?

Well, yeah. That had sort of been his MO since forever. But what was he trying to protect himself from anyway? The feeling of not being good enough? Of being left behind once he'd already invested too much of himself?

Because that had already happened. Charlie had walked away from him again, and Julian hadn't been able to save himself from that experience. And yet, he was still standing. He was hurt, sure, but his world hadn't crumbled, his heart hadn't stopped. He'd still gotten out of bed in the morning and dragged himself to work and put on a happy face for the people he cared about, because life kept demanding things from him, and it didn't care what he was afraid of.

So maybe it was time for him to push past those fears and take a chance on something new. Maybe it was time for him to choose himself.

"I think you'll find," Doris said, "that you have a lot of

people in your corner. An entire roomful of them, to be exact. And they want to see you succeed."

People who had chosen him, Julian realized with a start. Because the residents were more than just a job to him. They'd become his family. And there was nothing he wanted more than to continue to make a difference for his family.

Eighteen

Charlie

Charlie had forgotten how much she liked the Upper West Side.

Actually, she'd forgotten how much she liked New York City during the holidays. It had been several years since she'd been in the city around Christmas, and the streets were buzzing. Christmas lights hung from lampposts in the shapes of stockings and jingle bells and holly leaves. Shop windows had been decorated in fake snow, with the words Season's Greetings scrawled in reds and greens. Garland wreaths adorned almost every vertical surface.

Holiday cheer hadn't been high on her priority list since losing Tom, and that void in her chest flashed with warning as she treaded too closely to the memories. But it was hard not to get back into the spirit of things when she was voting on gingerbread house competitions and decorating trees in the common room and singing Christmas carols on repeat with the choir. All of which was Julian's doing.

A different kind of ache surfaced as she thought of him. Despite everything, she wished he was here now, if for nothing else than to enjoy the city with her.

Julian would have loved the way Christmas had crept across the boroughs. He would have marveled at the Rockefeller Center Christmas tree, towering beneath the skyscrapers. She could have taken him to Gingerbread Lane at the Chelsea Market. They might have gone ice skating or walked Fifth Avenue to see the holiday window displays in Macy's and Bloomingdale's.

Or none of that.

Charlie stomped on a pile of slush and gritted her teeth when some of it ended up in her boots. She needed to stop thinking about Julian and things that would never happen.

She told herself that he just didn't understand where her head was at, but maybe he just didn't understand her. Performing on this stage now could be her way to honor the dream Tom had for both of them. And maybe, in some way, it would help assuage some of the guilt she was still carrying around. If she could stand up there and say, *I did it, Tom*, then everything would hurt less. The loss would finally start to make sense. If Julian couldn't understand why she had to do that, then leaving what could have been behind in Elm Springs had been for the best.

She hurried across Columbus Avenue and down the sidewalk, careful of the slushy pavement under her feet. She passed the large silver block letters that spelled out LINCOLN CENTER and headed for the main entrance of the building, yanking on one of the glass doors, finding it unlocked.

Inside, she was greeted by a security guard in a pale blue

uniform. She showed him her ID, and he led her through a nondescript door before pointing her down a back hallway.

Charlie had only ever been in attendance here as an audience member. Now she was a guest. A performer!

A little thrill shot through her. A thrill she hadn't felt in a long time. The New York Philharmonic! She couldn't believe she was about to stand onstage with them.

Charlie navigated the long hallway to a series of offices, stopping next to an open door. The nameplate read Damien McGuire—Program Director.

She knocked.

Damien glanced up from his computer, and his smile immediately put her at ease. "Charlie Ward," he said, standing up to greet her. "You made it. I was worried you might have gotten caught in a bout of bad weather."

"Actually, I just managed to miss it."

He came forward, and she shook his hand. "Perfect timing. I think the orchestra was just starting to warm up."

Charlie would have liked to have had a couple days in the city to settle in before starting rehearsals, but being thrown into the thick of things brought her back to her days of covering off-ensemble roles and filling understudy parts. Sometimes these things were easier when you didn't overthink anything. All she had to do was pick up the sheet music and sing.

Damien guided her from the office. "I'll walk you out and introduce you to our conductor."

"That'd be great."

"I think most of our other performers are here," he said. "We'll run through the program a bunch between now and the end of the month, in between everyone's holiday time. That way you're all ready to help usher in the new year."

"I'm really excited," Charlie said. "Thank you again for the opportunity."

"We're glad to have you." Damien slipped through a door and onto a brightly lit stage filled with dozens of black chairs.

Charlie took a deep breath as familiarity settled over her. The strings were circled around the conductor's podium, the violinists tuning their instruments. Behind them were the winds and then the brass, with the timpani, percussion, piano and harp filling the space. Some of the musicians were already seated, reviewing their sheet music. Others stood and chatted casually, their conversations carrying in low murmurs.

In a way, it felt like no time had passed. Standing among the musicians was like putting on her most comfortable shoes.

Then she spotted a group of people gathered at the far end of the stage. It was the other performers. Charlie recognized every single one of them. Their combined star power made her stomach churn.

There was Eleanor Hardy, one of theatre's oldest and most endearing leading ladies; Dustin Brink, a former Phantom; the hilariously comedic Katie Parrish. And rounding them out was Annette McDonald, a soprano that Charlie had looked up to ever since she was a little girl.

She couldn't believe she was sharing space with this crowd. Breathing the same air. Standing in front of the same mic stand. She was actually going to pass out. But first she needed to find something for them to autograph. Would that be weird?

Stare less, she told herself. *Focus on the music. Be professional.*

Tom would have had a good chuckle over her fangirling.

"Just let me go find our conductor," Damien said, hurrying off.

Charlie waited there, taking everything in. But before she could get a hold of herself, Annette walked over.

Oh, God, Charlie thought. *Charlie. Charlie Ward. Remember your own name. Do not make a fool of yourself!*

"Hi there," Annette called. "I don't think I've introduced myself yet."

"Oh, trust me," Charlie said. "I know who you are." Annette reached her hand out, and Charlie shook it. "I am a very big fan."

Annette smiled sweetly. "Well, you've made a fan of me, too. I thought your performance with the Glendale Shakers was wonderful."

Charlie's eyes widened. "You saw that video?"

"Multiple times. My daughters showed it to me. What a special thing you were able to accomplish. I was so impressed. I hope I'm as vibrant and full of energy at their age."

"They are pretty special," Charlie agreed. She was touched by Annette's comments and a little amazed that they were having this conversation in the first place. She was also very aware that she had this opportunity because of the choir. She owed them a lot, and a flash of guilt surged through her.

But the choir was in good hands. They had Gram and Julian at the helm.

"How'd you get involved?" Annette asked.

"Oh, er... My grandmother moved into the retirement community," Charlie explained. "I was actually helping her get settled and ran into an old friend who works as the activities director there." Much more than a friend? "Next thing I knew I was directing a choir."

Annette laughed. "Isn't that how we stumble upon the best things in life? By chance?"

Charlie's answer got caught in her throat. She cleared it, but before she could say anything else, Damien was calling them over. He introduced Charlie to the conductor, the musicians took their places, and then they jumped right into the music.

Watching the others perform in this relaxed atmosphere was such a treat. Charlie did her best to soak up every second of Annette's soaring vocals and Katie's wisecracks to the conductor. She was so enthralled watching them perform that she almost missed her cue to center stage. She hurried out, adjusted the mic and gave the conductor a small nod when she was ready. He flicked his baton, and Charlie's insides trembled as the music swelled behind her.

It was nerves, certainly, and something else as she looked out at that nonexistent crowd. Empty theater seats stared back at her. Tom truly would have been in awe standing here, so why wasn't she more excited? Why had everything inside her suddenly gone cold? She searched for the thrill she'd had earlier, for the flutter of dancing butterflies. She reminded herself that she was performing alongside *the* Annette McDonald, but all she could find was the dull beat of her heart. Behind her, the music rang clear, and her voice soared. It should have filled that empty space inside her chest. This, here and now, was for Tom.

But her notes fell flat as the song came to a close. She winced at the mistake.

"Excellent," the conductor was saying, but Charlie knew it was far from excellent. She had to pull it together if she was going to stand onstage with this caliber of people and do Tom justice.

"Can we..." She cleared her throat. "Could we run it again? I just..." She gave an awkward smile. "It's been a minute."

"Of course," the conductor said, cueing up the orchestra again.

Charlie closed her eyes, letting the sound fill her until there was nothing else but the glide of the strings and the hum of the winds and the shimmering notes from the horns. The music echoed through her, seeping between her bones as she tried to latch onto the feeling of contentment she'd once found onstage.

"Let's get those lights tested," Damien called to one of the tech workers at the back of the hall.

Charlie's eyes flew open as a dazzling display of Christmas lights lit up the interior of the theater, reds and golds and blues and greens twinkling at her as the music reached a crescendo. A prickling chill ran up both her arms, something pinched tight behind her eyes, and suddenly, without warning, Charlie burst into tears.

She tightened her hand around the mic stand to keep it from shaking, feeling the tears stream down her cheeks and drip off her chin. *No... Not now!* Of all the emotions she'd stuffed away, this pain...this heartbreak had been shoved the deepest.

Charlie realized she hadn't let herself cry for a long, long time. Not when Gram had fallen and been admitted to the hospital. Not when she'd learned about Frank. Not even after her fight with Julian. She'd always managed to hold the tears at bay. To keep herself from feeling too much. Because those tears had been reserved for

Tom. But now, staring out at the dazzling brilliance of all that color, Charlie couldn't stop the tears because this was what she'd been missing these last two years.

She'd locked so many parts of herself away to try to protect herself from the devastation of Tom's loss that she'd packed all the color away with it. All the things that filled her with joy. And as the music faded behind her, Charlie realized with sudden clarity that she didn't want that anymore. She didn't want this colorless, music-less, joyless existence. She wanted to feel, to breathe, to just sit with the emotion, knowing it wouldn't drag her under because she had something else to hold on to—the world she'd started to rediscover at Glendale with Julian and the residents.

"I think that's a good time to break for a quick dinner," the conductor said, clearly trying to give Charlie a moment. "Then we'll run it all again."

There were nods of agreement.

The conductor checked his watch. "See everyone back here in a half hour."

The musicians jumped up, and a crowd of people surged through the side doors. Charlie waited for the stage to empty, frozen in that spot, the Christmas lights beating down on her, the mic stand rigid in her hands.

"Hey, stranger."

Charlie let out a strangled breath as she turned to see Alicia making her way across the stage. She surged into her arms. "What are you doing here?" They'd planned to meet up while she was in the city, but they hadn't settled on a time or a place yet.

"Damien confirmed the rehearsal time, so I figured I'd just pop by."

Charlie felt a fresh batch of tears along her eyelashes. "God, it's good to see you."

"You, too. Everything okay?"

Charlie laughed despite herself, pulling away and swiping tears from her cheeks. "I think I'm having a moment."

Alicia tilted her head. "Moments are allowed." She sank down on the edge of the stage.

Charlie sat beside her, feeling the polished wood beneath her fingers.

"You know, it's okay if you don't want to do this right now," Alicia said. "Or at all."

Charlie gave her a watery smile. "I think I've spent so long trying not to feel Tom's loss, that standing up here, it sort of scared me when I didn't feel him at all. If that makes sense?"

Alicia took her hand and squeezed.

"But I also think I've realized that it's not a matter of Tom not being here with me, but that *I'm* not supposed to be here. I put all this pressure on myself to get back onstage, to honor his memory and the dreams he had for us, but this isn't my dream. Not anymore."

"Dreams change," Alicia said, shrugging. "That's not a bad thing."

Charlie nodded, feeling as if she was free-falling. "I found a place where the music finally sings to me again, and it's not here."

She didn't want to run from her grief anymore. She wanted to let the feelings out of the box. All of them. Even the ones that scared her. Because she wanted to build something new with the residents at Glendale and with Julian, and she needed all of herself to do that.

"I'm happy for you," Alicia said. "Truly. And Tom

would understand. In fact, I think he'd probably ask what the hell are you still doing here?" Alicia climbed to her feet, reaching for Charlie's hand. "Don't you have a Christmas choir to direct?"

Charlie let Alicia pull her up, choking on a sob. It was time to let go of Tom's dream and the stage and this guilt she felt. She was allowed to want something new.

She was allowed to keep living.

Alicia hugged her again. "You want me to make your excuses?"

"No," Charlie said. "I signed that contract. I should tell Damien."

"Okay. But call me and let me know how the performance goes tomorrow. And how *other* things go."

"I will," Charlie promised. If she could make it back before the performance between the bouts of snow. If Julian even wanted her back. She gave Alicia one more quick squeeze, then hurried out stage left.

She made her way down the hall to Damien's office.

He waved her in. "All good?" he asked.

She sucked in a breath. Held it. Let it out. "Actually, no."

He looked startled. "Oh?"

"I'm really sorry to do this, Damien, and let me say again that I truly appreciate the opportunity. Really I do. But I can't do this performance. There's somewhere else I need to be."

"Your choir?" he asked.

She nodded. "I know it's last minute. It might be hard to fill the slot."

He waved her off. "We'll pull your song if we have to. Or maybe we'll get Annette and Eleanor to do a duet."

"The crowd will eat that up," Charlie said, smiling at the

idea. "Thank you, Damien. I know you probably don't understand, but this experience today has meant a lot to me."

He laughed a little uncertainly. "I guess I'm glad for that. And hey, maybe we'll get the chance to work together again someday."

"Maybe." Charlie turned to go, but something held her back: an idea, flickering at the back of her mind. "Actually," she said, "if you really mean that, I have something I'd love to pitch."

Nineteen

Julian

Julian bolted out of bed to the sound of a car alarm, his heart hammering in his chest. He padded across his room and peeled back the curtains, staring down at the street where the neighbor was cursing, trying to unstick his windshield wipers while silencing the alarm. Clearly the temperatures had dropped enough last night to create a nice layer of ice under all the snow. Even now, more snow fell, which felt fitting. He'd always been a fan of a white Christmas—or Christmas Eve.

Julian yawned and scrubbed a hand over his face. The choir competition started at 2:00 p.m., so that gave him about six hours to pull himself and the residents together before they had to leave for the community center. Based on yesterday's call sheet, the Glendale Shakers performed right after the Rockin' Six, a group of middle-aged dads, and before the Nightingales, a group of healthcare workers from the local hospital.

His thoughts drifted to Charlie, wondering if the Lincoln Center rehearsals were turning out to be everything she'd dreamed. Julian knew he'd been hard on her that morning in the kitchen and that he'd said all the wrong things before storming out. He'd been so desperate for her to stay that he'd tried to tell her how to live her life, and he'd been wrong. He should have been more supportive when she told him about the offer. Instead, he'd hurt her. Charlie didn't need anymore of that in her life.

He'd been online last night trying to buy tickets for her New Year's performance, but according to the Lincoln Center website, everything was sold out.

Perhaps that was for the best, though. After everything, a clean break was probably what she wanted and what he needed. The best thing to do was move on.

He picked up his phone, finding Diane's number. **Merry Christmas Eve.**

Do you have good news for me?

He laughed. Of course she was right down to business.

I'll take the job on one condition.

Diane sent back a question mark.

I want to have a say in who gets hired as the new activities director.

If by some miracle they managed to win this competition today and take home twenty thousand dollars, he wanted to make sure whoever took over his role was prepared to keep the choir going.

Deal. Consider it your Christmas gift. Now break legs and all that.

I think it's just one leg.

Julian grinned, stuffed his phone away and hurried through his usual morning routine—a shower, breakfast and then he was out the door with a thermos of coffee.

Much like his neighbor, he trudged through the snow to clear off his car, grumbling as his fingers froze around the snowbrush. The second the windows were clear, he hopped in the car and made his way to Glendale. He glanced at the sky, a mess of gray clouds, and hoped the weather cooperated long enough to get the residents to the competition.

A flutter of nerves surged through him as he pulled into the parking lot. He didn't know why he was nervous. He wasn't the one singing in front of half the town today.

Julian parked and headed inside.

Maggie pounced on him before he'd even cleared the lobby. "Good morning. You look refreshed."

Julian snorted. "I'm cold and was woken up by a car alarm."

"Okay, well, I'll just start with the first problem of the day."

"First?" Julian checked his phone. It was barely nine. This didn't bode well. "How many do you expect there to be?"

"At least three. That's how these things happen. In threes."

That was not what he wanted to hear. "Right. Hit me."

"The body glitter and antler headbands have arrived," she said. "Just in time, mind you."

"Body glitter?" His eyes widened.

"For our cheeks," Maggie confirmed. "You know, to give us that youthful, elf-like glow. Don't worry. We're not going to glitter up anything inappropriate."

Julian slurped his coffee. That was a relief. The antler headbands on the other hand had been his idea. He thought they'd add a nice touch to the "Grandma Got Run Over by a Reindeer" segment. "I'm not really hearing a problem."

"It's in regard to our matching T-shirts. I just realized that we forgot to include Frank in the count. He wasn't here the day we sorted the numbers."

"That's fine," Julian said. "He can wear mine."

"You're not going to be onstage with us?"

"You've got Doris leading on piano," Julian said. "I can't direct you anyway. Not like Charlie could. I'll just stick out like a sore thumb. But I will be waiting in the wings, cheering you on."

"I suppose that works," Maggie said. "Problem solved."

"Great." Julian stopped at the stairwell. "I'm going to swing up to my office and make sure the bus is sorted." He paused. "Should we gather the choir up in the music room? Get one last rehearsal in?"

"Oh, Doris is already on that," Maggie assured him. "Everyone's just finishing up their breakfast, then heading down."

"Perfect," Julian said. "I'll meet you there in about twenty minutes."

"Okay, remember when I told you these things happen in threes?" Maggie said, her lips flattening into a thin line.

Julian crouched down next to the bus where Walt was examining the rear tire.

"I just don't see how we'll get it changed in time," Walt said.

Doris stood next to Maggie, shivering. "What rotten luck. Of all the days to get a flat."

"It's these plows," Walt complained. "Pushing the snow, dragging all sorts of junk with them. I didn't see anything in the slush, but I felt the tire go."

"What now?" Maggie said, checking her watch. "If we don't get the choir to the community center soon—"

"I know," Julian cut in.

"We won't make our time slot."

"I know."

"And we won't get to perform!"

"I know!" Julian rubbed at his face. She sounded utterly heartbroken. This was all his fault. He'd gotten their hopes up, he'd encouraged their excitement, he'd somehow even managed to chase Charlie out, leaving the residents high and dry. Maybe he'd put too much pressure on everyone to win a competition that probably wouldn't change anything anyway.

He felt a hand on his shoulder.

"Let's not panic," Doris said, derailing his sour thoughts. "What are our options?"

"The bus is a bust," Walt said.

"Yes, thank you, Walter," Doris said. "I am aware that we will not be taking the bus."

Julian stood. Doris was right. He didn't have time to feel sorry for himself or to sulk about freak accidents. He had to get the choir to the community center.

"We could drive ourselves," Maggie suggested.

"The lack of licenses might be a problem," Doris said.

"No, I meant..." Maggie gestured toward Julian.

"I can only fit four people in my car," he said. "I'd need to make like five trips to the community center. With all the back and forth, we'd never make it in time."

"Too bad you don't know a bunch of dedicated Glendale employees who might also be willing to lend you a hand," Maggie said, failing to hide her grin.

God, she was right! Why was he being so obtuse? Julian whipped out his phone, texting Warren: SOS.

What's up?

I know it's Christmas Eve day and you're off with your family but any chance you could swing by Glendale for an hour? Bus has a flat and I need to get the choir to the community center ASAP.

A devil emoji. You will owe me big time.

Whatever you want.

A gingerbread house rematch.

Done, Julian typed, laughing. He'd buy out all the gingerbread kits leftover at the supermarket if he had to.

On my way, Warren replied.

Thank you. You're a lifesaver.

Warren sent through an emoji of a masked superhero. **Nurse by day. Chauffeur by day off.**

"Okay," Julian said to Maggie and Doris. "I'm working on alternate transportation. So far I've secured Warren. Let's get everyone gathered up in the lobby so we don't freeze while we're waiting."

Maggie took charge of that, ushering the rest of the choir back into the building.

Julian did some mental math. With Warren's van and some muscle, there'd be just enough room to accommodate Frank's wheelchair.

"Any chance you'd like to give some old folks a ride?" Doris asked Erin as Julian entered the lobby. "Our choir dreams have been bested by a flat tire."

"This is an emergency!" Harriet said, practically throwing herself over the lobby desk, picking up the phone as it rang and slamming it back down. "All hands on deck."

"Oh my gosh!" Erin said. "Of course. I'd be happy to. Let me grab my keys."

"That's another one secured," Doris said, turning to him.

"If Erin and I both make two runs, and Warren can accommodate Frank—"

"We'll just make it," Doris said.

Julian nodded. "You should come with me now in the first group. You can get us signed in while I run back for the second."

Doris bundled herself back into her coat.

"Maggie," Julian called, darting across the lobby. "You're in charge while I'm gone. If Warren gets here before I get back, explain the situation. Ask him to wait. He'll need my help getting Frank loaded into his van."

"Got it," Maggie said, stress painting extra glitter onto already glittery cheeks.

He turned back to Doris. "Okay, let's go."

They collected a few choir members, and all piled into his car.

"Not exactly how I saw the day going," Julian said as they drove through town, "but it could be worse."

"It could be a blizzard," Doris agreed. "Or we could have had a bout of laryngitis whip through the choir. Those would have been problems. This was a little hiccup."

"Well, according to Maggie, I've got at least one more hiccup coming."

Doris squeezed his arm. "I think we can handle it."

When they reached the community center, Julian let the group out. "I'll be back as soon as I can. Someone keep a lookout for Erin. She'll be bringing the next group. Doris—"

"I'll get us sorted. Drive carefully."

Julian did, only speeding a little as he made his way back to Glendale. When he arrived, Warren's van was parked in front of the building.

"You are actually the best," Julian said, hopping out of his car.

"It's my good deed for Christmas. Gotta make sure Santa still comes." Warren rolled the door of the van open. "Okay, what's the plan?"

"I think we get Frank situated in your passenger seat? The wheelchair should fold down and fit in your trunk. Then between the two of us, we should be able to take the rest of the residents."

"Sounds good."

Julian hurried back to the lobby to collect Frank. They

got him buckled into the van, then headed back to the community center with the rest of the choir. Warren helped Julian maneuver Frank back into his chair when they arrived.

"All right, I'm gonna head home to pick up the family," Warren said. "But I'll help you run the residents back after the show."

"I'm hoping Walt has the tire sorted by then."

"Keep me posted."

"I will."

Warren waved. "My kids are really excited for the performance."

"Just gotta make it onto that stage," Julian called.

"You've got this."

"I do," Julian said, hardly believing it. He turned and booked it inside the community center.

The energy was more frantic than the day of dress rehearsal. Choirs were lined up in the hall, dressed in various Christmas-themed outfits. Attendees had started to arrive, filling the auditorium with loud chatter. Heather was running back and forth, wearing a necklace of jingle bells, looking a little windswept.

"Julian!"

He twisted, spying Harriet, who waved him down the hall. She was all dressed up, reindeer ears with jingle bells on her head. Julian followed her through a door, up a short set of stairs and found the choir amassed behind the stage, spying on another group as they warmed up.

"One of the choirs didn't show," Doris whispered to him. "We've been moved up from our original timeslot."

Good thing we weren't late, Julian thought. "That should be fine. We're ready, right?"

"As ready as we can be."

"They're really good, aren't they?" Maggie said, and for the first time, Julian actually listened to the voices that were harmonizing backstage. "I didn't hear them at the dress rehearsal."

"I don't think they were there," Jim said. "We definitely would have remembered."

"There's no way they're an amateur choir," Harriet said. "They're too damn good. We should say something."

Doris tittered uncertainly. "To who?"

"It's not exactly like we can demand proof," Maggie added.

Harriet glowered. "Sure we can."

"I don't think we can do this," Elaine said. "We're not that good."

"It's not about being good," Julian was quick to say. "It's about having fun. Right?"

"But listen to them," Elaine continued as a volunteer popped by and hung up a sign next to the stage entrance. She darted forward to read it. "Are they on right before us? This is them, I think. The Markdale Music Makers." She pressed her hand to her forehead. "We're going to look ridiculous following that up. People are expecting something wonderful from us after that video went viral."

Doubts started to spin through the group. Harriet pulled off her reindeer antlers.

Maggie glanced at Julian. "Does this count as problem number three?"

Julian opened his mouth. Closed it. This was a problem he wasn't prepared to handle. He looked to Doris, but she didn't seem to have any words of wisdom.

Julian had never missed Charlie more. Wrinkled faces

stared back at him for reassurance, but Julian had nothing to offer them. All he knew how to do was write failed grant proposals and commit to things that never worked out.

They were right. They weren't ready for this. Not with him at the helm.

Defeat rang through him. "We're up soon," he said, not knowing what else to do. "Maybe take a quick walk? Shake out the nerves."

"Yes," Doris said. "Good idea."

The group trundled down the stairs and back into the hall. Julian hesitated, running through his options. Should he just pull them from the competition? That might be the easiest way to spare the residents the embarrassment of following up the Markdale Music Makers.

"There you are!"

He turned, and his jaw dropped.

Charlie? What the hell was she doing here?

She stood there on the opposite side of the stage. Julian felt like he was looking at a ghost. But the ghost of Christmas what? She hurried toward him, racing past the red velvet curtains that had been drawn across the stage.

"You're back," he said, staring down at her as confusion beat in his temple. He hadn't expected to see her... maybe ever again.

"I'm back," she gasped. She'd clearly been running. "I wasn't sure I was going to make it in time. Parts of the freeway hadn't been cleared yet and there was a car stalled in the middle of—"

"Why are you back?" he asked, bristling as the surprise wore off. "Don't you have important rehearsals?"

"Because I made a commitment," she said. "And I had somewhere else I needed to be."

Julian started to shake his head. "Charlie—"

She caught his hand. "Please. You were right about so much."

Julian's heart dropped into his stomach, the hurt inside him warring with his own regret. "I wasn't. I shouldn't have made you doubt yourself," he said. "Or your decision to go to New York. I should have been more supportive. I'm sorry for that."

"No," Charlie said. "You were just telling me hard truths I wasn't ready to hear. I thought I was protecting myself by closing off my emotions, shoving them away like old Christmas ornaments in a box. But I wasn't. All I was doing was cutting myself off from the experiences that really mattered… The music… The happiness that Tom would have wanted for me. The happiness I should have wanted for myself. Standing on that stage in the Lincoln Center, I realized that I didn't have to punish myself for being the one that's still here. And I'm sorry I had to walk away from you in order to figure that out. But I'm not going to do that anymore."

"What are you saying?" Julian said, his pulse rushing in his ears.

"I'm saying that you're part of what I want for myself."

Julian felt like his heart might punch through his chest. He barely forced the words out. "You're staying?"

Charlie nodded. "I'm choosing you and Elm Springs and this little life I think we could build. You gave me a safe place to rediscover myself again. And if you give me the chance to earn your trust back, I think I could make you just as happy. You're the place where the music sings to me, Julian. I love you."

"Are you sure?" he said, hardly able to believe it.

She laughed. "That I love you? Yeah, pretty damn sure."

"I mean, are you sure this is what you want?"

"It is. But is it what you want?" she asked.

"I've wanted nothing more," he said, surging forward to capture her lips. The feelings exploded inside him. Contentment. Relief. So much happiness he hadn't even realized it was possible. He kissed her again and again, until they were both dizzy. "I love you, too."

When they finally broke apart, he took in her beaming smile. He wanted to whisk her away from here and hold her in his arms, but there wasn't time for that now. "The choir's going to be so happy to see you."

He hugged her tight, knowing he couldn't spare the time, then he took her hand, tugging her down the stairs and into the hall. "I have a surprise for you."

"Frank!" Charlie exclaimed as Julian pulled her through an open door. "You're back!"

"Charlie?" Doris said, letting out a bubbly laugh. "What are you doing here?"

The choir jumped to their feet, eager to embrace her. Julian was loath to let her go, but he knew they needed her more than he did at this moment. Doris immediately wrapped her in a hug.

"How is everyone feeling?" Charlie asked the group.

"Better now," Maggie said, taking Charlie's hands. "Not that Julian hasn't been incredible," she was quick to add. Julian took no offense. "But it's good to have you back."

"It's good to be back," Charlie agreed. "And to see all of you. I know that me leaving so abruptly was probably difficult. But I want you to understand how proud I am to be here with you."

"The choir before us is pretty impressive," Doris said, cluing Charlie into the somber mood.

Charlie sighed. "And that's okay. The one thing I learned after all these years performing is that there's always someone better out there. Someone more talented."

"Harsh," Harriet said.

"I don't know if this is the pep talk you think it is," Julian muttered.

"It's the truth," Charlie said. "But people don't choose their favorite performers or artists because they're the best. They choose them because they connect with them. All those people out there who saw your video connected with you. With your joy and your spunk and your passion." She poked the antlers in Harriet's hand. "And maybe even your sassy sense of humor."

Harriet blinked down at the headband, slowly sliding it back on her head.

"So," Charlie said. "I say we go out there and give them the show they came to see."

Julian nodded. "Are we ready to rock this competition?"

"Yes," Maggie said, grabbing Harriet and Doris, looking determined.

"Hell yes!" Frank said and the group erupted into laughter. Frank wheeled himself toward the door, leading the way, and the choir followed.

"Guess this is it," Charlie said.

"Guess so." Julian stroked her cheek. "Break a leg. I'll be watching from the wings."

"Nice try." She picked up a pair of jingly reindeer antlers and fit them over his hair. "We're in this together, codirector."

Julian beamed. "The place where the music sings?"

Charlie nodded. "Like Frank said, hell yeah." And with that she darted off after the choir.

Julian hesitated for a moment, quickly pulling out his phone to text Diane.

So, I've had some thoughts on the activities director position.

Twenty

Charlie

"Merry Christmas," Julian whispered, snuggling against the softness of her cheek. "Did I forget to say that?"

Charlie bit her lip as Julian's hand tightened around her thigh. "I think it came up between 'Good morning' and 'are you my present?'" She moaned and shifted, curling her fists into the blankets.

"Good. As long as I mentioned it."

"You definitely did."

"We should get to Glendale," he said, breathing her in. Snow fell gently against the window, gray winter light highlighting the room in soft shadows.

"I'm not the one hard at work," she pointed out.

"You're right. Give me one more minute."

"Is that all it'll take?"

"I think I can be efficient when the occasion calls for it," he said, and she giggled as his lips ghosted down her chest and over her belly, nipping at her inner thighs. He teased the sensitive skin there, and Charlie tried to move her hips, tried to get his mouth where she ached, but he pulled back whenever she did.

"Stop that," she whispered.

"Stop what?"

"Teasing me."

"I like teasing you. I like all the little sounds you make. Like music to my ears."

Charlie snorted. "How long have you been waiting to use that one?"

"I've been saving it."

"Mmm," she hummed as he danced his lips toward her clit again. She stilled when he got close, anticipation coursing through her.

When his lips finally connected, Charlie saw stars. She groaned and canted her hips toward his mouth, wanting her release as badly as she wanted to draw this moment out. To savor it.

Julian licked and sucked and pulled the pleasure from her until her thighs trembled and her back arched and she came, riding the waves as they rippled across her body.

Julian left kisses everywhere as he crawled back into her arms. "Sorry I didn't get you anything for Christmas. Hopefully this suffices for now."

"Loveliest Christmas present I've ever received," she promised, still catching her breath. She ran her fingers through his hair, knowing right down to her bones that she'd made the right decision. She felt whole and settled and secure in his embrace. For the first time in years, Charlie felt like she was safe to simply *stay*.

"We'll continue part two later." He kissed her cheek.

"Oh, there's a part two?"

"There was a sale on wrapping paper supplies at the store," he said, giving her a wink. "They had lots of ribbon."

Charlie shook her head, catching her lip between her teeth, fighting off a grin. How had she ever considered walking away from this man when he made her so incredibly happy? "I wish I could have given you a better present," she said. Namely a twenty thousand dollar check and a first place trophy. She pressed her forehead to Julian's. "I know I've already said this, but I really am sorry we didn't win."

"The competition was fierce," Julian said, stroking his hand down her arm. "But I can't really say it feels like we lost either. At least, I feel like a winner." He kissed the curve of her jaw.

"You're okay with this consolation prize?" she asked.

"I'm more than okay with it." He kissed her, pressing their lips together until she smiled.

Standing on that stage yesterday had been the most fulfilling thing Charlie had done since performing with Tom. Her heart had warmed, watching the residents rock their performance as the audience jumped to their feet, cheering along. As she'd taken in Julian's joyous expression, standing among them onstage, and Gram's bubbly laughter, Charlie had known she was exactly where she was meant to be. Even when the winner had been announced, she'd still smiled, because none of it mattered. All that mattered was the looks on the residents' faces when the auditorium had erupted into applause.

Charlie didn't quite know what her future looked like in Elm Springs, but she wanted Julian and the choir to be part of it. Maybe she'd start teaching piano again or give voice lessons, volunteering at Glendale on her off days. She'd talk to Gram and her parents. If they could hold off selling the house for a while, she could get a little at-home business going. That would keep her flexible enough to fit in the choir. It might not be what she'd always imagined doing, and maybe it wouldn't be right forever, but it was right for her now.

"Come on," Julian said. "Now we really should get to Glendale. Celebrate with Doris and any of the residents that are around today."

"We should," Charlie agreed, actually finding herself looking forward to Christmas morning. They got up and dressed and made coffee in Gram's kitchen, unpacking mugs from boxes that had been destined for storage.

"Think your parents will make it back before dinner tonight?" Julian asked.

"Not sure," Charlie said. "I'm still waiting for an update from Mom." Their flight had gotten delayed once, and then when they'd finally gotten on a plane, they'd been rerouted through Toronto due to snow. "We can always video call them later. Gram will probably chat Mom's ear off and Dad'll end up snoring in the background, so it'll be just like any other Christmas." She caught Julian's eye, letting the flicker of sadness settle in her chest. Letting it linger. Letting it remind her of things she used to love. "Well...almost."

"Sounds perfect," Julian said, inclining his head in the direction of the door. "Ready?"

"Can you actually give me a minute?" Charlie asked.

"Of course. You okay?"

Charlie nodded. "Just one more gift to deliver."

The corner of his mouth curled. "I'll go start the car."

When the front door thumped closed, letting a drafty chill into the house, Charlie shivered and made her way to the base of the stairs. She latched onto the railing, nerves thrumming beneath her skin as she took one step, then another, dragging herself toward the second floor, toward that room. The place where Tom had decided to spend his last days.

The place where he'd last smiled at her.

Where he'd last laughed.

Her legs felt like jelly as she approached the open doorway. She exhaled in relief as she turned the corner, finding nothing but a silvery patch of sun on the bed, a few dust particles swirling like snowflakes. The room hadn't changed much since that day, frozen in a way that held Tom's memory. A picture of him—bright blond hair, smile caught mid laugh, a baton in his hand—sat on the bedside table. Charlie pressed her hand to her chest, took a deep breath, then walked into the room.

Emotion settled over her in waves, sometimes heavy, sometimes not, but she gave herself over to the feelings, riding out the current instead of fighting it, letting the tears gather along her lashes.

"Hi," she said, voice thick, chin quivering. She cleared her throat, pulling a program from yesterday's performance from her pocket. "I know it's been a while, and I'm sorry for that." She'd folded the program in half, showing off the photo of the Glendale Shakers as she laid it on the pillow. "I think you would have gotten a real kick out of this crew. They've been good for Gram." She lifted her shoulder. "Good for me, too, I guess."

She smiled, her finger drifting across the pillow. "Love you, Tommy. Merry Christmas."

★ ★ ★

A few days later, Charlie and Julian were greeted by whistles and cheers as they walked into the common room. Julian carried the tiny third place trophy in his hands, now engraved with the Glendale Shakers, presenting it like a wrestling belt, and the noise intensified.

Charlie made her way to Gram, perching on the arm of her wingback chair. Gram placed a hand on her knee.

"I wanted everyone here for this very special moment," Julian announced over the sounds of the choir. He lifted the trophy up and placed it on the mantel above the fireplace. "I think Glendale's first ever third place win deserves to be displayed here where everyone can see it instead of in my office."

Jim stuck his fingers between his lips and whistled so loud a few of the choir members winced and adjusted their hearing aids.

"I think there's enough room up there for a few more trophies," Gram called.

There were whoops of agreement.

Harriet crossed her arms. "I still think we deserve second place."

Maggie shook her head. "Let the children have it."

"They're lucky they're cute," Harriet muttered.

"With their little tambourines," Gram added. "And off-key singing."

Charlie laughed at the look on Harriet's face before catching Julian's eye. Harriet was never going to let this go.

"I believe my codirector has a little something to say," Julian said, gesturing for Charlie to take the floor.

She stood. She hadn't given them a proper goodbye when she left, and even though she'd made it back before the performance, she still wanted to make sure the choir really understood what they meant to her.

Charlie looked from face to face, trying to find her words. "So, I know we've only known each other for a short while, but I've had a really wonderful time volunteering here at Glendale, and I sincerely wanted to thank every one of you for always making me feel so welcome."

Maggie folded her hands over her heart.

"Before I got here, I was lost, drifting through life instead of actually living it." Charlie embraced the heavy emotion that gathered in her chest. "My brother passed away a couple years ago from cancer. He was not only my music partner but truly one of the brightest parts of my life."

Across the room, Gram's eyes watered. She lowered her head, wiping at tears.

Charlie continued. "For a long time I really didn't think I'd be able to sing again or find the same joy in music I once did. But then Gram and Julian cornered me in an elevator and roped me into this—"

Laughter echoed through the room.

"Because sometimes I know what's good for you!" Gram said.

More gentle laughter.

"You do," Charlie agreed. "Anyway, I guess I wanted to thank everyone for embracing me. I know you all think I was here to help you put this choir together, but I think you helped me far more." She cut off, her eyes glassy.

Maggie jumped up from the couch and rushed her, capturing Charlie in a fierce hug. Harriet collided with them next, and then Elaine and Dot and Jim and Frank. Pretty soon the entire choir was amassed in a giant group hug.

Charlie laughed and blinked a couple loose tears from the corners of her eyes. She plopped back down next to Gram as Julian took control of the conversation again.

"Well, I certainly don't have anything as lovely or as sentimental to say. But I do have an announcement to make," he said. "I wanted to take this opportunity to let everyone know that as of the new year, I will no longer be working at Glendale as the activities director."

Charlie frowned as the room erupted in gasps of confusion. He hadn't mentioned anything to her, and sure, maybe there hadn't been much time with the chaos of the competition and Christmas, but what about this morning?

There was a sudden outcry, the emotion in the room shifting dramatically. Gram stilled beside her, unusually silent. Frank shook his head, brow furrowed, clearly disliking the news.

"Why?" Harriet demanded at the same time that Maggie tearfully said, "You're leaving us?"

"No, no," Julian said, holding his hands up to keep their questions at bay. "I'm not leaving. Not exactly."

"What the hell does that mean?" Harriet demanded.

"It means... I've been given a promotion. Marlene is retiring in February, so Glendale needs a new general manager, and Diane has offered me the job. You all know I love what I do, but this is a chance for me to make new changes here. So I'm not leaving, just moving into a new role."

Harriet harrumphed. "You could have led with that."

"Sorry," Julian said, smiling.

Maggie dabbed at her eyes. "So all those visits to Diane's office demanding she give you a raise finally paid off?"

"Looks like it," Julian said. "And that's not all."

Maggie huffed. "Julian, I don't know if I can handle any more news."

"I have one more update," he said.

"A good one?" Harriet asked suspiciously.

"Hopefully." He pursed his lips for a beat. "I hesitated leaving this job because I didn't know who would take over this role after me. Who would be dedicated enough to try to keep the music program going? But I think I've found that person now. Someone who loves this place as much as I do, and who'll do everything they can to keep the music at Glendale." He gestured across the room. "And that's Charlie."

"Me?" Charlie sputtered, caught off guard.

He nodded.

What on earth was he talking about? "No. I can't... Julian, I'm not—"

Gram squeezed her leg. "Just hear him out."

"You knew about this?" Charlie said, searching her face.

Gram didn't seem at all surprised. In fact, she'd hardly reacted to Julian's news of a promotion. Gram gave her a wink.

"You basically put this choir together and ran it single-handed," Julian said. "This job would just make it official. No more volunteering. I know there are elements to the role other than music, but I can help you with those until you figure it out. And look, if this is not something you want, I'll find someone else," he said. "Or if your music dreams take you in a different direction, we'll support you. But right now, I'd really like it to be you. I think we'd all like it to be you."

There were nods and words of encouragement from the room.

Charlie's cheeks heated. Since she'd returned, she'd wondered how best to be a part of the community at Glendale, and here was Julian, offering her the perfect solution. She didn't know what to say. Tears gathered in the corners of her eyes again.

"Question is," Julian said, "do you want us?"

Charlie laughed. "I really do."

Gram wrapped an arm around her, hugging Charlie close in celebration. Then she was up in Julian's arms, wrapped in his warm embrace, her heart filled with so much gratitude she didn't even know what else to say.

"Sorry to put you on the spot again," he said.

She looked up at his cheeky grin. "No, you're not."

"Yeah, not really."

They shared a laugh, and her eyes fell to his lips. The only thing holding her back was the roomful of residents.

"Just kiss him already!" Maggie yelled, surprising them both.

Well, Charlie thought. She wasn't technically employed yet, which meant Julian wasn't technically her coworker. And who was she to refuse when they were being cheered for? She pressed up on her toes and gave Julian a chaste peck on the lips.

"Boo!" Harriet said. "You can do better than that!"

Julian laughed and wrapped his arms around Charlie, dipping her slightly before laying a rather unchaste kiss on her. She came up breathless.

"Oh!" she said, her eyes widening in excitement. "I have an announcement, too!" She pulled away from Julian, facing the group. "As my first official act as activities director, I'd like to propose a field trip."

Twenty-One

Charlie

Two months later

Charlie peaked out the slit in the door that led to the stage where the orchestra was prepping their instruments, dressed in their black formal attire. Her ears picked up the lingering notes as the strings were tuned. Violin. Viola. Cello. Double bass. Her gaze shifted from the stage to the audience where the lights were still bright, highlighting the audience, some already seated, others happily chatting as they clutched their programs.

Charlie held a program in her hand now, grinning as she took in the words on the front.

The New York City Philharmonic presents the Glendale Shakers.

She flipped open the first page to find an image of the choir taken by Julian in the music room just after Christmas. Beneath it were the words, *An evening of fun and fancy with everyone's favorite viral retirement home.*

On the next page, beneath the words *Our Story*, were more pictures. Charlie and Julian back to back with a blurb about both their professional careers. The choir at the community center with a QR link to that first viral video. The choir during their news segment. The choir just after the Christmas Eve performance, still donning their reindeer antlers. A write-up accompanied the photos, talking about the music program at Glendale.

It was hard to believe that so much had happened in such a short time.

And now here they were, about to perform onstage at the Lincoln Center.

Charlie wanted to pinch herself. Even though she'd pitched the idea to Damien before she left, part of her wasn't sure it would ever happen. But when she'd been hired on as activities director, she'd figured they had nothing to lose and reached out to him again after Christmas. To her delight, Damien had been eager to collaborate. A couple short months later, that idea was a reality.

Actually, it was a sold-out concert. Damien was already talking about inviting them back for a show in late summer. And of course the choir was already planning their comeback during the Twenty-first Annual Christmas Choir Competition. Harriet was determined to take second place at the very least and had been coordinating with Maggie's granddaughters on some more updated dance moves, which Charlie was certain she'd have to veto at some point.

"Ready?" a voice said, and Charlie turned to find Julian. His smile broke through the darkness that surrounded them.

"Almost," she said. "How's everyone?"

"Some nerves but mostly excitement. Doris has them warming up."

"Good. I was just about to do that."

"Enjoying the moment?" Julian asked.

She nodded. "Thinking about how far we've come."

"How far *you've* come," he added, stroking her face.

"That, too." She turned her head enough to kiss his palm. She wasn't the same person she'd been when she first met Julian. But she also wasn't the same person she was when she'd lost Tom. Time didn't heal all her wounds, but it certainly allowed her to grow strong enough to carry them.

"I'm very proud of you," Julian said.

"Thank you for coming tonight."

He tucked her hair behind her ear. "I wouldn't have missed this for the world."

"I know, but I also know how busy you are at work."

"Well, I had some very compelling emails from a certain activities director that I'd have been a fool to ignore."

Charlie hummed softly. "Sounds like she knows how to get your attention."

Julian wrapped his arms around her waist. "She certainly does. All caps. Lots of exclamation points." He lowered his head, and Charlie's heart raced.

"Get it together you two," Harriet said, sidling up next to them. "We've got a show to put on."

Charlie laughed as they broke apart, and the choir amassed in the tiny hall. She and Julian had gotten good at being professional at work for this exact reason. There always seemed to be eyes on them. "Everyone ready?"

A round of nods.

"Perfect," Charlie said, gathering them up in a circle. She took Gram's hand. "I know this is our biggest performance so far, but just like every other time, we're going to go out there and have fun. Because if we're enjoying ourselves, then so is the audience. And once again, I want to thank you all for being here. I couldn't have asked for better people to share the stage with."

"You're going to make us cry," Maggie said.

"Speak for yourself," Harriet muttered, huffing and turning away to discreetly rub at her eyes.

"Okay," Charlie said, hearing a round of applause as the conductor walked out from the other side of the stage. "That's all I'll say on the matter. We don't need tears onstage."

She squeezed Gram's hand, catching her eye. She might not be able to share the stage with Tom anymore, but she still got to share it with family. Charlie released Gram's hand, then pushed the door open, spilling light into the hall.

She took a deep breath, then crossed the stage to a second round of applause.

Charlie looked out at the audience, giving them a winning smile. She greeted the conductor with a hug, then took her spot onstage, raising her arms as the choir amassed in their two lines, facing the crowd. Julian wheeled Frank front and center, parking his wheelchair before hurrying back to the wings.

The swell of the orchestra music filled her. "Smile," she said, but the reminder wasn't necessary. The residents were already beaming.

Charlie nodded her head in time with the music, raising her arms. "Here we go! And one…and two…and…"

★ ★ ★ ★ ★

LET'S TALK
Romance

For exclusive extracts, competitions and special offers, find us online:

- **f** MillsandBoon
- **X** @MillsandBoon
- **◉** @MillsandBoonUK
- **♪** @MillsandBoonUK

Get in touch on 01413 063 232

For all the latest titles coming soon, visit
millsandboon.co.uk/nextmonth

A STYLISH NEW LOOK FOR MILLS & BOON TRUE LOVE!

Introducing

Love Always

Swoon-worthy romances, where love takes centre stage. Same heartwarming stories, stylish new look!

Look out for our brand new look

OUT NOW

MILLS & BOON

FOUR BRAND NEW BOOKS FROM
MILLS & BOON MODERN

Indulge in desire, drama, and breathtaking romance – where passion knows no bounds!

OUT NOW

Eight Modern stories published every month, find them all at:

millsandboon.co.uk

MILLS & BOON

THE HEART OF ROMANCE

A ROMANCE FOR EVERY READER

MODERN — Prepare to be swept off your feet by sophisticated, sexy and seductive heroes, in some of the world's most glamourous and romantic locations, where power and passion collide.

HISTORICAL — Escape with historical heroes from time gone by. Whether your passion is for wicked Regency Rakes, muscled Vikings or rugged Highlanders, awaken the romance of the past.

MEDICAL — Set your pulse racing with dedicated, delectable doctors in the high-pressure world of medicine, where emotions run high and passion, comfort and love are the best medicine.

Love Always — Celebrate true love with tender stories of heartfelt romance, from the rush of falling in love to the joy a new baby can bring, and a focus on the emotional heart of a relationship.

HEROES — The excitement of a gripping thriller, with intense romance at its heart. Resourceful, true-to-life women and strong, fearless men face danger and desire - a killer combination!

afterglow BOOKS — From showing up to glowing up, these characters are on the path to leading their best lives and finding romance along the way – with plenty of sizzling spice!

To see which titles are coming soon, please visit

millsandboon.co.uk/nextmonth

MILLS & BOON
A ROMANCE FOR EVERY READER

- **FREE** delivery direct to your door
- **EXCLUSIVE** offers every month
- **SAVE** up to 30% on pre-paid subscriptions

SUBSCRIBE AND SAVE

millsandboon.co.uk/Subscribe

OUT NOW!

THE ITALIAN'S BILLION-DOLLAR *Christmas*

SHARON KENDRICK   CAITLIN CREWS   SARAH MORGAN

3 BOOKS IN ONE

Available at
millsandboon.co.uk

MILLS & BOON